SACRIFICE LOVE

SAINTS PROTECTION & INVESTIGATIONS

MARYANN JORDAN

Cover design: Cosmic Letterz

ISBN ebook: 978-0-9968010-9-6

ISBN print: 978-0-9975538-0-2

1

The blue sky peeked occasionally between the pillowy, white clouds as the large group gathered around the casket at the cemetery. Chad Fornelli stoically said his last goodbye to his long-time friend and former ATF bomb squad team member. *Fuck, Adam, what the hell happened?*

The minister stepped up to the head of the casket and looked out on the gathering. He spoke of Adam, regaling them with his heroics, as well as his antics. Adam was known for both, and no one understood that better than his ATF buddies. The minister nodded toward Adam's mother and step-dad, sitting in the front, pain etched upon their faces, calling Adam a dutiful and loving son. Adam's mother leaned heavily on her husband, her hands clasped in his. Chad knew Adam's biological father walked out on the family when Adam was young so he was raised by his mother alone. Several years ago, she found love again and Chad remembered Adam speaking respectfully of his mother's husband. He remembered they were older, but they appeared much more so at the side of their son's coffin.

The minister then turned toward Danielle, Adam's wife. *Dani.* Chad sat next to her, his large hand clasping her much smaller one. He glanced to the side, taking in her profile. Her wavy auburn hair was tamed into a sleek ponytail at the base of her neck instead of flowing wildly down her back. Dark circles underneath her green eyes accentuated her pale face. The slightest smattering of freckles across her nose drew his gaze. A dash of lipstick gave the only color to her features. She held a tissue in her free hand, but she appeared to have no tears left. Her eyes, slightly puffy, were dry.

As the minister talked about Adam's love for his wife, Chad wanted to put his arm around Dani and pull her in close. He wanted to tell her that her grief would not last forever. He wanted to assure her that he would help with anything that needed to be taken care of. He wanted to tell her...his biggest secret...and biggest regret.

That even though she married my best friend...she was the only woman I've ever loved.

Two hours later

The mourners gathered at the local pub, closed to the public, for the wake. The crowd was subdued at first but became lively after a few beers were consumed, all knowing this was what Adam would have wanted. Chad held his beer, toying with the sweat droplets sliding down the sides. Smiling at friends, listening as they shared their stories and memories of Adam, his eyes continually searched for Dani. She spent time with her and Adam's parents until they left to go back to their hotel. Now, even with her friends circling around, she still appeared as a lost waif in the middle of a crowd.

She lifted her eyes to his and the familiar punch to the gut hit him. Those eyes...*I wanted to look into those eyes every day for the rest of my life.*

She shifted her gaze to one of the women sitting next to her and Chad turned back to the bar. Seeing his reflection in the mirror behind the bartender, he allowed his mind to slip back in time once again...to the first time he saw her.

I loved the ATF picnics. We'd gather at a local park, mingling around food-laden tables, playing volleyball in the sand pit, and enjoying the brilliant summer day. For the Explosives Enforcement Officers, it gave us a chance to blow off steam while enjoying the company of other ATF agents from different local offices.

Jerking off my ATF t-shirt, I tossed it to the ground before jogging over to enter the volleyball game. I towered over many of the other guys with my height, but my agility surprised them. Laughing as I dove for a low ball, I collided with one of my best friends.

"Fuck, man," Adam Turner growled, pushing me off him. "You're like running into a goddamn freight train."

I stuck my hand out and Adam took it, allowing me to give him a pull to his feet. We grinned at each other, dusting off the sand before continuing the game. Twenty minutes later, we walked toward the food tables, the game successfully won by our team.

Slapping me on the back, Adam said, "Well, look who's at the table. If it's not the hottest ATF investigator in the office."

My eyes swept across the tables and landed on the object of Adam's proclamation. He's not wrong...Dani is the prettiest—

"I swear I gotta tap that."

"Come on, Adam, show some respect," I growled, uncharacteristically irritated with my friend. "Not every woman is the kind to try to fuck over."

Throwing his hand over his heart, Adam pretended to be wounded. "I don't fuck 'em over, bro. I just fuck 'em...and they always want to come back for more."

"You're impossible, man," I accused, my eyes still on the beautiful redhead. "She's too damn good for you."

Hoping she would not fall for Adam's cheesy pick-up lines, I walked over, keeping my gaze on her and watched her eyes shift between me and Adam. The three of us had met at an ATF training a few months ago, but I had no idea if she would remember me. It seemed she did. She turned her brilliant smile, complete with dimples, and green eyes toward me...and I was a goner.

Over the next couple of months, we three forged a bond, spending many weekends drinking beer, watching bad movies, and eating pizza. Dani resisted Adam's advances—it didn't take her long to realize his womanizing ways. And after evenings of drinking, when Adam left to find his next ass to tap, she and I would sit and talk. But I never made a move...fear of losing their friendship always won out.

One night, the three of us were sitting in Adam's apartment and I looked up as Dani brought the re-filled chip and dip bowls back in. Setting them on the coffee table, she stepped over Adam's feet and situated herself between us. Closer to me. Adam's eyes were glued to the football game. Dani's eyes were facing the TV but I noticed she would glance my way often. I was always hyper-aware of her. Where she was, what she was doing, what she wore...everything.

"Damn quarterback," Adam grumbled, standing up. "I'm losing money on this shit." He walked out of the room, shouting about taking a piss before I heard the bathroom door slam.

Alone, my awareness of Dani skyrocketed. The way her hair, pulled up in a messy bun, had tendrils falling about her face. The way her white tank top showed off her tan, as well as her breasts. Her jeans cupping her ass and how when she leaned forward to dip her chips, her heart-shaped ass looked even more amazing. Her pink painted toenails peeking out from the bottom of her jeans. Everything snagged and held my attention.

As she leaned back, she twisted her head to gaze at me. Smiling, she shoulder-bumped me as she pressed her body into mine. "Hey, big guy. You're kind of quiet. Whatcha thinking?"

I wanted to say, "That I think about you all the time. That I've decided that for me, you're it. You're the one." Gazing into her eyes, I believed she wanted me to say those words. Her wide green eyes pierced mine as her tongue darted out over her bottom lip, wetting its dryness. Leaning in, my mouth a whisper away from hers, I held her gaze, looking for any indication that she did not want this as much as me, and all I saw was acceptance...and desire. My lips barely brushed hers—

"That was one fuckin' long piss," came the loud voice of Adam as he walked out of the bathroom.

Dani and I jumped apart, our eyes darting around nervously. She shoved a chip into her mouth and I leaned back heavily on the sofa, hating the missed opportunity. But the almost-kiss was close and she wanted it, I was sure.

My phone vibrated in my pocket and looking down to see who was calling, I recognized the number. Stepping out on the balcony to take the call in private, I re-entered the apartment a few minutes later, trying to mask my frustration.

Adam's eyes were once more glued to the game, but Dani's sharp expression was pointed at me. Shaking my head, I offered a smile, but knew it didn't reach my eyes.

The good news was that my request to serve a six-month tour in Afghanistan as an ATF representative with a Special Forces unit had been approved and scheduled. I left in one month. The bad news, as my gaze stared at the beauty sitting on the sofa, was that we would be separated for six months. And that killed my desire to start a relationship now. But when I got back, I vowed, I would do everything possible to show her how I felt. Because I'd fallen. And fallen hard.

"Hey," a soft voice jerked him from his memories as a delicate hand touched his arm.

Looking down, he smiled seeing Dani. "Hey back," he said. His eyes roamed over her face. "How're you holding up?"

Lifting her shoulders in a little shrug, she replied, "Okay, I guess. It still doesn't seem real." Her gaze drifted over the crowd, hearing the laughter and comments about Adam, and she smiled. "He would have loved this."

Chuckling, Chad nodded. "Yeah, he would have. Forget the formalities—a wake in his favorite pub would be just what he wanted." He peered at her for a moment, seeing the effects of the past several days written on her face. "Can you tell me any more about what happened? These guys," he nodded toward several of Adam's teammates, "told me some."

Grimacing, Dani replied, "I don't know much more, Chad. The official story was that they were called to check out a suspicious house. Seems the neighbors had called the cops numerous times on the comings and goings. Even the ATF won't give me too many details since it appears to be possible terrorist activity." She tucked an errant strand of hair behind her ear as she looked up into his face. "It seems the house was rigged much more so than anyone anticipated. And you know Adam...he was the first one in."

Chad did know Adam—fuckin' fearless. But smart.

"I can see the wheels turning," Dani said, her eyes piercing his. "I haven't heard anyone say he was careless." She sighed, "They were just unprepared for the destruction."

Chad had read the report and understood the entire house was destroyed by the bomb that was set off. *Peroxide based shit—unstable, easy to make, and fuckin' destructive.* In fact, the two houses next door suffered substantial damage as well. Several ATF team members were injured, but Adam was the only one killed. *Why did you not send a robot in first, Adam? What was going through—*

"You know, we missed you," Dani's soft voice once more interrupted his churning thoughts.

Guilt shot through him as he captured the questioning expression in her eyes and struggled with his reply. "I...I'm...oh fuck, Dani," he struggled through his reply. "I'm sorry. Jesus, so fuckin' sorry. It was...hard...when I got back and you guys had married."

The uncomfortable silence lay between them, making him feel miles away from her instead of just a few feet.

Sighing deeply, she said, "Yeah." She appeared as though she wanted to say more, but closed her mouth as she blinked hard, moisture pooling in her eyes. "You were always such a good friend...to both of us. I'm sure...the situation was difficult...um...if things could have been different, I—"

Just then, the door to the bar slammed open as a tall, heavily made-up blonde walked in. While wearing all black, her attire could hardly be described as funeral appropriate. The dress was too short, the heels were too high. Chad did not know who she was—but he had a bad feeling. Dani stepped over a few feet, peeking around others in her way, to see who had arrived.

"Oh fuck," Chad whispered to no one in particular.

"You can say that again," one of the men standing next to him said. "Why the hell would she come?"

Looking at Adam's current team member, he asked, "Who is she?"

The man looked up at Chad, an incredulous expression on his face. "You used to work with Adam...you knew him. That's his latest piece—"

"Why the hell didn't anyone tell me where Adam's wake was?" the woman slurred, the effects of her previous drinking already showing.

Chad's eyes flew around, landing on Dani. *Shit!* Dani was approaching the woman, questioning in her eyes.

"I'm Dani Turner, Adam's wife."

The blonde teetered on her heels, her drink sloshing over the sides of the glass. "Wife? Wife? He never told me he had a wife!"

The silence in the room rivaled any tomb. Every person's eyes stayed riveted to the unfolding disaster playing out in front of them.

Dani's face hardened as she lifted her chin in defiance of what was coming. "This is a private wake. How did you know...my husband?"

The blonde snorted, a poor attempt at a giggle and said, "He was my...well, my very *intimate* friend, if you get my drift." The woman attempted a wink, but the effect fell short.

Chad knew he needed to do something. Toss out the blonde. Rush over to Dani. Anything. Something. But like everyone else, he stood rooted to the floor. This was the reason he had stopped communicating with Adam. He had no respect for a man who could not keep it in his pants, and couldn't bear to see Dani with Adam. Like a coward, he separated himself from them, thinking that would be easier.

"I don't see how he could be your *intimate* friend, as you say, when he had a wife," Dani said, her voice finally beginning to strain.

"Well, I guess having a wife didn't matter to Adam when he was fucking me," the harsh reply came. The blonde looked around, recognizing some of Adam's team members. "Y'all know me," she sneered. "You've seen me with him and none of you fuckers let me know he was dead. I had to find out from the news."

Dani turned slowly, piercing the crowd with her pain-laced gaze. "Did you? Did you know about her?"

Some of the men looked down at their feet or suddenly found the ceiling to be of utmost interest. Then her eyes came to Chad's and he couldn't look away. She walked over slowly until she stood directly in front of him, his height causing her head to lean way back as she kept her eyes pinned to his.

"You knew?" she asked, her voice as soft as a whisper.

"I didn't know about *her*," Chad answered honestly.

"No, you couldn't, could you. I wondered why you became a long-distance friend over the past year, Chad. So tell me...did you know about others?"

He felt choked, as though someone had grabbed his tie and pulled it tight. *What the hell do I say? Yes, I knew your husband couldn't keep his dick in his pants whenever he went out?* Once more, Chad froze, unable to answer her.

"And I thought you were my friend as well," she said, blinking back tears.

Dani turned a slow circle, staring at the people gathered. "So you all knew?" She drew herself up to her full height, which at five foot five inches was not significant, and yet her regal bearing bespoke of dignity. "Well, fu—," she stopped, her face full of agony as her body shook, swallowing deeply. "I'll leave you to mourn with his…" she looked over at the blonde, whose drunken, lipstick-smeared mouth smirked, and said, "*his latest piece of fun.*"

With that, Dani walked stiff-backed toward the door. Several of her girlfriends immediately hustled to follow her, but with her hand in their faces, they stopped. Others tried to call out to her in support while others attempted to get the blonde to leave. None of their efforts worked. Dani left and the mourners soon followed, Adam's wake officially ended.

2

Chad lay on the hotel bed, still wearing the now wrinkled clothes from yesterday. He had come from the wake, driven to his hotel and immediately thrown himself down on the bed after kicking off his shoes. His mind whirling, he slept little. He thought of Adam. He thought of Dani. He thought of missed chances. And finally, his mind stayed on his regrets.

The dawn was still an hour away when he got up and walked over to the window. The high-rise hotel offered a view of Washington D.C. in the distance, the slight morning fog blanketing the city. Leaning his forehead on the cold pane of glass, he remembered the first time he met Adam.

At the introductory training the ATF required everyone to go through, regardless of their knowledge and background, Adam was one of the instructors. He had picked me out as a weak link because of my size. At six feet five inches, I towered over most of the others in the room. It didn't take them long to realize that as a former Green Beret with weapons and detonation experience, I was the man to watch out for.

Adam, ever the jokester, added extra weight in the Advanced Bomb Suit given to me. The other new employees in the training assisted me into the suit and I felt the difference immediately, having worn an ABS in the Army. Glancing up at Adam, I knew what he was up to. Without missing a beat, I performed the physical training of jogging up and down stairs with a better time than anyone else.

"Fuck me, big guy," Adam said, his shit-eatin' grin plastered on his face.

Taking off the helmet, sweat pouring off my face, I grinned right back. "Just a walk in the park, asshole."

The two of us bonded over that introduction and Adam made sure I was assigned to his team with the Washington, D.C. field office. It didn't take long for our team to become the one others aspired to be with.

The sun was now rising over the tops of the distant buildings. Moving away from the window, Chad walked to the bathroom. The reflection in the mirror did nothing to still his unsettling thoughts. His dark hair was trimmed neatly, but his five o'clock shadow was now a six o'clock in the morning beard. His eyes latched onto the medallion hanging around his neck. A St. Chad medallion. A saint known for self-sacrifice.

He bought the pendant after the funeral of one of his Army ordnance disposal buddies who had been killed. The priest officiating the service told him of Saint Chad; saying it was such an unusual name, he wondered if Chad was familiar with its meaning. Wearing the medallion helped him remember death could come to any of them at any time on the job. The old truck he drove belonged to his buddy, given to him by his grieving mother. It was a jalopy, but Chad kept it running.

Grimacing, he reached up grabbing the pendant in his large fist, wanting to jerk it off. *Self-sacrifice...yeah, right. More like, selfish bastard!* He stilled his hand, unwilling to dispose of the medallion that had come to be a part of him. Sighing heavily, he turned from his reflection.

Turning on the shower, he stripped from his well-worn and slept-in clothes. Standing under the hot spray of water, he let the warmth pound his muscles in an attempt to pound out his thoughts. It did not work.

"You've got to be shittin' me, man," Adam bit out. "We're a fuckin' team."

"This is something I've got to do," I explained. I'd been offered a chance to return to Afghanistan to work

with some Special Forces teams in a non-combat capacity. The ATF had new robots that the Army would be using and I was going to have an opportunity to work for six months in the field, reviewing and testing the new equipment. "It's only for six months, guys."

"Yeah, yeah," Adam groused. "And while you're over there re-living your glory, Army days, I'll be stuck here with some new-ass partner."

"They were hardly glory days, I'm sure," Dani spoke softly, her voice laced with recrimination...and sadness.

Adam and I, along with Dani, were sitting in a bar as I discussed my plans. Looking into Dani's green, somber eyes, I added, "I'll be back in six months and it'll be as though I never left." I hoped my expression conveyed to her what I really wanted to say—wait for me. I'll be back. Then I'll make a move and see if you and I have something special.

But when I got back...Dani and Adam were married.

Shaking the excess water from his head, Chad dried off and prowled to his suitcase to retrieve clean clothes. Worn jeans, a navy polo that stretched across his wide chest and was tight on his arms. Grabbing all of his belongings, he glanced around the room once more before heading out.

Jesus, I'm a goddamn explosive expert. Not some coward. Time to man the fuck up. Exiting the elevator, he placed a call to his boss, Jack Bryant. No longer with the ATF, Chad worked for Saints Protection & Investigations, a private firm not constrained by the governmental bureaucracy. For his new co-workers, from the FBI, CIA, SEALs, Special Forces, police, and other agencies, the Saints provided a chance to work without the bullshit regulations that often tied their hands. For Chad, it gave him a place to do his job...while running away from the couple that unknowingly broke his heart.

"Jack, I'm taking a few extra days to help Adam's widow. We were close at one time and I'd like to assist her if I can." Leaving the message, he counted on Jack not minding his extra days off. He sure as hell had earned them.

Sitting in his old truck, he pulled out of the hotel's parking garage and headed to Dani's house. As he thought earlier, *time to man the fuck up.*

He had only been to Adam and Dani's rental house once, but the GPS quickly navigated him through the early morning traffic. Forcing himself to not arrive too early, he killed some time at a local diner, but found the food sitting on his plate, his eggs congealing, as his coffee churned in his stomach.

It was now almost nine thirty a.m. and he figured it was not too early to arrive, even unexpectedly. Pulling onto their—*it's now just her*—street, he caught sight of a large moving truck in one of the driveways. Approaching, he realized it was in her driveway and from the looks of things they had an early start. *What the hell?*

Chad parked his vehicle in front of the neighbor's house and began walking to the front door. Dani came out, her formal clothing of yesterday now replaced with black yoga pants and an oversized grey t-shirt. Her long hair was pulled up in a bun on top of her head, errant tendrils falling about her face. He observed as one of the moving men's eyes followed her as she walked back inside her house and fought the urge to land his fist into the man's face.

He made his way around the truck, glancing into the open back as he passed. Filled with boxes, bags, and furniture odds and ends, he was certain the move was unplanned. Stalking toward the front of the house, he stopped short when Dani came back out, her arms full of a few smaller boxes.

Her eyes landed on his, almost at eye level as she stood on the porch with him several steps below. "What are you doing here, Chad?" Her voice was laced with a mixture of surprise and irritation.

All the congenial words he had practiced saying flew out of his mind. Jerking his head back toward the moving truck, he growled, "I was going to ask you the same thing."

"With your powers of observation, I would assume you could deduce I was moving out of this house."

Taking a deep breath while counting to five, he put his hands up in front of him. "Come on, Dani, let's not make a hasty decision that you'll regret. Let's talk about what you're doing. Making this kind of decision when you've just—"

"What Chad? Just buried my cheating, lying, husband?" Her emerald eyes flashed in anger as she continued down the steps by him.

He reached out and stopped her with his hand on her arm, taking the boxes out of her hand. "Dani...look, I know yesterday was—"

She interrupted him once more. "You don't know anything, Chad. You left us a long time ago and disappeared for God knows why." She looked into his face, battling tears of anger as well as frustration. "You walked out of our lives. You did that. You became a Saints Investigator and chose to not come around anymore, so do not pretend to care about what's going on now. I can take care of myself. I have for a long time. And we are not having this conversation. Understand?"

He watched her walk back inside the house before he handed the boxes to the mover who approached. The realization hit him that Adam and Dani's marriage had not been what he assumed. She was right—he had distanced himself because the friendship was too painful to maintain once he came back to claim her, only to discover they had married.

He followed her inside, noticing the large furniture was still in place. Sofa, end tables, and dining table. *The rental house must have been furnished.* He recognized Adam's old recliner sitting in the corner and wondered if it was going to stay. *Who the hell am I kidding? No way's she taking anything of his right now.*

Chad heard banging in a back room, the sound of slamming doors echoing through the small house. Sighing, he sat on the sofa, putting his head in his hands for a moment. The morning was not going the way he planned at all. He arrived, expecting to comfort his grieving friend, promise to help her with anything she needed to deal with and, hopefully, forge ahead in rebuilding their friendship. What greeted him was a furious woman, determined to separate herself from her deceased husband's memory the day after he was buried. He heard footsteps coming down the hall and lifted his head as she rounded the corner.

"You're still here?" she asked, her calm voice belying her anger.

"Dani, you're right," he began, watching her eye him carefully, waiting for a verbal misstep. "I did walk away but for reasons that were needed at the time. Now, looking back, they may not have been the best reasons. But I'm here now and I want... want..." he faltered, looking around at the room that was decimated of personality. The little mementos that make a house into a home were gone—packed away or thrown away, he was not sure. Standing to his full height, he said, "Regardless of what you think, I do care. We need to talk. You need to tell me what you're doing. I want to help, Dani."

She had lifted her head as he stood, maintaining eye contact. Now she glanced toward the open front door and the movers still packing her belongings into the back. Swallowing hard several times, she stood stoically, as though any movement would cause a breakdown.

He recognized stress...anguish...utter desolation, and stayed perfectly still so as not to disturb her thoughts. *Come on, Dani. Talk to me.* The silent minute stretched interminably. Just when he thought she would not speak, she turned her gaze to his. No longer anguished...but resolute.

"You don't know what my life has been like for the past year. You left for six months, a year and a half ago, to go on a mission and while I understand your reasons for leaving, when you came back, you came to see us once and then that was it. So my *marriage*," she stumbled over the word, "and my life is no longer your concern. You made that choice, Chad."

"This is so sudden, Dani," he replied. "This move. How the hell did you even get it arranged so quickly?"

Barking a rude sound, she admitted, "The guy who owns the truck is a neighbor. I helped out a few months ago when his mother had a stroke, and he told me that anytime I needed assistance to give him a call. I left the wake yesterday afternoon, walked into this house, and knew I didn't want to spend one more day in it. So, I gave him a call yesterday evening, and he had his crew here at seven a.m."

"What are you going to do?"

"He's taking everything and putting it into a storage unit outside of Richmond and I'm moving back to my parents for a few weeks until I can decide what to do."

"But—"

"I've told you more than I should have, Chad. I meant it when I said that you are not welcome here. My life and my decisions are not up for debate."

He stared at her for a long minute. The sun coming through the front window glistened in her hair, causing the auburn to appear more red than brown. Her eyes, greener from yesterday's crying, were large in her pale face. Even with no makeup and her hair pulled up haphazardly, she was still the most beautiful woman he had ever seen. *And used to be the sweetest. What the hell happened?* He was afraid of the answer, knowing it revolved around Adam.

He wanted to drag her over to him and demand she tell him everything. Why had she and Adam rushed a marriage? Why had she intimated her marriage was not happy? Why, even with Adam just buried, was she getting rid of everything that belonged to him? But she was right. Because of his selfish desire to protect his heart from seeing them together, he had separated himself from their friendship.

He walked to the door before turning and piercing her with his stare. "You're right, Dani. I fucked up big time. In more ways than you know by not telling you what was in my heart when I went overseas. And then again when I selfishly stayed away once I came back." He noticed her head cocked to the side in confusion as she listened to his attempted confession. "Right now, you're hurting and my being here only seems to make it worse. So I'll leave." Stepping back to her, stopping only when his large cowboy boots were right in front of her small, grey sneakers, looking down at her upturned face with the little row of freckles across her nose that made him want to nuzzle her, he said, "But this isn't over. You need time. Time to figure out what all you're feeling right now. But babe, I'm only a phone call away. And whether or not you like it, I'll be keeping an eye on you."

Before she could reply, he leaned down and kissed the top of her head, then turned and walked out of the front door.

Dani stood motionless, watching Chad walk away. Her heart pounded a staccato in her chest as she lifted one shaking hand to brush back a strand of hair falling across her face. As his retreating back moved toward his truck parked on the street, she battled the desire to run after him, begging him to stay and make the fucked up situation better. Or at least more tolerable. *My gentle giant. At least he used to be.* But her head won the battle over her battered heart, and she remained motionless until his truck drove away.

Her neighbor came through with another box and glanced her way. "You okay, Miss Danielle?"

His words jolted her out of her inner war. Looking over at him guiltily, she mumbled, "Yes. Yes, I'm fine. Are we about finished?"

"Yes, ma'am. This is the last box from the bedroom. My men packed things according to your instructions and we've labeled them accordingly. All of Adam's personal belongings have been boxed separately. We boxed your clothes and everything in the bathroom you set aside and put them in your car, just as you said. We loaded the mattress and box springs, and the upholstered rocking chair, since you wanted to take that with you. Kitchen items are labeled as well so that once we've delivered everything to the storage unit you've directed us to, then you should be able to find things quick enough."

Attempting a smile, she nodded and replied, "Thank you, Mr. Tibbons." While she gladly walked away from the mattress she had shared with Adam, the one in the guest room was hers before the marriage. She planned on using it when she found a new home. The cushy rocking chair had been in her family for three generations. Her mother had been rocked in it, as well as she. She hoped to use it some day, so it was staying with her.

All the other furniture was part of their rental agreement.

The man looked at her closely, causing her to fiddle awkwardly with her hair again. She hoped he would not say anything else, but luck was not on her side today. *Hell, luck hasn't been on my side in a long time.*

"I hope you know what you're doing, Miss Danielle. Packing up the day after your husband's funeral sounds a mite hasty to me. Are you sure you won't regret this?"

Fighting the urge to tell him to mind his own business, she forced herself to smile. "No, Mr. Tibbons. I promise you, I won't regret this. To be honest, I was never very happy in this house." *Or marriage,* she wanted to add, but refrained. "I have called the storage facility in Richmond. Actually, it's on the western side of town, near where my parents live so it should be convenient for you to get to. Once there, just place all of Adam's belongings toward the back, if you will. The odds and end furniture can go in next and then anything labeled kitchen, books, or mine can be near the front."

Nodding, Mr. Tibbons stuck out his hand. "Will do."

"Thank you so much," she said sincerely, her hand still grasped in his.

"Miss Danielle, you don't have to thank me. You did my family real good when momma had a stroke. My wife always said you were a saint." With that, he turned and walked back to the truck. After securing the load, he climbed in. He and his assistant pulled out of her driveway, leaving her very much alone.

Dani closed the front door before walking into the kitchen to pull out a lone water bottle from the refrigerator. The cold liquid poured down her raw-from-crying throat and soothed her nerves. She wandered through the house one last time, glancing into each room to make sure everything was gone. It was. *Who am I kidding? I just want one more tortuous walk through to remind me of what I thought I had...and what a mess I've made of my life.*

She glanced out onto the small wooden deck, complete with an old gas grill provided by the owners of the house. Adam had sworn they would have lots of cookouts, but she only remembered one time he invited some buddies over. *He preferred going out.* The spare bedroom had rarely been used for anything other than storage. The bathroom had been cleaned—she threw his toiletries away last night in a fit of rage after the wake.

She looked into the master bedroom, her eyes naturally going to the bed, stark and bare without the colorful comforter she had loved. *Adam had been a gentle lover, if somewhat unadventurous. Must have saved that for his women on the side.* She closed her eyes for a moment, the agony of what went on in that room threatening to overwhelm her to the point of falling, catatonic to the floor. *In...out... in...out.* She breathed deeply until the emotion passed, once more replaced with resolution.

Checking the closets, she walked to the front of the house. The living room, kitchen, and dining room looked the same as the day they moved in. Adam had been full of promises. Shaking her head, she almost smiled. *Why did I expect a leopard to change his spots? He had been full of it alright...just not full of promises he could keep.*

Closing the door behind her with a resounding click, she walked to her car refusing to look any more at the memories and regret slamming into her. Pulling out of the driveway, she sucked in a deep breath once again battling the threatening tears. Dashing them away, she maneuvered to the highway taking her to her Richmond, and her parents' house, until she could find a new place to live. *One devoid of any reminders of the past...and that includes Chad.* At least the last part of that wish was what she tried to convince herself.

3

Two days later Chad arrived at the Saints' compound located on Jack's property. Driving through the security gate after entering the code, he breathed deeply as the first peace in almost a week slid over him. The familiar long driveway through mature trees, then coming into the clearing where Jack's house stood with the Blue Ridge Mountains in the background, eased a tension headache he had sported since leaving Dani. Late winter gave way to early spring and the green buds on the trees mixed with the evergreens gave the land a fresh coat of green paint. Parking his old jalopy next to the other trucks and SUVs in front of Jack's house, he bounded up the front steps to the wide porch.

Jack's wife, Bethany, looked up in surprise as he entered. "Chad, I didn't expect you back so soon. Welcome home." The pretty blonde, exuding a girl-next-door beauty, moved from her desk in the corner of the living room toward him, arms outstretched. She wrapped her arms around him in a genuine hug. “I’m so sorry about your friend,” she said, looking up into his face, her eyes searching. “I can tell how difficult this is for you.”

Giving her a squeeze, he shook his head. “Just tired from a long, and not very pleasant, journey.”

She moved to the kitchen where she plated some cobbler. “You can take it on down. They’ve already had theirs,” she grinned.

Smiling in return, he took the offered treat and made his way down the stairs to the secure working area for the Saints. The compound consisted of a spacious conference room complete with computer equipment, monitoring screens for the security aspect of the business, secure video conferencing equipment used for the many virtual meetings with government officials, and then Luke’s station where he managed to hack into most systems needed. Smaller rooms were filled with ammunition, weapons, safety equipment, and just about anything else they might need. A locker room, complete with bunk beds, was in another area for times when they worked around the clock at the compound. The back stairs led to a garage entrance.

The other Saints looked up as he came in. Jack, their no-nonsense leader, cocked his head in Chad’s direction. “You okay? You didn’t say much when you called to say you were back and would be here today." The normally taciturn boss gazed at Chad with concern in his expression.

Chad slid into his seat, his face filled with honest emotion. Raw. Painful.

Cam, a former undercover police detective, leaned forward resting his forearms on the table as he peered at Chad. "Don't play poker, bro. Your face tells a story and it's not a good one."

Chad nodded, saying, "Yeah, well, when trying to defuse a bomb, you don't exactly have to hide your intentions from it." He chuckled as he thought of the different roles they played. Cam's face gave away nothing. The large, Hispanic man had grown up in the gangs of El Paso and could break into any place needed. In contrast, his best friend Bart's, easy-going manner belied the former SEAL's stealth and strength.

Luke poured Chad a cup of his potent coffee and, sitting it down in front of him, said, "Looks like you need my special brew."

"Jesus, Luke. That strong shit'll keep him up for days," Marc joked, "He looks like he needs sleep." The former CIA pilot was at home in the wilds and had no trouble cooking over an open campfire, but he was awed and a little intimidated by Luke's complicated coffee maker.

"You're just jealous because I brew the best shit, as you call it," Luke retorted, his hair already ruffled from running his hand through it as the caffeine did its job. The former CIA computer analyst and resident hacker could find anything the Saints needed when it came to information. His people skills were slightly off kilter, but with a computer, he was a genius.

Chad looked at Monty, the dapper, former FBI agent. "You and Angel okay?" When the call had come to Chad about Adam's death, the Saints were just finishing an assignment involving three murdered women and the attempted murder of a fourth—Monty's girlfriend.

"Yeah, thanks, man," Monty responded. "Her new bakery is up and running, and she moved into my place...for now." The others laughed and Monty continued, "I know, I know. But we'll wait a bit before looking to buy something."

"Glad to hear it," Chad acknowledged. He looked around at his friends and co-workers. Only six months ago, they had all been single. Now Jack was married to Bethany, the cabin rental owner next door. Cam married Miriam, a nurse who was his rescue mission from last fall. Bart was now engaged to Faith, the pretty woman with the gift of sight that helped them on a kidnapping case last Christmas. Jude, another former SEAL, was engaged to Bart's cousin, Sabrina. And Monty, the serious one of the group, was living with Angel, his exact opposite and owner of Angel's Cupcake Heaven.

Not many of us still single. Don't think that'll change for me anytime soon.

Blaise walked into the room, his hands up in apology. "I'm sorry to be late. Daisy's close to giving birth and I wanted to make sure she was fine before I left." He looked over, seeing Chad. "Hey, man. Sorry to hear about your friend."

Chad nodded once more, glad his friends truly cared, but thought, *I'll be glad when the condolences are over.* Plastering on a smile, he acknowledged, "Your dog doing okay?"

Blaise, a veterinarian, formerly with DEA, more at ease with animals than people, smiled. "Yeah, for a mutt found abandoned on my street, she's a sweetie. Seems to be doing great and I should have puppies in the next day or so."

Jack, turning the conversation back to business, quickly went over the new assignments. When they were not involved in a case large enough for all of them to be working on, they divided the security installations and monitoring. The Saints did not handle personal or small-business security. They left that for the numerous other companies with the ability to perform the task. The Saints were called in when large companies or government agencies needed computer, building, or personnel security.

"After solving Senator Creston's daughter's murder and the subsequent murders that went along with that case, we have some down time. Work on your assignments as they come and we'll meet back here at the end of the week."

Chad spoke up, "Before we leave, Jack, I wanted to ask if you had an objection to me investigating a little into the explosion that killed my friend." He hastened to say, "I know the FBI and ATF are on it, obviously, but I'd like to keep up on their investigation."

Jack eyed the Saint with the biggest heart, seeing the pain etched on his face. "I've got no objection at all. I've read the preliminary report..."

Chad nodded, continuing, "The initial investigation puts it squarely in the terrorist camp. It's one thing to know ISIS has a long arm into this country, with cells everywhere. But it's different when someone you know was killed by them. And in this country. The agencies are looking to find out what they can about whoever was in that house and what other places they may be located waiting to blow the shit out of the next unsuspecting person." His passionate speech over, he leaned heavily back in his chair, rubbing his hand over his face.

"You mentioned your friend had a wife. How's she holding up?" Marc asked.

Chad looked around the table seeing nothing but concerned faces. He shook his head, "I honestly don't know. I fucked things up a long time ago with her and it doesn't look like I'll be unfucking them anytime soon."

The others wisely kept quiet, knowing Chad would share more, if and when, he decided to. Walking over to Luke as the group headed up the stairs, he asked, "Can you set me up with some general surveillance on my laptop?"

"Sure," Luke answered, not questioning why Chad made such a request. "What do you need?"

"I'd like to be able to keep tabs on Danielle Houston Turner. Nothing too intrusive, just..." he shook his head, "I guess that's an oxymoron, right? Non-intrusive surveillance."

Chuckling, Luke agreed. "No worries, man. You want to make sure Adam's widow is okay. What are you looking for?"

"Just her address and if she changes her phone number. And employment. Our friendship is...I guess you could say strained at best. I want to make sure she's okay even if I'm the last person on earth she wants to be around."

Luke peered closely at his friend, seeing grief as well as regret. "You got it, man. I'll get it set up today."

Slapping Luke's shoulder in thanks, Chad headed up the stairs after the others.

"Honey, are you sure you don't want any dinner?"

Dani closed her eyes for a moment, loving her parents' concern...and hating her parents' concern. She would have never considered moving back into her childhood home if she had not been desperate to get out of the house she shared with Adam.

Taking a deep breath, she replied, "I'm sure, mom. I'll eat a bite later when I feel like it." The truth was her stomach had been churning since she first received the call about Adam's death. Moving from the den, out to the sunporch, she sat on the glider letting the swaying motion ease her tension.

She loved the glassed-in porch, the sun beating down creating a warmth enveloping her even though the early spring day was cool. It seemed she was unable to get warm. The cold of the funeral had seeped into her bones and nothing gave comfort. Sipping a cup of hot tea, she closed her eyes, allowing her mind to flow with thoughts...memories.

Had it only been less than two years since she, Chad, and Adam met and formed the odd Three Musketeers? At first, it was so obvious Adam wanted to get into her pants and equally as obvious Chad did not want him to. Once she made sure Adam knew that was not going to happen, the three became friends. Her office was not in the same location as theirs, but she lived close enough for them to hang out whenever they could.

Turning her face up to the sun, she remembered the day Chad told her he was going to take a six- month overseas assignment. Sighing, the crushing weight of the day he left, as though it was yesterday, pressed down on her.

Taking him to the airport that morning, my heart ached. Six months! Why did that seem like forever? He turned and smiled, giving me that endearing expression of his. I cared for him as a good friend. As a fellow ATF agent. And more? Yeah, I wish there was more. Some-

told he did not suffer but had died instantly. *Thank God.* As angry as she had been at him the past week, she still cared for him. He was a good agent and deserved better than to be blown up in a terrorists' home-making bomb lab.

Swallowing hard, she opened her eyes again, now focusing on the tall, dark haired man with his arm around her. Chad. Her gentle giant. His face had been memorized over time, once dreaming it would be hers. *What would my life be like if I'd told him what was in my heart before he left to go to Afghanistan? If only I'd told him that I was in love with him? If only he'd said the words back to me?* Sighing, she traced his face in the photograph with her finger slowly. *What was it grandma used to say? Oh, yeah. The two saddest words in the world are...If only.*

Placing the picture back into the box, she tiptoed to her bedroom, crawling into bed. Sleep still did not come for hours and when it did, dark dreams followed her into slumber.

4

THREE MONTHS LATER

Chad had checked his watch as he walked into his kitchen to turn on the coffee maker. Unlike Luke, he was fine with the coffee pods. He stood at the kitchen sink, staring out into his back yard, watching the sunrise over the tops of the trees. Hearing a noise, he turned and walked to the front door. A quick look confirmed what he assumed and he threw open the door to Marc.

"Come on back," he called out, as he moved into the kitchen.

"I see you cut a few trees," Marc commented as he reached for the travel mug of coffee. "Looks good."

"Yeah, I've been trying to take care of some work on the house on our down days. The last winter storm really took a toll on a few of them."

Chad had bought a fixer-upper when he began working for the Saints and between the house and the yard, he always had a project going. Marc had bought property not too far from Jack's and began building his own home. Chad had not been that enthusiastic about starting from scratch, but loved the projects on the old farm-style home situated on five acres.

"Let me know the next time you're cutting trees," Mark said. "I'll come over and help."

Chad knew Marc was making an honest offer. The natural outdoorsman would love nothing more than spending a Saturday cutting trees. Setting the alarm, the two men got into Marc's truck and drove to the Saints' compound. The conversation was easy, mostly sports and what the group had been working on recently.

"Any idea why Jack called the meeting?" Marc asked.

Chad shook his head, and said, "Not sure, but I've got a bad feeling with all that's going on." The intelligence community news was rife with the new ISIS cells popping up all over the country. "I wouldn't be surprised at all to find us being tasked for investigations by either the FBI again or even ATF." Looking over at Marc, he continued, "Can't say as that would bother me since I was looking into it anyway."

Pulling up to the large house, the two went inside and hustled down to the command center, finding most of the others already there. Small talk ensued until the last of the Saints arrived and Jack immediately got down to business.

Jack nodded toward Luke, who patched them

into a video-conference with Mitch Evans, the local FBI agent that had worked with the Saints on several cases. Greetings were made and then Mitch began.

"The FBI and ATF have been working together to ferret out the ISIS cells that are cropping up everywhere. One of the new things that the terrorists are doing is using houses in normal neighborhoods, some in Virginia, and setting up bomb building centers. Chad, I understand that this used to be your territory before working for the Saints."

Luke panned the camera around and focused it on Chad. "Yes, I've been with the Saints for almost a year now, since I came back from the assignment in Afghanistan."

Mitch nodded and added, "I know your former partner was killed by one of these setups. I'm sorry."

Chad accepted his condolences. The grief over losing Adam was still very real.

"My contact at the ATF, Roscoe Barnes, has alerted me to the fact that more and more setups, like what killed Agent Turner, are cropping up all over the place. But that's only part of why I'm here. It's the newest development that has both the FBI and the ATF concerned. Terrorists are becoming more sophisticated in how they detonate these bombs. Remote detonation is nothing new, but they're getting their hands on more sophisticated technology making it easier for the bombs to be detonated from a distance. On top of that, they are using newer explosives that are easy to make, but highly unstable...and very hard to detect."

The Saints, always alert, became even more so. Chad, his nerves tight, leaned forward, eager to hear how Jack's company might be of service.

Mitch continued. "The FBI has discovered that ISIS is recruiting computer loners...geeks if you will...to develop munitions detonation software that will work from a distance. It appears they're aggressively recruiting a particular profile of person."

Luke sent the information to the Saints' tablets, as Mitch added, "They're looking for computer software experts, often still in college, or just out and without employment. They're targeting the loner, non-social person who needs money."

"How are they targeting these people?" Monty asked. The former FBI agent had worked on murder cases, but not terrorist threats.

Mitch shook his head and said, "You wouldn't believe it."

Monty, quick-minded, bit out, "Dating sites. They're using dating sites."

Nodding, Mitch agreed. "Yep, they're looking at on-line dating sites and finding just the type of person they want to recruit. At one time we just had to worry about the Chinese fucking with us by using the internet to gain information and access... now, even the smaller terrorist groups are gaining this information from social media."

"Hell," Bart said, leaning back in his chair. "I

never thought about what those sites could be used for."

Luke piped up, "The internet is going to be used as a way of mass destruction one day if the terrorists have their way."

"So what exactly are they doing?" Chad interrupted. He knew Luke, who lived and breathed computers, could go on a rant, for hours, about the lax security most companies had.

"They find those that fit the profile they're looking for. They engage them in online discussions, then usually rope them in with money or promises of women. We don't have hard evidence about their operation, but that's why we've contacted the Saints."

Jack looked at his group and said, "I've accepted a contract with the US Government, through the combined FBI and ATF task force. We'll be working on gathering intel on these new operations and when we find them, visit recruits to obtain the computer information that's needed to shut them down. We'll also be getting surveillance on some of the sites that may be used for bomb making."

As usual, when Jack announced a new major mission the room resounded with a chorus of *fuck yeahs,* and this time was no different. Jack turned back to the cameras, saying, "Mitch. Looks like you're working with the Saints again."

The agent chuckled before adding, "Good to be working with you again. I've sent my preliminary intel to Luke."

The Saints looked to Jack for instruction. "To begin with, you'll be going out in teams to cities where the newest identified persons that have been recruited are located. Luke will stay here, working on a program to scramble some of the dating sites they have been known to use. It appears they avoid the major ones and use lesser-known sites. Once they've made a contact, then the terrorists begin the integration."

"What does that entail?" Cam asked. His background came from police undercover experience with gangs, not terrorists.

"Once a contact has been brought into the fold and begins to work on a project or accept any money, then it's hard for them to stop because of the threats held over their heads," Monty explained.

Mitch rubbed his chin, looking disconcerted for a moment before saying, "Chad, I need to ask you about your former partner. I know this may seem public, but I thought this was easier than bringing you in for questioning."

At that, Chad sat up straight in his chair, senses alert. "What do you need to know?"

"We've come into some intelligence that indicated Adam was involved somehow. We don't know how, or to what extent, but wanted to ask you about it."

Chad's face grew red with controlled anger. "Are you implying Adam Turner worked for terrorists?"

"No, I'm not. But I'm telling you that his name

came up in the investigation. We don't have proof he was involved, investigating things himself, or what. We simply know at this time that his name came up from one of the cells we're investigating."

"Adam Turner was many things, but a traitor was not one of them!" Chad growled. "He could be rash, a jokester, and..." he almost said *a man who couldn't keep his dick in his pants*, but chose to not divulge that bit of personal information. Sucking in a deep breath, he continued, "I'd stake my life that he was not involved in anything untoward."

Mitch nodded, saying, "I've read reports on him and think you're right, but he could be a loose cannon at times and the fact that his name was mentioned in an intelligence report...well, it didn't look good."

The video-conference came to a close, but Chad's mind rushed with thoughts. *Adam? Why the hell would his name come up in conjunction with a terrorist? Was it because he'd been killed?* Running his hand over his face, he heaved a sigh. *Whatever Adam was as a man...working with terrorists certainly had not been one of them!*

Looking up, he realized the other Saints had grown quiet staring at him. "You okay, man?" Marc asked.

"Yeah." Grunting, he amended, "No. I mean, what the fuck?" He looked around the table and said, "Adam was like a brother. We were the closest of friends for almost three years. Trained together. Worked together. Drank together. ATF agents working on bomb diffuses were just like a team in the military. Tight. No way would he be involved in anything like this."

Blaise, with his typical anti-social aplomb, said, "You indicated when you came back from the special assignment overseas, you separated from your friendship with him. Maybe you sensed something then?"

"No!" Chad growled, then shook his head in frustration. "It had nothing to do with his work...or mine. It was...I needed a change and...oh hell."

The silence in the room was strangely comfortable. Chad knew the other Saints were not judging...only waiting. For the right words to come from him in their right time. He let his gaze roam around the table and saw nothing but good men. Men he trusted with his life. Like Adam.

"The short and dirty story is there was a fellow female agent and the three of us were good friends. Only I screwed up and fell in love with her. There wasn't time, before I left, to explore what might have been since I agreed to take the overseas assignment. But I thought there was still time when I came back. I thought her feelings leaned that way too, but I pussied out and never told her."

He paused and realized that he should feel embarrassed by talking about this to his co-workers, but these men were also friends. And he felt their acceptance. "You probably don't have to guess where the fucked up story goes next. I came home and Adam had married the woman I loved. I was blown away, but since I never told her before I left, I can hardly say I was betrayed. I visited with them when I got back, but just couldn't handle it." Emitting a chortle, he shook his head. "I realized I couldn't continue to be his partner and see them together every day, so I quit the ATF and found the Saints."

He pierced Jack with a hard stare. "You asked me in the interview a year ago why I wanted to leave the ATF. What I told you was true. Almost three years in and I was tired of the bullshit. You thought I only meant the bureaucracy...I did, but I was also speaking of the personal relationships that were fucked up. I never regretted the move...best goddamn decision I made."

He then moved his piercing stare around the table to every single Saint before continuing. "But I'll stake my reputation and my life that Adam Turner was not working with terrorists."

The silence continued for a few seconds before Marc proclaimed, "Good enough for me, bro." The others followed in unison.

Taking the meeting back under control, Jack said, "Let's work the problem, men. We've got assignments to divide among the group and to do some reconnaissance." The meeting continued, but Chad had to force himself to focus. His mind was still on Adam's possible involvement...and what that would mean for Dani.

Dani walked out of her office to head to a meeting down the hall. Leaving the ATF and working for the Marsden Energy Systems and Munitions Plant had been a good decision. The job did not pack the immediate punch that her ATF investigator position had, but the pay was good, work was steady, and they were thrilled to hire the former officer. With her background and knowledge in explosives and detonators, she was hired to work in their Military sales department.

In the past couple of months, she finally came to grips with Adam's infidelities. They had started as friends and she knew they should have left their relationship that way. She missed his company...his smile...but realized her heart was only wounded, not broken.

"Hey, Danielle," Aaron greeted.

She turned and smiled at her counterpart, the person in charge of the Industry sales department. While she worked with the military side of the business, he was responsible for selling the explosives to private companies, such as road constructions, mines, quarries and others who needed their products.

"Hi, Aaron," she returned his friendly smile. The tall blond, with his ready grin had quickly become one of her favorite co-workers. He and his wife had invited her out a few times and she appreciated the offer of friendship. The past three months had not been easy, starting over. She thought when she left college and began working at ATF her lonely days were over. Now here she was, in her late twenties beginning a new life... again. New home, new job, new career.

Only a couple of former girlfriends from her past were still friends...the ones she believed did not know about Adam's philandering. Even if their marriage had not been one of great love, he had sworn to be faithful. And failed.

As always, her mind wandered to Chad, torn between hating him for not being there for her and wishing—

"You're lost in thought," Aaron said, laughing.

Blushing, she responded, "Oh, I'm sorry. You're right, my mind is all over the place right now. What did you say?"

"I was wondering if you had any experience, when you were with the ATF, with the detonation studies for the latest SMC's robot model. I thought I'd read where the ATF did some studies with the company. I've got a meeting with them next week and I wanted your input."

Dani scrunched her face in thought before admitting, "That sounds familiar but the reports would be about five months old. I...well, I have a bunch of things in storage from when I was with the ATF. I'll search for you."

"I don't want it to be a bother," he said.

"Oh, no bother. To be honest, I've needed to get into the storage unit for a while. I can easily go after work."

"By the way, Melissa wanted me to ask if you'd

like to meet us for dinner this Saturday night. We're going to Stella's, to celebrate our tenth anniversary.

Dani smiled, secretly envious of their successful relationship. "I hardly think you want company on your anniversary," she joked.

"Oh, this'll be some friends getting together. She and I'll celebrate alone later."

She eyed him suspiciously. "Friends? Why do I get the feeling that's code for trying to fix me up with someone?"

Throwing his hands up, he laughed. "Hey, don't blame me if Melissa is a secret matchmaker. But honestly, it's just some friends. It'll be fun."

"Okay," she finally agreed. "I'll run by the storage unit today, but it may take a day or two before I can locate the information for you. The studies would be public record, but I'd need to look them over again before I can give you my personal take on them. This gives me the push to do what I've needed to do anyway. I need to move the rest of my boxes to my house."

"Perfect," he said, "We'll see you tomorrow."

Continuing down the hall, Dani walked into a large conference room for a meeting. Her discussion with Aaron made her a few minutes late and she slid into the closest chair. Todd Marsden, president of Marsden Energy Systems, smiled her way. His daughter, Cybil, was presenting a report and Dani quickly began taking notes.

The door opened again and Jahfar Khouri

slipped into the seat next to hers. Glancing over with a smile, she continued to take notes. He seemed flustered, having not brought his tablet with him...or even a pad and pen to write with. Leaning over, he whispered, "Can I acquire the notes from you later? I forgot we had this meeting today."

She nodded silently, wondering what had the usually unflappable man so distracted. Looking to the other side of the table, Cybil's fiancé, one of the plant managers, Ethan Petit, was staring at Jahfar. Dani's mind wandered momentarily, thinking, *I wonder why Ethan is glaring?*

As the lights came back up after Cybil's presentation, Dani startled and looked down at her notes. *Thank God, I paid attention to most of the speech.* She turned to Jahfar, blushing, and admitted, "My mind wandered at the end, but I can email the notes that I have to you later today."

He smiled, saying, "That's perfect, Danielle." His dark eyes cut over toward Ethan's and he said, "I've...um, I need to be going. Talk to you later." He stood up with the others and hustled out of the room.

Staring at his back, she jumped when a hand touched her shoulder.

"You okay?" Ethan asked, concern in his eyes.

"I'm fine," she smiled up at him, as she pushed her chair back to stand. He was handsome, in a stylish way, and she could see why he had caught Cybil's eye.

"I wanted to tell you that you're doing a really good job here. We were glad to get you."

"Thank you," she replied, her gaze moving to Cybil and Todd as they made their way over as well.

The group of four chatted for a few minutes before Cybil and Ethan headed down the hall. Turning to Todd, she smiled, saying, "I want to thank you for allowing me the chance to be a part of Marsden Energy Systems."

Taking her hand, Todd replied, "Danielle, I will echo what Ethan said—MES was lucky to employ you. How are you settling in?"

"Two months in and I've learned a lot," she answered. "Just when I think I know what I'm doing something new crops up."

Laughing, Todd admitted, "I'm the one who took this ammunition business over from my father and grew up in the trenches...and I still learn things."

"Then that definitely makes me feel better," she said, smiling as they walked out of the room. Saying goodbye, she walked down the hall to her office. Her heels clicked on the tile floors and she smoothed the pencil skirt over her legs. She enjoyed dressing up for work, something she never did with the ATF. *But for how long?* she wondered.

Entering, she sat down in her chair, leaning over with her keys in hand to unlock the bottom drawer where she left her purse. The drawer was partially open. Pulling it all the way open quickly, she breathed a sigh of relief seeing it still there.

Lifting her large purse into her lap, she dropped her wallet into it then noticed her cosmetic bag was opened and the contents spilled out.

Her years as an investigator with the ATF had her on alert. Carefully going through her purse, she did not find anything missing, but the idea that someone had gone through it took root. She hesitated but hated calling security, since nothing was missing and her desk lock did not appear tampered with. *Maybe I really am losing my mind!*

5

Chad's feet pounded the ground in a familiar rhythm as he ran along the perimeter of Jack's property. A great place to keep in shape, it also doubled as a way to keep a check on the expensive security equipment in place. Having trained for the ATF bomb squad, he had run in full gear, weighing over seventy-five pounds, so running with no extra weight felt light as air.

Winding through a dense copse of trees, he glanced down, easily maneuvering the protruding roots. The back of the acreage sat at the base of the Blue Ridge Mountains and he began to climb slightly. The oak and maple trees created a complete canopy overhead. Moss and fern grew beside a small stream and he heard steps directly behind him. Jude came alongside and, without speaking, the two ran companionably together for several more minutes.

Jack kept his property in top shape, so the

weekly runs were good for maintenance of both body and mind, as well as scoping out the perimeter. The two came upon Bart and Cam as they rounded the bend heading back to the house.

"Weather's great for this," Cam remarked, enjoying the spring sunshine. "Although the humidity sucks."

"You wimp," Bart joked. "Hell, me and Jude would have considered this to be a walk in the park when we were SEALs."

Jude laughed his agreement, his blond curls plastered to his head with sweat.

"Well, fucking sorry I wasn't in your Navy," Cam said jokingly. "But growing up in El Paso, hell, the heat there makes this seem like heaven."

The banter continued as they made their way around the house and toward the deck, seeing the others already there. Water bottles sitting in an ice chest pulled their attention. Guzzling the refreshing liquid, the group cooled off in the shade as they reported their perimeter checks to Jack. Chad leaned over the railing and poured some of the water over his head to cool off, before giving his head a shake. A few of the others followed suit, dousing themselves to combat the heat of the day.

"You've got a tree down on the east perimeter, about five klicks due east," Blaise reported.

"Camera in the west corner needs to be checked. Some kind of ivy shit is growing on the tree. Not interfering yet, but by summer, it'll be a problem," Marc added.

Jack made notes on his tablet. "Got it. I'll grab the chainsaw and we'll work on it after the briefing." He looked around the group. "When I first bought this place, I wanted to set up a state-of-the-art security system around it. Figured to some it was overkill, but I knew that, one day, it would be needed. Up till now, the biggest threat was some hiker getting lost and strolling around where I didn't want them."

"Like Bethany?" Blaise asked, his eyebrow raised and a smirk on his face.

The others laughed, having been witness to Jack's first meeting with his now wife. "Yeah, no more wanderers." Jack looked into the distance, taking in the various greens covering the mountains. The flashes of color from redbud and dogwood trees broke through the almost solid greens. Sucking in a deep breath of fresh air, he said, "Change is coming, men. I understood it then. I feel it now."

The others, quietly listening to their laconic leader, knew what he was saying. They felt it too.

"The world has changed. Gone are the days when we knew our enemies. Gone are the days when those of us in the military fought overseas against the ones who would threaten our country. Now the enemy has slipped into our borders and creeps toward our very foundations."

"Something new come in?" Monty asked.

"We've got the official go-ahead to pursue whatever threats we uncover. I anticipate within a week or so, some of you will be flying to different cities to bring back the proof of what some of the new recruits are working on. Not going over that today, but just know it's coming." Slapping his hands on his knees, he stood and said, "Tomorrow night, we'll be at Stella's, celebrating Bart's upcoming wedding. Now...we cut up a fallen tree."

With *hell yeahs* ringing through the air, the men headed off to work on the grounds. Soon the sight of shirtless, muscular, sweating men filled the view. Bethany looked out the window, nearest to her computer, where she continued to work on the marketing of her wedding venue next door. Smiling at the sight of her husband, Jack, and the other Saints had her thinking she must have the best job in the world.

Dani used her security code to drive into the All-Safe Storage facility. As she walked past the office to make her way to her unit, the manager called out.

"Miss? Miss?"

Turning around, she saw the young, scraggly young man hustle over to her. "We've got a memo that I've been working on but don't have it out yet."

She waited patiently while he jogged over to the desk. Picking up a piece of paper, he walked back to hand it to her. Her eyes scanned the letter first, then lifted them to him for further explanation. He simply stood, smiling at her.

"Um, do you want to explain further?" she queried.

His brow furrowed in confusion. "Don't that letter tell what happened?"

"It says that there was an attempted break-in to the facility and the cameras showed the person making it to Section 2B before the alarms sounded and they left."

"Yep, that's what happened," the young man said proudly.

Lifting her eyebrow, she counted, not so patiently, to ten. "My unit is in Section 2B. Why was I not notified about this?"

"But you are being told. That's what I'm doing now," he said, confusion mixed now with irritation on his face.

"Yes, but this letter doesn't say when it occurred. I should have been told immediately."

"But it just happened last night," he protested. "I can't do nothin' without the big guys at corporation telling me what to do."

"Last night? Did you turn the security tapes over to the police?"

"Huh? Well, yeah, I guess," he answered. "Some man came this afternoon and got 'em. But they were messed up, so I don't think the tapes'll do 'em much good."

"Some man? Did he show identification?"

"Huh?" he asked again.

Oh, fuck. Save me from incompetence. Sucking in a deep breath, she asked, "How do you know who you turned them over to if the person did not show you a badge?"

"Well, why would someone come in and ask for the tapes if they weren't no police? Anyway, I ain't seen no regulation that says I can't give it out."

I'm pretty sure there's a regulation, buddy, but realizing she was getting nowhere with her investigative, suspicious mind, she smiled and thanked him for the letter. *I'm checking my unit and then I'll call the police myself. Or maybe one of my FBI buddies.*

Her heels clicking along was the only sound heard as she made her way down the long, empty hall of the indoor, climate-controlled storage facility. Turning onto Section 2B, she looked up at the security cameras in the corners. *Unless they are state-of-the-art cameras, my unit in the center of the hall would not be very protected.* Arriving at the door, she realized she had nothing of real value in the unit. *So, why the hell am I concerned? A thief could walk away with everything and I wouldn't care!* Convinced it was just the investigator in her, she unlocked the unit and raised the garage-like metal door.

The scent immediately hit her. The smell of musty cardboard...and Adam's aftershave. She had her possessions and the few bits of furniture moved to her new home last month after two months of living with her parents. The only things left were the few boxes, labeled Adam or Work; she had not been emotionally ready to deal with them then. But now? *I need to go through them, but not here. I need to do this in private.*

She pulled her phone out and called the front desk. “I need you to bring a cart to unit 236 in Section 2B, please. I want to take my last boxes and close out my account.” She paused, listening. “Yes, I’m the lady you just spoke to. Please bring the cart now.” Disconnecting, she pinched the top of her nose in frustration.

In a few minutes, she heard the loud sound of squeaky wheels on tile and was grateful to see the young man rolling a long, flatbed cart toward her. As he arrived, he said, “I’m real sorry, but I ain’t supposed to help with any of your stuff. It’s against corporate policy.”

“No worries,” she assured him. “I’ve lifted much heavier boxes than these. Thank you, though, for bringing the cart.”

She walked in and lifted the first box to place it on the cart, then suddenly it was taken from her hands.

“Oh, hell, miss. My momma didn’t raise me to let a lady lift boxes while I stood around with my thumb up my ass.” He set the box on the cart and went back to get the next one.

She smiled and, between the two of them, they made short work of the six boxes. Thanking him, they pushed the cart together and she stopped at the front desk to complete the paperwork to cancel her rental agreement. Tipping him handsomely, she took the boxes to her car. Using the trunk, back seat, and passenger seat, she managed to pack them in.

She pushed the cart back into the office and the young manager looked up sheepishly. "Sorry, you worked faster than I thought. I was gonna come out and take the cart."

"It's all good," she replied. Thanking him once more, she got into her car and headed home. Appreciating the warm, late spring day, she pulled into her new rental home driveway. Glancing at the box sitting next to her, she thought, *Okay, Adam. Time to go through things. For better or for worse...*

The next morning, glad for the weekend, Dani sat down in the living room filled with Adam's boxes and opened the first one, marked **Clothes.** Assaulted by his scent when she began to pull out the articles of clothing, her throat grew tight as she held back the tears. Sucking in a deep breath, she proceeded to pull them out and place them into piles. One for giveaway; one for throwaway; and one for keeping.

His clean pants, jeans, shirts, and suits went into the giveaway pile. Belts, ties, and shoes went there as well. Underwear, socks, and worn-out clothes went into a garbage bag to throw away. She buried her nose in his soft, ATF t-shirts, remembering times she slipped them on to sleep in.

Keeping a couple of them, she put the others in the giveaway pile.

Hauling the garbage bag to the trash can outside, she dumped it in without a second glance, before returning to the living room. She sat on the floor for a few minutes, amidst the clothing. Leaning her back against the sofa, she opened her mind, allowing the memories to flood. The ones she normally kept dammed, knowing if she did not the emotions would overtake her.

"We'll be fine, you and me. I'll take care of you and it'll all work out," Adam promised, taking her hand.

I rolled my eyes at him, wondering how he thought getting married would make things better. After all, he was hardly the marrying kind. "Adam, this is nuts. You can't be faithful and I can't accept anything less."

He leaned in and kissed my forehead. "Dani, for you, I promise to stop chasing skirts."

I peered into his face and, to my surprise, saw sincerity. "Adam, this isn't how we planned anything to go. I feel like one day you'll wake up and hate me for tying you down."

"Nope, not going to happen. Hey," he joked, "I wanted to bang you the first time I saw you. Now, I get to do it anytime I want."

"God, you're incorrigible," I groused.

"Come on, Dani girl," his voice softened. "Let's do it. Let's make it all legitimate and get married."

I thought about my options. I had some, but what

he was offering made sense. At least at the time. If only I'd waited for a while to see how things would work out. "Okay," I agreed. "We'll get married. But," poking my finger into his chest, "no more girls for you."

"Promise," he whispered just before kissing me.

"Oh, Adam," Dani said in the stillness of my house. "You just couldn't keep that promise, could you?" In the three months since he died, she had come to the conclusion that she was not as pissed at him as she was pissed at the situation. *We fucked up, Adam, you and me. We tried to make something work when there was nothing to build upon.*

Standing up, she rubbed her aching back. Taking the bags of giveaway clothes, she put them inside her car to be dropped off later at the Re-Sale Store. Walking back inside, she grabbed the saved t-shirts off the sofa and carried them to her bedroom. Placing them in the bottom drawer, she did not plan on sleeping in them. *No, they're for memory-keeping. And one day to give to—*

Her phone sounded, alerting her to a text from Melissa, Aaron's wife. **Don't forget tonight. Meet at 7pm at Stella's.**

Going out tonight is the last thing I want to do, she thought, but then realized that after a day of memories she needed to get out of the house. Texting back, **see you then**, she sighed heavily and began to get ready. *Time to learn how to move ahead.*

6

Stella's Restaurant and Bar was in the newly renovated downtown area of Charlestown. When Dani moved from her parents, she thought about moving into Charlestown, but with her new job northwest of Richmond, she wanted to split the difference. Finding a small home in a modest neighborhood near work, she was about twenty minutes from work and about twenty minutes from Charlestown.

Catching a ride with another co-worker, they arrived on time, finding parking easily. Entering the restaurant, Dani immediately appreciated the warm interior. The wall sconces illuminated the reddish tones of the cedar plank paneling. The long bar to the right was of a deeper wood and polished to a high gloss. The crackle glass mirror behind the bar caught the light and refracted it creating a soft glow. She recognized Aaron and

Melissa at the far end of the bar, standing with another man. *Not bad looking...if I was in the market for another man.*

Plastering a smile on her face, she walked over. Greeting Aaron and Melissa, the introductions followed. "Danielle, this is Simon, my cousin."

They shook hands and she noticed his eyes lit up at their introduction. Moving to a table already filled with a few of Aaron and Melissa's other friends she sat down, hoping the evening would go quickly. Ordering a sparkling water, she caught the strange expressions from her tablemates. "Sorry, I've had a...stressful day, and feel like the water will be easier on my stomach." As the conversation flowed, she relaxed. A rather loud group was occupying the back area making hearing difficult. Leaning forward to catch what Melissa was saying, her gaze roved behind her. And caught sight of Chad...staring straight at her. Shifting back rapidly, she tried to still her racing heartbeat, irritated that even after so long the sight of him affected her.

Reminding herself why she was so angry with him, the reason now seemed ridiculous. *If I can separate myself from Adam's betrayals, how can I not do the same with Chad?* Sliding her gaze back to him, she was assaulted with the realization of how handsome he still was. Broad and muscular, compared to the men at her table, she noted he appeared to fit right in with the others at his table.

Suddenly realizing Simon had been speaking to

her, she blushed. "I'm sorry. I seem to be such poor company this evening."

"No worries," Simon said smoothly. "We'll just have to make sure to go out again sometime when you are less stressed."

Offering him a wan smile, she forced herself back into the conversation with her tablemates.

Chad had seen her walk into Stella's. He would recognize those titian colored waves anywhere. Her dress was modest although did nothing to hide her figure. A figure he had dreamed about for almost two years. He watched her move to the bar, where it appeared she was meeting her date for the first time. *Good, he's not a boyfriend.* He had kept up with her secretly. He knew when she landed the job with Marsden Energy Systems and Munitions. He knew it was a good job and she would do well there with her ATF background. He knew when she moved out of her parents' house and into the rental outside of Charlestown. A drive-by assured him, while the neighborhood was modest, it was safe. *Maybe I can't have her, but I can sure as hell try to take care of her from a distance.* He watched as she laughed with her friends and grimaced at the emotional kick in the gut. *Shit, who am I kidding? I want to be the one to make her laugh.*

The Saints and their women were rowdy as they laughed, talked, and celebrated the upcoming marriage of Bart and Faith. Jack, Bethany, Cam, Miriam, Jude, Sabrina, Monty, Angel and the other Saints, some with dates, rounded out the group.

The wedding reception would take place at Bethany's Mountville wedding venue and Angel was providing the gourmet cupcakes in place of the traditional cake. The men could care less about the venue, but knew that Bart's wealthy family would spring for great food and free-flowing alcohol. Chad tried to keep his attention on the Saints' conversations but to no avail. Dani had his full attention.

Faith, sitting next to him with Bart on the other side, leaned over. "I see you're staring at the beautiful woman over there. I sense she's someone important."

Chad looked down at the dark-haired beauty and smiled. "An old friend, you might say."

"I think she's more than that."

Chad stared at Faith, wondering what she saw. Her gift of sight had helped them before on a case and, while she never exploited it, they all learned it was important to listen to her. Sighing, he said, "Yeah, Faith. She was the proverbial one who got away. Or, rather, I let get away. It doesn't matter anymore, I'm afraid. She married someone else and is now a widow, but it didn't end well for us."

"Her eyes keep glancing this way, so I wonder why that is, if she has no interest in you," Faith added. "Perhaps you just need to try harder."

Nodding slowly, he agreed, but had no idea what that *trying harder* would entail. He jolted when Faith put her hand on his arm and realized she had been speaking again. "I'm sorry, Faith. I must be preoccupied."

She laughed gently. "I could tell." Her face sobered as she leaned in, "I sense danger around her, Chad." Her face scrunched in thought as she rubbed her forehead. "Or at least…risk."

By now, the other Saints were listening intently to their conversation. Bart had his arm around his fiancé, pulling her close, recognizing the headaches that appeared after the images took hold of her mind.

Chad jerked his head around, staring at Dani once more, her gaze back on her date. *Danger? Risk?* The idea that Dani could be at risk resonated through him. *If Adam had been involved in something...fuck what am I saying? But if he was, would that now put Dani in jeopardy?*

Miriam's voice pierced his thoughts as the other Saints sat quietly. "I think she may need a friend… now more than ever, Chad. And there's no friend like an old friend." Cam also threw his arm around his wife as her words moved over the group.

Chad asked, "What makes you think she needs a friend, Miriam?"

"There's just a look about her. And even though there could be lots of reasons, I do notice she's drinking water at what appears to be a celebration."

"Huh?" Chad looked over at Miriam in confusion.

She glanced down at the drink in front of her. Water. When everyone else was drinking alcohol.

Then her hand moved over her pregnant belly as Cam's hand landed there as well.

Once more staring at Dani, the idea she could be pregnant slammed into him. *Oh, God. If she's a pregnant widow, she does need help. She does need me... or at least I want her to need me.* Sucking in a deep breath before letting it out slowly, he pushed his seat back. *No more avoidance. We're gonna talk. And we're doing it tonight.* Standing, he bent to kiss the top of Faith's head, then winked at Miriam. With a nod to the rest of the group, he turned and stalked over to Dani's table.

Stopping next to the breathtaking woman, his heart pounding, he called out, "Dani?"

She jumped at the sound of her name from right next to her. She had convinced herself Chad was ignoring her the way she was attempting to ignore him. Plastering a smile on her face, she turned toward him. "Chad," she said in a voice that indicated her politeness was a pretense.

"We need to talk, Dani." He hated the way his words sounded curt, but was not about to back down now. Not this time.

A flare of anger shot through her eyes as she replied, "As you can see, I'm out with friends tonight."

Simon was about to intervene when Chad leaned down and whispered, "Do you really want to have the conversation here? I know your secret, Dani." He knew he was taking a chance, by insinuating she had a secret, but it was worth it when he observed her startle. If he had any doubt about what Miriam intimated, it disappeared the instant he saw Dani's reaction to his words. Her eyes flew open, their green depths wide with surprise...as her hand flew to her stomach.

"How...what..."

Taking her by the elbow, he assisted her up. Reaching for the sweater hanging on the back of her chair, he was halted by Simon's hand.

"Now wait just a minute," Simon said, his face flush with anger. "You can't just come over here and disrupt the lady's evening."

Dani felt the sizzle pouring off Chad and immediately turned to Simon. "No, it's fine. We're old friends." Turning to Aaron and Melissa's surprised faces, she said, "I'm so sorry to leave in a rush, but I do wish you a happy anniversary."

With Chad's firm, but painless, grip on her arm, she was propelled out toward the front door. Glancing back at the table he had left, she noticed the grins from every person sitting there, which only made her angrier. *Who the hell does he think he is?*

"I can hear your thoughts as loud as if you were speaking," Chad said, as he led her to his old truck. "Did you drive?"

"No, I rode with a co-worker. Why?"

"Cause we're taking my vehicle and now I don't have to worry about yours."

"You know, this caveman act isn't quite the

Chad I remember," she quipped as he assisted her into the passenger seat.

He walked around the front and pulled himself in. Turning to look at her face, he recognized the irritation plainly written in her expression, and replied, "A lot has happened in the last year, Dani. Time to get used to the new me."

7

The ride was silent—uncomfortably silent. Dani stewed as she worried her bottom lip. Chad drove with a purpose, and with her mind in a whirl, she barely paid attention. Suddenly, sitting up straight, she noticed he turned into her neighborhood.

"How did you know where I live?" she bit out, surprise overriding her concern.

"I've been keeping tabs."

"Keeping tabs? What the hell does that mean?" She glared as he turned into her driveway, parking behind her car. Jerking her head around, she said, "Oh, yeah. You work for a fancy security company now. I guess spying on people is commonplace to you. Well, listen up, budd—"

He exited the driver's side, slamming the door in the middle of her tirade, walked around and jerked open her door. "Let's go, Dani," he ordered. Seeing her sitting with her arms crossed over her chest, he softened his voice. "Please, Dani. Let's go in and talk. We owe each other at least that."

Secretly agreeing, she nodded. Glaring at his proffered hand for a moment, she relented, allowing him to assist her down from his tall truck. Walking stiffly to the door, she ignored his upturned hand, unlocking the door herself and walking in. Tossing her purse onto the table by the door, she kicked her shoes off, wiggling her toes. She bypassed the living room and walked straight into the kitchen. Continuing to ignore the large man leaning against her kitchen counter, she took out her frying pan and opened the refrigerator. Cracking a couple of eggs, she popped a piece of bread into the toaster.

Looking over at him, she said, "Since you interrupted my dinner before it was served, I assume you don't mind if I eat something."

Sighing, he walked over to the refrigerator and grabbed three more eggs, adding them to the frying pan. "I'm sorry, Dani. I would never keep you from eating. Here..." he gently moved her over to the stool, "let me finish."

Irritated at his take-charge attitude, she mentally shoved it aside as the smell of food wafted through the kitchen. *Hell, it's only scrambled eggs and toast, but I'm starving!*

Looking into the refrigerator again, Chad found the bacon. Grabbing several slices, he placed them on a paper towel and put them in the microwave. Within five minutes, he set the buttered toast, crispy bacon, and cheesy scrambled eggs in front of her with a glass of milk. He smiled, watching as she dug into the food. Taking his plate to the counter, he joined her.

Neither said anything while they ate. Quickly polishing off the simple meal, he made sure she finished the milk before taking her plate to the sink. With a rinse, he put them in the dishwasher before placing the frying pan in the sink.

Dani contemplated, still stunned that Chad was in her house, in her kitchen, and about to delve into her business. *He said he knew my secret. How could he know?* She wanted to be angry, but the sated feeling in her tummy eased her temper. Her thoughts swirled so fast in her mind she missed him walking over to her stool.

"It's time, Dani," his voice caressed.

Sucking in a deep breath, she nodded. It had taken a while, but she had finally come to grips with Adam...his life, their marriage, everything. Her world could hold no more secrets. She led him into her living room and sat down on one end of her sofa. Tucking her legs up under her, she turned to face Chad as he sat on the opposite end. Considering her sofa was not very large, she realized they were actually very close to each other. She could see his blue eyes staring deeply into hers. His strong, clean-shaven jaw. His large body dwarfed her furniture, but he seemed strangely at ease in her house.

"Dani?" he said, watching her jump. Smiling, he

perceived she had been staring at him as much as he could not take his eyes off her.

"Sorry," she mumbled. Looking down to pick at imaginary lint from her dress, she said, "You're the one who wanted to talk, so talk."

Chad sat for a long, silent minute. *Hell, she's right. I wanted to talk and now have no clue what to say.*

"I'm not going to bite, Chad."

He looked up, her face a window to her sadness and the realization stabbed through him. "Dani, I've thought of what I wanted to say to you for so long, but you now make me realize I've been such a horrible friend to stay away from you."

"I didn't exactly make it easy for you when I walked away after Adam's funeral. I was just so... ugh...pissed!"

The silence stretched out once more, this time as both fell back into memories. Finally, Chad spoke, "I need to start back a long time ago. Will you give me that chance?"

Nodding, she shifted to a more comfortable position, finding herself curious to hear what Chad had to say.

"I remember the first time I laid eyes on you two years ago," he began with a smile. "I thought you were the most beautiful woman I'd ever seen." He watched as her face relaxed and her lips curved up slightly. "Adam wanted to fight me for you, but I think he quickly realized you weren't going to be his typical...uh..."

Rolling her eyes, she cocked her head to the side. "If we're going to have this talk, Chad, we're going to have to be totally honest with each other. You forget, I was friends with Adam for a long time before we married. So, believe me, I recognized he was a player when we first met."

Chad nodded, although wistfully at the thought of the trio's friendship several years ago. "We did become good friends, didn't we?"

Dani smiled, the first honest smile she had in a long time. "Yeah, we did."

"That was my first screw-up," he admitted. "While we were friends...I fell for you."

At that, she jerked back, stunned at his words. "You...but you...you never said...anything. Nothing."

"That was my second screw-up. At first, I was afraid to ruin the friendship. Then, when I was about to kiss you that night we were watching the game and Adam left the room, I got the call and was offered the chance to go overseas to help out with the Special Forces again. I knew it wasn't fair to start something with you and then leave for six months. I thought we'd have time when I got back. I figured we'd slip back into our same old friendship and then I'd make my move." Heaving a heavy sigh, he admitted, "Like I said, I screwed up. Then, when I came back, you two were married. I was... shocked. I mean, I never saw that coming. I didn't figure Adam was the marrying type and...damn, it was a punch to the gut."

Dani blinked back tears at the memory of her and Adam meeting him at the airport when he returned from overseas. The two men bear-hugged before Adam let him go and she got a chance to hug him also. Chad had leaned down and whispered in her ear that he had something to share with her, but before he said another word, Adam blurted out that they were married. She remembered the look on Chad's face—stunned...and hurt. And now she understood why.

"Oh Chad, I wish I'd known. I had feelings for you too, but never had a chance to act on them. I was selfishly angry when you left to go overseas. I felt you were walking away from me. I know that wasn't what was really happening...but it felt that way."

"I never asked, Dani, but when did you and Adam fall in love?"

She held her breath, observing his blue eyes carefully as she answered slowly. "We didn't. We were never in love."

She watched as his face registered confusion, followed by disbelief. "I don't understand. If you weren't in love, why did you marry?"

Her gaze shifted to the side, staring at nothing, her mind racing over the past. Sighing, she moved her eyes back to his and admitted. "A reason as old as time." Seeing his still confused expression, she added, "I was pregnant."

This time, Chad reared back, the information overload almost too much to bear.

Before he had a chance to ask more questions, she decided to rip off the emotional Band-Aid. *Painful, but no holding back.*

"I was lonely after you left, Chad. And so was Adam. Oh, he'd joke about it, but I knew deep inside, he missed you. And honestly, I think he was a little hurt that you chose to go back to work with your old military unit instead of staying with him. I know that sounds childish, but he was really envious of your previous military background. You possessed that certain...calm, leadership quality he lacked." She looked up, but saw his jaw was tight, so she plunged ahead.

"We went out one night, drinking. It was stupid," she admitted, her hands twisting in her lap. "We drank too much and made a really bad decision. I don't remember much of the night, but the next morning I woke up in his bed. I did the walk of shame and we tried to pretend it didn't happen. And then? Yep, we were so irresponsible, I got pregnant. My first fear was catching something from one of his many one-night stands, so I got tested immediately." She gave a rude snort, admitting, "Who am I kidding? I was one of those girls."

Chad reached out touching her arm lying on the back of the sofa. "No matter what, Dani...you were never one of those girls. You were miles above anyone else Adam had ever been with. And he would have known that."

She gave a little shrug, sighing once more. "So, I told him about the pregnancy and he suggested we get married. I thought it was crazy. We weren't in love. He wasn't a one-woman man. It was wrong on so many levels. But he kept saying that he didn't want his kid to grow up without a father." After blowing another errant strand of hair out of her face, she leaned over, grabbing her purse and dug around for a moment, finding a hair elastic. With a few sweeps of her hands, she twisted her long hair up into a sloppy bun.

The action appeared to give her peace and he could not take his eyes off her beauty. He tried to imagine her pregnant, confused, upset, and dealing with Adam, who had the emotional maturity of a child at times. He realized what a predicament Dani had been in. *And I, one of her best friends, wasn't around for her to talk to. Hell, if I'd been around, they wouldn't have slept together.*

She continued, "Adam's dad abandoned them when he was very little, and he was adamant we marry. I even told him that I'd never keep him out of his child's life and we didn't need a piece of paper, but he presented a good argument. Or, at least it sounded good at the time. Now, looking back, it sounds pathetic." Seeing Chad's attention still riveted on her, she said, "He said it made sense to get married because he'd never planned on getting married and if he was going to do it, it might as well be with someone he was friends with. And he pointed out that my chances of finding a man who was willing to take on a child were not great." She observed Chad's incredulous expression and grimaced. "Yeah, I know. Hearing myself say that now sounds ridiculous."

"But you got married," he stated simply.

Sighing, Dani nodded. "Justice of the Peace. No church. No fancy dress. No reception. Just two of the biggest idiots in the history of the world getting married." Before he had a chance to argue, she threw her hand up. "I'm not looking for sympathy. We were adults and made a decision."

They were quiet for a moment before she spoke again, her expression full of resignation. "Chad, I've come to accept that there are times in life when we make decisions...based on what seems right at the moment. Sometimes, it's only later when we look back with clarity and see where we made a mistake."

She discerned the emotions cross Chad's face, taking in all of the information. "Since there's no child, you can figure what happened. We were married a month. I was about two and a half months pregnant and had a miscarriage. It was devastating," she choked, losing the battle of the tears. "I was at home, alone. I'd already gone to bed when I started bleeding." She stopped, breathing deeply as she pulled herself together. "I drove to the ER myself since Adam was out late that night. By the time I got ahold of him and he arrived...it was over."

Chad closed the space between them, engulfing her in his embrace. Holding her head against his massive chest, he murmured into her hair while stroking her back. She did not sob. Just silent tears that fell wetting his shirt. After a few minutes, she pulled back and looked up at him. Her moist, green eyes glistened brilliantly. Kissing her forehead, he did not ask any more questions, showing her he would listen when she was ready to talk.

Taking a shuddering breath, she said, "That was one month before you came home. I talked to Adam about getting a divorce since the reason for the marriage was now no longer a necessity. He insisted that he wanted to be with me. Said I made him a better man. Said we could try again for children." Shaking her head, she looked up at Chad, anguish in her eyes. "I know what we did makes no sense. But he really was good to me...or at least I thought so. We didn't fight. We enjoyed the same things. Living with him was actually easy. I was worried about when you came home, wondering how you would take the news, but then I'd convinced myself that you only felt friendship for me. I figured I'd blown any chance with you anyway."

"And I didn't take it very well did I? Dani, I'm sorry. You're right, though. The thought of seeing him with you killed me. There was no way we could go back to being the fun trio again...not when I cared for you the way I did. I assumed you two were happily in love and Adam never let on that you weren't."

The two sat, both reflective in the silence.

"Did you change jobs because of us?" she asked

softly, grabbing a tissue from the end table and wiping her face.

Keeping his arms around her, he said, "Not entirely. It's true that when I came back, I couldn't stand the thought of seeing you two together all the time, so I guess that makes me just as selfish as you said you were. But, it wasn't the only reason. The time back in Afghanistan was...different. I was close to death every time we got near an IED. But it also made me realize that I wanted a change. When one of the Special Forces team members found out I was in Virginia, he told me about a former SF who started his own security business when he got out. I planned on talking to Jack anyway, feeling that my life needed a change. You and Adam being married just made that decision easier."

This time the silence was more comfortable, as though they had slipped back into the same easy camaraderie as before. He squeezed her slightly to regain her attention. "That's my story, Dani, but you've got more to tell me."

"Yeah, I guess I do." She shifted out of his arms and stood, blushing. "I...um, I'll be right back. I need to take a quick break." She walked down the hall to the bathroom and took care of business. Needing to pee often was something she was getting used to again.

Coming back into the room, she stopped in the kitchen, grabbing two water bottles. Walking into the living room, she handed one to Chad as she stepped around his long legs and settled back onto the sofa. Twisting off the cap, she took a sip.

"We stayed married, as I said, because I think we were both too scared to actually admit we'd made a mistake. Adam was good company and I honestly believed that we might make something of our marriage. Friendship, companionship...it didn't sound like a bad basis for us. We fell into a routine, like most couples, though. Work, household chores, yard work. You know, the mundane things that make up life. The problem was that without the love holding it all together, we fell into boring and you know Adam...he never did well with boring."

Shaking her head, she admitted, "I feel like such a fool though. I was the epitome of the wife is always the last to know."

"I had no idea Adam was cheating, Dani, until right at the end. He and I never talked anymore and I had moved to Charlestown. It wasn't until about a couple of months before he was killed. I ran into an old ATF buddy when I was in D.C. interviewing for a case. Adam came up in casual conversation and the guy said Adam was back to his old tricks."

She looked away, pain slashing across her face again. It did not matter that it was old news...it still stung.

"Sorry, babe," he said, hating his words had caused her pain.

Giving her head a little shake, she continued, "I told him that I needed him to be faithful. That I couldn't stand the idea of him being with me after having been with someone else. I told him that he needed to make sure I wouldn't catch anything." Jumping off the sofa, she paced in front of the mantle. "Was that too much to ask? Was marriage to me so horrible that he couldn't keep it in his pants? Jesus, how many people knew and laughed behind my back? Poor little Dani who can't even keep her fucking husband happy so he has to go out and fuck his bar bimbos?"

Chad jumped up, stalked over, stilling her pacing with his hands on her shoulders. "Dani, stop. Honey, you're going to make yourself sick talking this way."

She looked up, her eyes filled with anguish. "What was wrong with me?" she whispered.

"Nothing," he promised. "Absolutely nothing." Pulling her into his chest again, he held the back of her head with one hand while the other wrapped around her back. "The fault was entirely on Adam. I don't know why...maybe it was his lack of a father figure. Maybe it was his lack of maturity. But baby, you were the best thing that ever happened to him." He felt her shoulders droop and he continued. "Whatever it was that made him have a need to be sexually promiscuous, baby it had nothing to do with you."

"He hid it well," she admitted. "I had no idea. Or maybe I just didn't want to see it."

"Come on, let's sit back down." He led her over to the sofa, making sure she was settled before he sat right next to her. He glanced down to her still flat stomach and when he lifted his eyes, he saw her staring at him.

"Yeah, life can be crazy, right?" she smirked. "I get the visit by the ATF Chaplain to tell me that Adam was killed. It didn't matter if we didn't have the greatest love story in the world…we were husband and wife. We cared for each other." Squeezing her eyes tightly together as though to ward off the agonizing memories, she sat still, the only movement the quivering of her chin. Finally, taking another deep breath, she opened her eyes to see Chad's gaze holding hers tenderly.

"And then the funeral…" he prompted.

"Oh yeah, let's not forget my brilliant performance at the wake." Shaking her head again, she blushed as she admitted, "I just lost it. I was grieving my husband and friend and then to have that blonde fuck come in and…and…I just totally lost it. The realization that Adam had been fucking around behind my back and everyone seemed to know it…" She pushed herself away from Chad, piercing him with her gaze. "I was livid at everything and everybody at that moment. I got out of there, drove back to our house and knew I had to get out. I called my neighbor and well, you know the rest."

"Not all of it, honey," he said, dropping his eyes to her stomach again.

"How can you tell?"

"One of my friend's wives noticed you were only

drinking water and your hand kept drifting down to your stomach. She's pregnant and just got a feeling."

Dani's hand slipped down to her flat stomach again in the unconscious, but timeless, movement of mothers-to-be. "I missed my period that was supposed to be right after he died. I figured it was stress. With moving and getting a new job, I kind of forgot about it. Then when I got morning sickness, I took a pregnancy test. Positive. Can you believe that?" she implored, her smile genuine. "I know most people would assume I'd be horrified...pregnant by my deceased, philandering husband." Placing her small hand on Chad's much larger one, she said earnestly, "But honestly? Once the shock was over, I was happy. I love this baby. Having lost one, and terrified until I can make it to the next trimester when the chance of miscarriage is much lower, I really love my baby."

Linking fingers with her, Chad smiled back at her. Her eyes were puffy and red. Her hair was falling out of the sloppy bun. Dark circles underneath her eyes accentuated her pale complexion. And she never looked more beautiful.

8

Dani's head rested on Chad's shoulder, with his arm around her protectively, as they sat on the sofa. Neither spoke for several long minutes, having exhausted themselves with the conversation. Her fingers splayed over his chest, the steady heartbeat pounding underneath. He pulled her in tightly, kissing the top of her head. The silence settled, blanketing them in a tentative peace.

Finally, she lifted her head and peered into Chad's eyes. "What now?" Her tongue darted out to moisten her dry lips and she trembled. "I mean, we've just had this big emotional talk...both realizing we should have said things to each other before you went overseas...and now...I...well, I... uh." Flopping back, she huffed in frustration. "I don't even know what I'm saying."

"No, no, you're right," he consoled. Shifting her body around so that she was facing him, he tightened his embrace. "We can't change the past, Dani. But we sure as hell can change the future."

She cocked her head to the side, her hand once more on her stomach.

He saw her expression of confusion and continued. "I wasn't there for you the way I should have been before taking the mission. I wasn't there for you when I came back. And I wasn't there for you when you found out about Adam...both his death and...well...other things."

She glanced down but Chad lifted one hand and cupped her cheek. Rubbing his rough thumb over her delicate cheek, he raised her head so she was once more looking into his eyes. "No more leaving things unsaid or uncertain." He noted as she sucked in her lips, her face a mask of question. "I'm here, Dani. Right here. And I'm not going anywhere."

"Chad, I'm having Adam's baby. That takes precedence over anything I might want...or feel for you."

He slid one hand from around her back to her stomach, laying his hand over hers. "You're having the baby of a man who at one time was one of my closest friends. I still cared for Adam. Dani, he can't be here for you and the baby...but I will be."

He wasn't sure what he expected her reaction to be, but the flash of anger in her green eyes caught him off guard.

"I'm not some poor charity case," she bit out. "I don't need you to sacrifice yourself for me. Hell, that's what Adam did and look where it got us! Women have been single mothers for a long time and I don't need your sympathy. I made that mistake once and won't be making it again!" She wiggled to move away but found herself held tighter.

"I don't pity you," he groaned, her movements causing his dick to stir. "I'm saying that we've wasted almost a year and a half by not telling each other what was in our hearts. As long as you were married to Adam, my feelings were secondary and I'd never act on them. But Adam's gone. And you're still here. And honest to God, Dani...we'd be having this same conversation if you weren't pregnant!"

Holding her gaze, he moved in closer. "I want to be with you. The fact that you're pregnant doesn't matter to me as far as that goes."

She sat perfectly still, the only sound in the room was their breathing. Gazes held, each taking the measure of the other. The sting of tears hit the back of her eyes and she hated the idea of crying... one more time. "When you say it doesn't matter—"

"No, no...I said that wrong," he rushed, his fingers still brushing her cheek. "I meant to say that it's just an added bonus." Catching her expression, he continued. "Adam was my friend and you know how I feel about you. Even Adam knew that a baby needs a father figure. I'd be honored to be that father figure for your baby."

Sucking in a ragged breath, Dani slowly moved

from his embrace, stood and walked over to the window overlooking her yard. Her outside lights illuminated where the previous renters had attempted to plant a flower garden but their efforts had been overshadowed by the myriad of weeds and unraked leaves from the past fall. A few twigs littered the ground. *I hate yard work. Or at least, I used to always hate yard work. A toddler will need a safe place to play so I suppose I'd better start thinking about those things.*

"Dani?"

She startled at the pressure of Chad's hands on her shoulders. *Jesus, was I that deep in daydreaming that I did not even hear him walk over?* She dropped her head, realizing she was thinking about yard work when the man she cared for had just told her he wanted to be a part of her and her baby's life. *This must be mommy brain...or I've completely gone over the edge.*

"I can hear your thoughts whirling even though you're saying nothing," he said. With his large hands still on her shoulders, he gently turned her around and pulled her body in close to his. Neither spoke for a moment as their heartbeats pulsed in rhythm.

Lifting her head from his chest, Dani looked up into his face, pondering her words carefully. "I'm not sure exactly what you want me to say, Chad," she began. "I'm glad we talked today. I'm glad you told me how you felt about me and why you stepped away from both Adam and me last spring. I..." she hesitated, her gaze dropping to his chest.

"I hear a *but* coming," he interjected, hoping he was wrong.

"No, not really a *but*...more like a *slow down*."

He lifted her chin with his fingers, wanting to see her face. "Dani, we both screwed up a year and a half ago when neither of us clearly expressed what we were thinking or feeling. I don't want to make that same mistake again. So, I'm going to speak plainly and I need you to do the same, okay?"

She nodded, looking into his eyes once more.

"I want to be in your life. I want to get our friendship back on track, but I'll be honest...I plan on showing you just how I feel because I want more than just friendship."

The corners of her lips curved slightly as a small smile crossed her face. Her hands, holding on to his massive arms, gave a little involuntary squeeze as his words sunk in. "I'd like that too," she agreed. "But slowly," she quickly amended. Seeing his eyebrow lift in question, she explained, "We've changed in the last year and a half, Chad. I've been married and widowed. I've trusted and had that trust betrayed. I lost you, my best friend, and had to learn to live without you. I've been pregnant twice and miscarried once. I've changed homes, cities, and jobs. To say that my life has been a whirlwind of change would be an understatement." Sliding her hands over his chest and down to his waist, her fingers gripping for emphasis, she implored, "So, yes…I'd like you in my life again. But slowly," she repeated. "I'm not about to jump one more time into a situation that hasn't been well thought out because life's not just about me anymore."

His fingers flexed on her hips, warring between wanting to argue that they had wasted enough time and knowing her caution was right. His eyes dropped to her stomach and he smiled. He leaned down to kiss her forehead, holding his lips there for a moment. Her scent drifted to him—floral and fruity. Sighing heavily, he leaned back, holding her green-eyed gaze. "You're right. Slow and easy is good. I've got to rebuild your trust in me, and babe? I'm gonna do just that."

The next morning, Dani wandered into the kitchen, thankful it was Sunday and she did not have to go to work after having such a restless night. After their long talk Chad left, but his words played over and over in her mind. Desperate for coffee, she fixed a cup of herbal tea knowing she had to avoid the caffeine. The flavorful tea brought peace but hardly the alertness she needed. She moved to her purse to take out her phone and found the padlock from the storage facility as well as the letter she had stuffed in there. It was obvious the padlock had deep scratches on it where someone had attempted to cut it. *Why didn't I notice that the other day?*

She walked back to her second bedroom where she had stacked the remaining boxes from the storage unit and looked at them. Staring at them for a moment, she pondered why someone would have attempted to break into her unit. Convincing herself that she must have been just one of many they tried, she went back to the kitchen and grabbed a marker. Walking back to the guest room, she made her way around, re-labeling the boxes. Now that most of Adam's items had been disposed of or given away, she was just left with books, old CDs, a box of some of his things that she was giving to his mom, and out of season clothes for her.

Walking back to the kitchen to toast a bagel, she was interrupted by a knock on the door. Looking through the peephole, she glanced at the mirror by the front door. *Oh hell, who cares what I look like!* Throwing open the door, she stared at Chad, looking handsome as ever. Dark t-shirt stretched over his arms and chest, leaving her to wonder how lucky the soft material was to be so close to those muscles. Faded blue jeans that showcased his hard thighs and that mouth-watering ass. Even his booted feet screamed to her girlie parts. And in his hand was a bouquet of flowers.

"Chad? Um...I wasn't expecting you." Fiddling with the long t-shirt she was wearing, she hoped it covered her ass, which seemed to have gotten larger with this pregnancy. Cocking her head to the side, she added, "And you just left here late last night."

Grinning, he handed her the flowers while

placing his hand in the middle of her chest, gently pushing her backward. Kicking the door closed with his booted foot, he leaned down to kiss her cheek. "Don't want the neighbors getting a glimpse of your gorgeous body." Seeing her standing in the doorway wearing a t-shirt, her hair piled on top of her head in a sloppy bun with tendrils hanging haphazardly down, and dark-framed glasses perched on her nose...his blood began running south.

She snorted as she turned, walking into the kitchen to put the flowers in a vase. Standing on her tiptoes, she reached up to grab a glass vase from the top shelf of a cabinet.

Chad watched, mesmerized, the t-shirt lifting as she reached, offering a glimpse of the bottom of her ass-cheeks. Blood now rushed to his dick and it took all his control to make it to her in time to take the vase from her hands. Standing right behind her, he groaned as her ass moved against his cock. Stepping back, he said, "Here, let me get it."

"I'm pregnant, not incapable," she said, turning to look at him. Now that she was close, she noticed the circles under his eyes, mirroring her own. "Did you not sleep well?" she asked.

Hanging his head, Chad chuckled. "I was up till the wee hours this morning looking up some things on the internet."

"A case you're working on?"

"Uh...kinda," he replied.

Stepping away from him, she moved to the

stove wanting to put some distance between them. Having him so close made it hard to think—and feel anything other than his strong masculine presence. "I was fixing some breakfast. Would you like some?" she asked.

"You haven't eaten yet?"

His voice sounded strangely sharp. Looking at him over her shoulder, she saw his brow knitted as he frowned at her. "No. It usually takes a while for the morning sickness to pass."

"Oh, right," he said, the frown instantly replaced with a look of concern. "Have you seen your doctor? When do you go next? Have you had any other problems besides morning sic—"

"What are you going on and on about?" she asked, turning to face him, the spatula lifted in her hand as she stopped stirring the eggs in the pan.

"I just wanted to make sure you're all right and taking care of yourself properly. Um..." he hesitated, "I know you need protein...and vitamins."

Staring at him for a moment, she cocked her head to the side. "And just when did you become such an expert on pregnancies?"

"Well, I wouldn't say I was an expert," he muttered.

"What exactly were you looking up on the internet last night, Chad?"

He stepped forward, closing the distance between them, placing his hand on her shoulders, pulling her in closer, a sheepish expression on his face. "Okay, I was up most of the night looking up information on pregnancies...and birthing procedures...and babies."

Nervously chewing her lip, she stood still. Stepping back again she found her process halted as his hands did not leave her shoulders. "Why?" she asked, her voice barely a whisper.

"I wanted to know," he admitted, shrugging his wide shoulders. "I want to know everything that you're going through. Everything that's happening."

Putting her hand upon his chest, she felt his heartbeat pounding steadily through her fingertips. "Chad," she began tentatively, shaking her head back and forth. "I don't think tha—"

"Dani, I can tell you're getting ready to throw up a wall. I told you last night that I want to move forward. Friends for now...if that's all you'll give me. More as we build the trust back up. And I want to be involved."

"I thought we agreed to go slowly?"

"I know we did, but I can't go at a snail's pace when it comes to the pregnancy. If I'm involved, then I've got to catch up!"

Smiling, she bent her head forward until it rested on his chest as he wrapped his arms around her body. Kissing the top of her head, he said, "This is going to seem weird, but I actually came over to ask you to have dinner and here I am telling you how I spent last night learning all I can about the pregnancy."

"Like a date?" she leaned her head back, pondering his request.

"Only if you want it to be. I'd like to take you out tomorrow night."

She hesitated, wanting to agree. "I don't know. I don't usually go out on work evenings since I have to get up so early for work the next day."

"How about if I told you it was an early evening? I can pick you up about five and I promise to have you home by eight?"

"Then I'd say I'd love to accept your formal invitation," she laughed.

"Good," he said. "I've got to go but I'll see you tomorrow."

9

"Aaron," Dani called out, seeing her co-worker walking down the hall after coming back from the company's cafeteria. "I found the information you were looking for."

Smiling, he flipped through the report. "This is perfect," he confirmed. "Just what I need to add to my presentation."

"Good. That's a copy so you're welcome to keep it."

"How did your evening turn out on Saturday?"

"Oh, that. I should apologize, Aaron. That man was an old friend and I know I left abruptly, but well...we had a lot to catch up on."

Throwing his hands up, he said, "Hey, it's all good by me, but I promised Melissa I'd find out the story."

"Are you sure only your wife wants the gossip?" she laughed. "Well, tell her I'm fine. And it was nice to catch up with Chad."

"So I take it you want me to tell Melissa that she doesn't need to try to set you up with anyone else?" he inquired, barely able to hide his smile.

Tapping her cheek with her finger as she pretended to ponder his question, she grinned. "Tell her that I'm off the market...still not looking for anyone."

The Saints gathered around the conference table, poring over the intel provided by Roscoe Barnes from the ATF and Mitch.

"Right now, they've identified a recruiter in our area. Habib El-Amin. Male, thirty-two years old. American, although his parents came over from Iraq."

Luke sent Habib's information to the large white screen on the wall as well as to each man's tablet. "Here is his account profile with the Geeks2Gether dating site."

The silence around the room was thunderous, until the laughter broke out. Cutting through the tense meeting, the name of the dating site drew chuckles from most around the table.

Luke looked offended, saying, "Hey, you have no idea how hard it is being a computer nerd in an alpha world. I should know."

The others looked over at Luke, seeing his tall, muscular frame. Built more like a runner than a football player, he was nonetheless not what they would describe as hard-up when it came to dating.

"You hardly fit that category, bro," Bart laughed.

"Yeah, easy for you to say," Luke grumbled. "Who used to go home with the most gorgeous woman from the bars…or more than one?"

Remembering his life before he met Faith, Bart had the grace to blush. "Aw hell, man. Don't remind me."

"I'm just saying that there are a lot of geeks, many introverted, who don't have the same ease of meeting women that some of you do. It makes them much more susceptible to look for online dates. Add on to that, they have the skills these terrorist recruiters are looking for."

Cutting through the jocularity, Jack asked, "His profile is male, so I assume he's recruiting female computer experts?"

Wiggling his eyebrows, Luke replied, "Not necessarily. He also has this profile." With a click of his fingers on his laptop, he brought up a female's profile, complete with false picture and personal information. "He uses this one as well, to look for males."

"Okay, I gotta ask the question, Luke," said Blaise. "If these recruits are such computer geniuses, how is it that they can't figure out he's not who he says he is?"

"I wondered the same thing, but it appears that Habib is using state of the art encryption programing. Anyone trying to see if his profiles on the dating site are real are going to come up with the information that he wants them to."

"So what do we do with this?" Marc queried.

"The latest recruit he seems to be going for is Robbie Carter from St. Louis." Putting up the info on Robbie, Luke continued, "The problem is that I can see from the site what Habib is doing, but I've got no idea if anything's happened yet. I've gotten into Robbie's financial account and can see where some money has been transferred in. But then it gets buried in encryption again."

Chad asked, "What does the ATF want us to do?"

"Once we get a lock on who Habib is targeting, then we'll go pay a visit to the recruit. Luke will be able to decipher their computer codes if we can obtain the info directly from their units."

"I take it those trips aren't exactly sanctioned officially," Cam laughed, fist bumping Bart, both loving clandestine missions.

"We'll take the first one," Bart grinned.

The others chuckled as Jack just shook his head. "We'll divvy them up when we get the go-ahead to proceed." Looking back at Luke, he said, "Who else is in our sights?"

Luke, caught in the middle of a swallow of hot coffee, spluttered as he tried to speak. After his coughing fit, he looked up sheepishly and answered, "It appears that Habib works with Fazan Darzi and Abdul Nagi. Who they work for is still a mystery but I'm trying to unravel it with Mitch's FBI assistance."

"Do Fazan and Abdul do the same thing that Habib does with the dating sites?" Blaise asked.

"Yep," Luke agreed. "I'm working on finding the other links between them all and who the hell is the leader they are reporting to."

"And Adam Turner? How does he fit into all of this?" Chad asked, his jaw tight with irritation.

Every pair of eyes turned toward him. "Not sure," Jack answered honestly. "But it appears that his name was mentioned in conjunction with Habib. Only once, but still...it bears investigating." Jack pinned him with a glare. "And Chad...you're not working on that angle. I'm having Blaise and Monty follow up on anything related to Adam."

"What?" Chad exploded.

"You know you're not able to be objective," Marc said, putting his hand on Chad's shoulder.

Blaise spoke up, "Monty and I'll work to find out what was going on, man. Don't worry...we're not out to get him."

Sucking in a frustrated breath before letting it out slowly, Chad nodded. He was not happy, but understood this was the way the investigation needed to go.

The Saints moved to their workstations, each delving into unraveling the links between Adam, Habib, Fazan, Abdul, and the Geeks2Gether website.

Pulling into her driveway, Dani parked close to her house knowing the grocery bags were heavy. Reaching into the back seat, she grabbed the four bags, looping them on her arms, along with her purse and briefcase. Lugging them to her front door, she wondered why she did not just make two trips instead of carrying them all together.

Opening the door, she stumbled in, managing to set the bags on the floor as she went down on her knees in a pile. "Dammit!" she cursed. Pushing her hair from her face, she sat on her ass and pulled her black pumps off her feet. Tucking her feet under her, she pushed off the floor and stood. As she bent to pick up the bags, her eyes moved across her living room. *Something's wrong.*

The furniture stood in place, the pictures on the walls, the knick-knacks on the mantle. It looked undisturbed...only not quite right. Leaving the grocery bags on the floor, she walked in her stocking feet into the room. Glancing down at the rug under the sofa, she noted the deep impressions in the carpet where the sofa had been moved and not put back exactly in place. She looked at the pictures hanging precisely straight on the walls. Adam's voice came back to her from the first time he was in her apartment. *Girl, you can't hang pictures straight to save your life. Every picture in your house is slightly skewed.*

Someone had looked at her pictures...or behind

them, and then straightened them before leaving. Tip-toeing back to her purse, she bent and slipped out the handgun she kept with her. Moving to the kitchen through the small dining room, she noted the straight pictures on the wall there as well. Opening her drawers, she ascertained they had been rifled through as well. The scissors she used last night were pushed to the side, not in the front where she remembered she left them.

Her heart pounded as she quietly sucked in a deep breath. Holding the gun steady, she moved to the hall by the kitchen leading to the two bedrooms and bathroom. Checking first to make sure there were no intruders, she tucked the weapon into the waistband of her skirt as she carefully looked into her bedroom. Same thing. Pictures hanging perfectly straight. Bedcovers tucked neatly. *I'm neat, but not that neat.*

Anger burned into her at the thought of someone in her house, pawing through her things. *What the hell were they looking for?* As she opened the second bedroom, used for storage, she stopped short, her mind whirling. The boxes had been opened even though they still had tape on them. She observed the tape was loose as though pulled opened and then pressed back. Lifting the tops, she noticed the books and notebooks were not stacked as orderly as she had left them. *Storage unit searched? House searched?* Thoughts of calling the police flew through her mind but she dismissed them.

Nothing was taken. No real evidence that someone has been here other than my intuition. Yeah, the cops'll love that. She thought of Chad, biting her lip in indecision for a moment. *He's an investigator...at least he'll take me seriously.*

Walking to the front door, she grabbed her purse and placed her gun inside before pulling out her cell phone.

"Hey, Dan—"

"Chad? I've had an intruder in my home," she blurted out.

"What the fuck?" he roared. "Where are you?"

"I'm here. I've checked it out. No one is here now."

"Babe, get the hell out of the house and drive somewhere public," he ordered.

She heard people's voices in the background and wondered if he was still at work. "I'm not leaving my house, Chad," she argued. "It's clear, but I—"

"Then lock yourself in and we're on our way," Chad bit out.

Disconnecting, Dani walked into the kitchen after dumping the grocery sacks on the dining room table. She wanted to get a drink but, unwilling to touch anything, she grabbed a water bottle from one of the bags. Sitting down on a kitchen stool, she looked around, tossing her long hair over her shoulder. Stewing, she sat, her left leg crossed and swinging wildly. The fury was overwhelming at the thought of intruders. *Well, they snooped in the wrong house,* she vowed.

Chad's tires squealed in the driveway as he barely stopped the truck before hurtling himself out. Marc, on Chad's heels, with other Saints right behind, pounded up the front steps. Throwing open the door, they charged in. Not knowing what to expect, Chad came to an abrupt halt seeing Dani sitting on her kitchen stool, legs crossed, wearing a sexy-as-fuck black pencil skirt with a pale blue blouse, sipping water as though she were at a bar tossing down a martini.

"Babe?" he said, crossing the room to her.

Tilting her head to look at him, she glared. "Chad, I'm so fucking mad someone was in my house, I could spit nails!"

Laughter sounded from the doorway and when her eyes looked at the men standing behind Chad, she lifted her eyebrow in question.

Marc threw up his hands in supplication, saying, "I'm sorry, Mrs. Turner, but you are no damsel in distress, are you?"

Taking Chad's hand as he helped her down from her stool, she cocked her head to the side as she approached the wall of men. Big men. *Wow. Are all the Saints this big?*

She saw their eyes assessing her living room, seeing it appear normal. "Before you ask, no, I did not touch anything. But someone has been here and I'm the only one who would have noticed."

A tall, bearded man approached, his hand outstretched and shook hers firmly. "Jack Bryant, Ms. Turner. I own the Saints. This is Marc, Jude, and Bart."

She nodded at each man and then turned her eyes to Chad. "I didn't know who else to call. I knew the police would blow this off."

Chad walked over, pulling her in into an embrace. Resting his head on the top of hers, he felt the warmth of her body close to his. "Okay, Dani, tell us what happened."

"This is not actually the first thing that has occurred…it's actually the second."

"What the hell? And you're just now telling me—"

"Whoa, buddy," she said, pulling back away to look at his face. "Until a couple of days ago, we weren't even speaking."

Taking a deep breath, he nodded. "You're right. Sorry. Please tell us what's going on."

"I'll start with today. I confess that when I got home from work, I wasn't paying attention to my surroundings, so I didn't realize anything untoward until I entered. One of the things my husband used to say was that I always hung pictures crooked on the walls. I never really thought about it, but he was right. My pictures always hang a bit crooked. I notice it now, but still never straighten them. Every picture in this house is straight. Every single one.

As though someone looked behind each one and then without realizing they were crooked to begin with, they straightened them when they finished.

She watched as the men's gazes roamed the room...and the doubt they had. "Your reaction is exactly why I didn't call the police."

Tiptoeing over to the sofa, she pointed down. "The sofa was moved and not placed back exactly where it had been so the dents in the carpet show."

Chad and the others moved into the living room to see what she was talking about and she saw the dawning in their expressions.

"In the kitchen, my drawers and cabinets are not exactly the way I left them. I went to the grocery store today because I was low on some items. I was looking in my cabinets this morning to check my canned goods. I had the vegetables in the front because that was what I was focusing on. If you care to look, you'll see that my soup cans are closer to the front."

"Every room the same?" Chad asked, anger pouring off of him at the idea of someone in Dani's home.

"Yeah. I armed myself and searched the house first. Once I knew it was secure, I did a more thorough search and discovered that whoever was here, did a good job of covering their tracks...but not to me."

"You did an armed search?" Bart asked, a grin of admiration on his face.

Dani looked at him, seeing his panty-melting

smile. He would turn many heads, she guessed, but had a feeling the big guy was now spoken for. She often found herself thinking of what people's lives were like...especially after several of her unwise decisions.

"Dani?"

Startling, she jumped then guiltily looked at Chad. "Sorry, my mind wandered." *Be professional, girl, and stop daydreaming!* "Uh, what did you say?"

"You said there were two incidents," Chad repeated, taking her hand and leading her to the table and ushering her into a chair. The five men sat down, as well, and appeared to be ready to listen to whatever she had to say.

"I was handed this letter on Friday when I went to the storage unit to close out my account with them. There were just a few more boxes that needed to be brought here and I retrieved them." She handed the notification of the intruder to Chad and let him read it before he passed it around to the others.

He finished and lifted his gaze back to hers, a questioning expression on his face.

"It just so happens that my unit was on Section 2B and on top of that, look at my padlock." She walked over to her large handbag and pulled out the padlock. Handing it to him, she watched as curiosity crossed his face only to be quickly replaced by anger.

"Which facility? We need to get their security tapes."

"The kid that works there said someone came to pick up the video, but couldn't tell me who. Do you think you can get a copy?"

Grinning, he said, "Babe, this is what we do for a living." With a nod from Jack, Chad placed a call to Cam. "Hey bro, I'm at Dani's and we've got a job for you. I need the security video feed for All-Safe storage unit on Lansom Street. Yep, for last Thursday night. Jude'll meet you there and distract the manager and let you take care of the rest. Thanks, man. I owe you."

Dani watched, impressed as Chad took control. Irritated that someone had been in her house, she knew the situation was out of her hands. In the middle of an investigation surrounding her, she smiled inside at the feeling that someone wanted to help.

10

Jude left to meet with Cam as the other Saints continued to question Dani.

"What do you think they were after?" Jack asked her, his eyes warm, but alert.

Sighing, she said, "I'm embarrassed that I haven't really thought about it. I was too busy being angry." She looked over at her small living room, her mind processing the facts. "It has to be small, or there would be no reason to look behind pictures. In fact, it would have to be small and flat for that to be where it was hidden."

The Saints observed as she continued. Her eyes found Chad's and she said, "The problem is...I've got no idea what they were looking for."

"Anything you're working on at Marsden Systems?" Marc asked. "Anything work related or secure?"

"I've only been at the job for about two months but yes, I come in contact with confidential documents every day. I work in a highly secure area and have a top security clearance. But I assure you, I don't bring home materials from work."

She sat thoughtfully for a moment, then looked around. "Now that I think about it, this is actually the third thing that seems odd. I can't be sure, but I think that my purse was searched when I was out of my office the other day."

"What?" Chad bit out, followed immediately by similar curses from the other Saints.

Hustling to add, Dani said, "Now I can't be sure. But when I got back from a meeting, my desk drawer was not locked. My purse was intact and all the contents were there...but I had a feeling someone had rifled through it. My cosmetic case was opened and the contents spilled out in the purse. Any of these things individually would be nothing...but all together? I'm either completely paranoid or someone is trying to find something they think I have."

"Was there anything your husband was working on before his death?" Jack asked, drawing a glare from Chad.

"Adam?" She shook her head, with a slow smile on her face. "No, Mr. Bryant. Adam was with the ATF, like Chad. His specialty was explosive disposal. He wasn't an investigative agent."

The room became quiet, the silence eerie as she looked around at the faces of the men sitting at her table. Seeing the darted glances between them, she turned her attention to Chad. "What's going on? Why the questions about Adam?"

Just then, they were interrupted by a call from Cam, who reported he had the CD in his hand.

"Any problems?" Chad asked.

"Don't insult me," Cam pretended to growl. "I'll deliver it to Luke and have him analyze the tape before we turn it over to Mitch if needed."

"Thanks," Chad stated, knowing Cam would be able to obtain anything they needed...and not get caught.

"Good enough," Cam called out, before disconnecting.

Chad turned back to Dani and ordered, "You need to pack your stuff so that I can take you out of here."

Turning to stare dumbly at him, she said, "What? Why?"

Leaning over to her, he placed his hand on her shoulder and said, "Come on, Dani. Someone was here in this house and if they didn't find whatever the hell they were looking for, they'll come back."

"Chad, I'm not leaving my house," she declared, her eyes flashing her defiance. "I just started to get settled here."

"Don't make me beg because I will," he said softly, moving in close so that his words were for her only. "Think of the baby, honey."

Her face fell as resignation set in. A sense of fear slid in next to the anger she felt. "I've had so many changes in the past three months...how many more can I take?"

Wrapping his huge arms around her body, he pulled her in tightly. "I'm so sorry, babe. Honest to God, I am. But I can't take a chance on someone coming back and finding you here. We've got no idea right now what could be going on, but I want you safe while we investigate what's happening."

Looking over her head, which was pressed against his chest, he noticed the other Saints had discreetly moved to the other room while he talked to her. Pulling her head back slightly so he could gaze into her eyes, he said, "Look, how about this. What if I stay here for a couple of nights? That way you don't have to move again...at least not now. And I promise to do everything in my power to make you, and the baby, safe."

She peered into his eyes, remembering how they made her feel almost two years ago when they met. Safe. Secure. Cared for. All the things that no matter how much Adam wanted to offer, he never could. "Okay," she whispered, resignation settling.

"But for now, you and I are heading to Jack's to check out the CD, talk about anything else that you can think of, and Jack'll have a couple of buddies come in this evening to dust for fingerprints and set up a preliminary security system. Then, tomorrow, we'll have a full installation."

An hour later, Chad sat staring at Luke's computer screen, his anger growing by the minute. He watched as a person dressed all in black with a hoodie pulled up over their head walked down the Section 2B hall, moving directly to one storage unit, not stopping at any others. Taking out lock cutters from underneath his jacket, he began to cut the padlock. Suddenly an alarm sounded and the person ran back down the hall, keeping his face away from the cameras at all times.

"I knew your computer equipment would enhance the non-existent quality most of these businesses have with their crap security systems," Chad said. "But damn, there's nothing to enhance."

Jack looked over Luke's shoulder as well, his face unreadable. "And this is the only unit he went to?"

"Cam got them all from that night, so yeah. This unit is the only one singled out."

Looking down at Dani's padlock in his hand, Chad showed the Saints the cut marks on the lock. *Fuck! What did she have in that unit?* Pondering the situation for a moment, he wondered if any of Adam's belongings had been there?

Standing up straight, Chad said, "What if whatever they were looking for had to do with Adam?"

"You didn't think he was involved in anything," Jack said, meeting his gaze.

Running his hand over his face, Chad answered, "I don't want to believe that he did, but

I'm not willing to risk Dani's safety just because of my possible false hope."

Luke spoke up. "If they were unable to break into the storage unit because an alarm went off, they won't be deterred. There's a good chance they'd go back and try again...this time making sure the alarm system is disabled."

"She said she emptied it out on Friday," Chad said, then the realization rushed over him. "Shit, if they realized the unit was empty, that's why they tried her house next."

"What I don't understand is how this could be tied into her feeling that someone at Marsden Energy Systems rifled through her purse," Blaise said. "Anyone with access to where her office is located would have to have a security clearance."

Chad ran his hand over his face in frustration. "And if whatever the person was looking for did have to do with something cocked up that Adam was involved in, then that would have nothing to do with Marsden Energy System. Her job at MES came after Adam was killed."

Monty looked over at Chad, and asked, "Not trying to get in your business, but how involved are you now? Will it be a problem to have her on our radar?"

Chad looked around at his friends. "Told you I fucked up. I was in love with her before I went back overseas, but never told her. Not making that mistake again." He hesitated but understood they needed all her information to keep her safe. "She found out a few weeks after the funeral that she's pregnant."

"Fuck," Marc said, then chuckled. "And she pulled out a weapon and searched her house."

"Yeah, well don't tell a former ATF investigator that she can't protect herself," Chad said, shaking his head. Sighing, he added, "You might as well know now...I've already told her that I want us to see if we can move forward as a couple and that includes the baby."

He saw the smiles of the men around the table. "Adam was my closest friend at one time and while I moved away from them when I got back...well, that's on me. But I plan on being with Dani and I want to be the man in her baby's life. I owe that to Adam. I owe it to her. Hell, I owe it to me."

"Fuckin' yeah," Cam said, his thoughts on his own impending fatherhood palpable.

Jack looked at his men all earnestly working the problem. "Chad, Ms. Turner is now on our radar and her security is of ultimate priority. We're working the problem for the ATF and FBI, now just adding her to our mission as well."

Gaining nods from around the room, they went to work.

Dani waited upstairs in Jack's house while the Saints were in the compound's conference room looking over the surveillance video. She was floored when they drove down the long driveway, through the forest of maple, pine, and oak trees. The redbud trees were just blooming, giving the spring green a flash of purple color.

When they reached the main house, she stared in unabashed awe. "Good grief, his log cabin is like a mansion," she exclaimed.

Chad smiled, glad she agreed to come with him. Entering the house, she was greeted by Jack, who introduced his wife, Bethany. After meeting the other Saints, her eyes followed them as they moved down the hall.

Hearing a laugh from behind her, she turned to see the pretty blonde smiling. "I can see you're impressed with the Saints eye candy, aren't you?" Bethany asked.

"Oh, yeah," Dani admitted while secretly thinking that Chad had them all beat in holding her attention.

Just then the front door opened and several more women walked in. "Hey," the petite, dark-haired woman, wearing maternity nursing scrubs, called out. "Cam called and asked if I would come over after my shift."

Dani met Miriam, Cam's visibly pregnant wife. She noticed Miriam's gaze drop to her stomach and when she lifted her eyes to hers, she smiled. Dani smiled in response but wondered if Miriam knew she was pregnant, even though she was not showing.

Before she had a chance to think about it, she

was introduced to Faith, Bart's fiancé, another petite, dark-haired woman. Dani was unable to hold back her grin. *I just knew Bart was with someone special.* A few minutes later, a curvy woman walked in, her blonde hair streaked with pink, purple, and teal. The woman carried a white box tied with colored string and Dani instantly recognized the Angel's Cupcake Heaven logo on the box.

The beautiful blonde introduced herself as Monty's fiancé, Angel, and the women immediately tore open the box to enjoy a cupcake. Just as Bethany served the herbal tea, in deference to Miriam's pregnancy, another blonde walked in. Jude's fiancé, Sabrina, tossed her designer bag onto the counter and grabbed a cupcake.

It only took a few minutes of tea and cupcakes for Dani to bond with the other women. Each unique, like their Saint, they appeared to understand the special careers the men worked in. Not upset at the late or odd hours, interrupting phone calls, or travel. It was obvious to Dani, these women were special...and adored. *And after seeing their men...I bet the sex is amazing!* Then her mind shifted to what sex with Chad would be like. *Oh, Lordy,* she thought as she squeezed her legs together. Shaking her head, she blamed pregnancy hormones on her thoughts.

Muhammad Hakim walked into the room, his dark eyes quickly moving over the others. "What did he get?"

"Nothing," came Abdul Nagi's frustrated voice. "The idiot did not cut all the alarms at the storage unit and was interrupted before he could get in and search. Then she came the next day and removed everything."

Muhammad said nothing but kept staring, expecting the rest of the story. Abdul continued, "Then he went to her house. Easy break in and he said he left no traces of being there and that he found nothing. The boxes he searched did not contain anything of importance."

"And?"

"The bitch returned and must have noticed something because when he drove by later, the driveway was filled with trucks and a group of security-type men were around."

"He came back with nothing?"

"Nothing," Abdul confirmed. "Whatever Adam Turner had, we haven't been able to find."

Muhammad's lips thinned in anger as he turned away from Abdul. His mind calculating, he ordered, "Get rid of the incompetent. We'll find another way to get what we want."

11

After getting back late from Jack's, Dani and Chad walked into her house. Tossing her bag onto the dining room table, she looked toward the living room. Remnants of fingerprint dust were still visible, but Chad had already informed her that no prints turned up other than hers and his. Sighing heavily, she stood completely still. Chad moved behind her, wrapping his arms around her middle and chest as they both let the emotions of the day wash over them.

"Whatcha thinking?" he asked, his voice soft and his breath warm against her ear.

"I now think this was a bad idea," she replied, exhaustion evident as her body slumped back against his.

Not knowing what she was implying was the bad idea, he stayed quiet.

"I so wanted to stay in my house. It's not a great house, but I was making it mine. I was trying to build a life here...for me and the baby. Now I look at those goddamn straight pictures and the knowledge that someone was in my home...touching my things." Suddenly she jerked out of his arms and ran into the living room, whirling around with her arms flung out to the sides. "Augggh!" she screamed. "My. House. My. Things!" she yelled, thumping her fist against her chest.

Chad stalked over, pulling her into his embrace as she let her weight drop against his. He bent and scooped her up into his arms, moving to the sofa. Sitting down, he arranged her so she was draped over his lap, still enveloped in his warmth. Holding her close, he murmured words of comfort as she cried out her frustration.

Spent of all tears after a few minutes, she rested her head on his shoulder. "I guess I don't look so badass now, do I?" She felt his chuckle as it rumbled in his chest.

"Dani, you were always one badass and this little breakdown doesn't change that. But you feel violated by someone being here in your house, and we need to think about what's the best thing to do."

Using her free hand to wipe her tears, she nodded. "I hate the idea of one more change in my life, Chad. I'd hung up my pictures...a little crooked, but still, they were mine." Her gaze latched on his beautiful smile and she continued. "I suppose, for safety's sake, maybe I should stay at your place for a few days until we have a better handle on what's going on." She looked into his face, seeing the worry lines ease a bit. "But not tonight," she hustled to say. "I'm really tired right now."

Nodding, he said, "I'll be here tonight. We'll be safe."

She laid her head back to his chest. "We'll...," she murmured.

"What, babe?"

"You said *we'll be safe,* not *you'll be safe.* I like that. I like the word *we.*"

Smiling, he stood with her in his arms as he walked into her bedroom and set her feet gently on the floor. "That's what we are now."

Dani smiled up at the handsome man she cared for and sudden shyness overtook her. Here he was in her bedroom, where she wanted him, and she now had no idea what to do.

"Hey, baby," his gentle voice broke through her tangled thoughts. "Why don't you get ready for bed and I'll check the security again."

She stood still until his hands nudged her toward the bathroom. Jolted out of her musings, she hustled into the bathroom, her nightgown in hand. Washing her face, moisturizing, brushing her teeth and then slipping on her nightgown, she stood staring into the mirror over the sink. Auburn hair with fiery red streaks, brushed to a shine, framed her pale face complete with the smattering of freckles across her cheeks and nose.

Her eyes roamed down to her breasts, now fuller and her stomach with its barely-there baby bulge. Splaying her hand on her tummy, she said, "Okay, baby. I love you and I promise I'll make sure you know your daddy. But out there is a really good man...a man I had loved before I cared for your daddy. And he wants both of us. What do you think?"

A knock on the door startled her out of her musings. "You okay in there, Dani?"

"Um, yeah," she said. "Just...uh...finishing up." She opened the door and saw his eyes move slowly from her hair to her face and down her body before roving back up again.

She stared unabashedly at him. He stood shirtless, his massive muscles on display, his strength overwhelming. His jeans hung low on his hips, the top button undone. His arms were outstretched, resting on the doorframe, and her eyes moved from his thick arms, over his defined pecs and down over the six-pack abs, to the delicious muscular V that ended below his waistband. At the bottom, peeking out, were his naked feet looking as sexy as the rest of him.

"I thought I heard you talking," he said, his eyes finally landing on hers.

"I was...just...uh...well, talking to..." she stopped muttering, her hand protectively on her stomach.

His eyes dropped to her hand and his face softened. "You do that a lot?"

"Yeah. They say the baby can hear voices. I want it to know me. And sometimes I'm less lonely when

I think about it being here with me." She rolled her eyes, and continued, "That sounds pathetic, doesn't it?"

"There's not one thing pathetic about you, Dani." Stepping closer, he reached out and placed his large hand on hers. He noted her eyes dilated with lust. Her chest heaved as she stared at his eyes before dropping to his mouth. He heard his heartbeat echoing in the small room and felt sure she could hear it as well. Leaning down, he lowered his mouth to a whisper away from hers. "Dani?" he asked, his warm breath washing across her face.

No words of rejection came. No thoughts of recrimination filled her mind. Nothing but the desire to know his touch. His feel. His heartbeat against hers. His lips on hers. Standing quickly on her toes, she wrapped her arms around his neck as she molded her lips to his. They were just as she imagined. Soft. Strong. Just like him.

Chad pulled her body tightly to his as he moved his mouth over hers. Gently...for only a few seconds until the tinder flamed and the white-hot passion overwhelmed any thoughts of going slow. Picking her up, she wrapped her legs around his waist as he angled his head, taking over the kiss, owning it, claiming her.

Walking to the bed, he lowered her carefully onto the mattress, handling her like fragile glass, careful to keep his body from crushing hers. "What do you want, Dani?" his voice gruff with desire. "I only want to do whatever you want."

"I want everything with you," she confessed, pulling him as close as she could.

That was all he needed to hear. Owning her lips again, he poured his soul into the kiss. Past times together. Past chances missed. Now a future. Everything he was. Everything he thought he lost. Everything he hoped for was now lying beside him and giving herself to him.

He devoured her lips, his tongue plunging in, tasting the essence of Dani. Warm, minty, delectable. Her tongue tangled with his, both discovering the sweet secrets of each other. He moved his hands down her waist to her hips, digging his fingers in as he rolled her toward him, his erection now firmly pressing against her stomach. Hearing her moan, he intensified his movements. Sliding his hand back up her waist, he cupped her full breast, his rough thumb flicking over the taut nipple. Palming the soft mound before moving to the other one.

She grabbed his cheeks, her fingers splaying over his strong, stubbled jaw and held him tight as the electricity zinged from her nipples to her core. She slid her right hand over his shoulders and down his arm, feeling the muscles bunch and flex underneath her fingertips. He had no idea, but she used to watch him at the ATF picnics when he would take off his shirt while playing volleyball, basketball, soccer—whatever he was doing. She would watch the play of muscles in his upper body and wonder, even then, what they would feel like as he lay over her making love.

She realized he had stilled his hands and stopped kissing her. Lifting her eyes, she saw him gazing at her, a puzzled look on his face.

"Where'd your mind go, baby?"

Blushing, she admitted, "I was thinking of how amazing you looked playing sports back when we first met, and even then, I wanted to know what you felt like."

He touched her nose with his, then slid it to the side, his whisper warm against her cheek. "You used to think about us doing this?"

"Oh, yeah, Chad. All the time."

"God, I wish I'd known. So much time wasted," he moaned.

"No, no, honey. Time apart just makes this so much sweeter. We understand now what we lost. What we gave up. It makes this, right now, just right."

He grinned down at her, latching onto her lips once more. Groaning as she sucked his tongue into her mouth, he moved his hand to the bottom of her gown, grabbing it by the hem and tugging it upward.

She let go of his kiss and raised to a sitting position. Her gown was now bunched around her waist and she pulled it over her head in one sweeping motion, tossing it to the bedroom floor. Now completely naked, she lay back where she had been, letting his fiery gaze roam her body.

"Jesus, Dani," he groaned, as though in pain. Leaning forward, he latched onto a distended nipple, first sucking it deeply before nipping it with his teeth and then soothing it with his tongue.

Her hand attempted to work his zipper over his erection, but there was little room to maneuver. He pulled away from her chest and rolled onto his back, quickly shucking off his jeans and boxers. His erection, now free, moved toward her as though it had a will of its own and knew exactly where it wanted to go.

Her hand wound around his fullness, drawing a hiss from his lips. Smiling, she moved her fingers up and down his girth, wondering for a moment how the hell it would fit. She had partners before Adam, but none very endowed. Adam had been a fun lover, certainly proud of his prowess and with good reason. But her husband had nothing on Chad. *In fact, I'm sure no other man in the world has anything on him.*

"Babe?" his voice cut into her thoughts.

Her eyes jumped up to his as a blush rose from the tops of her breasts to her forehead. "I'm so sorry, Chad. I swear, I'm not sure if it's the pregnancy hormones or just stress, but my mind goes everywhere nowadays."

"Not sure I'm comfortable about your mind wandering when your hand is wrapped around my dick," he admitted.

Grinning slyly, she said, "Don't worry. My thoughts were purely complimentary."

Lifting one eyebrow, he laughed. "Well then, daydream on, baby. But how about we make them come true?"

"My thoughts exactly," she enthused.

Chad slid his hand between her legs, slowly teasing her wet folds apart, slipping a thick finger into her entrance. She was so ready for him as her hips moved involuntarily, needing more friction. Keeping his finger in her, working her into a frenzy, his thumb applied pressure to her clit, driving her wild. Sucking her engorged nipple deeply into his mouth again, she clung to his shoulders, her fingernails digging into his flesh as her orgasm ripped through her. Shuddering, she fell motionless back onto the bed, his name having been screamed from her lips.

Lazily she opened her eyes watching as he brought his finger, wet with her juices, to his mouth and sucked on it. Then he leaned over, kissing her deeply, allowing her to taste herself on his lips. Intoxicated with the scent, she slid her hand back to his cock, lightly spreading the pre-cum around the head.

Groaning, he rolled over making sure to keep his body weight off hers by resting on his forearms. Maneuvering so his legs were between hers, he placed his eager cock at her entrance. Stilling, he peered into her eyes. "I've never gone unwrapped, Dani. I swear I'm clean and the same testing we had to do for the ATF, I do for Jack's. I'm clean."

"I told you I got tested after finding out about

Adam's indiscretions and then again when I was hired by MES." Smiling, she added, "And I can't get pregnant...again."

Chad stilled for a moment, thinking of Adam. "Total, complete idiot," he said.

Her eyes, warm with lust, quickly cooled. "Excuse me?" she bit out.

He jumped, suddenly aware of the change in mood. "No, no, baby. Not you. Adam. He had all this beauty, all this that makes you who you are... and he fucked it up."

Hating to think about Adam, she nodded. "But don't focus on him, honey. It's just us right now. Just you and me."

Nodding, he lowered his mouth to hers as his cock entered her waiting sex. Warm. Tight. *So amazing.* He had never fucked around like a few of the other Saints had...until they met the right women. But, still, he was unprepared for the emotions slamming into him as his cock thrust in and out of her. *So right. So fuckin' right.*

Her arms around his neck, her legs around his waist, Dani felt his fullness as she climbed the summit again. She had wanted him, wanted this a long time ago and gave it up when she thought there was no choice. But now that she had him back in her life, she could not imagine a world where he did not wake up with her every day.

He lowered his head to her neck as he powered into her body. Her slick channel tugged his cock as he sucked on the pulse beating wildly. His balls tightened and he mumbled, "You close? I want you coming with me."

She lost the ability to speak so she simply nodded her head against his forehead. His mouth found hers again as his tongue began to thrust in rhythm to his cock's movements.

Her legs grabbed his waist harder and he realized she was close. Keeping his considerable weight balanced on one arm, he slid one hand down her waist, over her mound and lightly pinched her clit. That pressure forced her to the summit and over the edge. Flying apart in his arms, she cried out his name while her inner clenched his throbbing dick.

Feeling her walls squeeze him, his orgasm pulsated out of him over and over until he was wrung dry. Panting, his arms weak, he rolled to the side pulling her with him.

She lay partially on top of his body, their sweat mingling as the coolness of the room slowly beat back the heat pouring off them. Her chest lay against his, their heartbeats erratic at first and then beginning to beat as one. Sucking in a ragged breath, she was not sure she could move even if she wanted to.

Shifting her slightly to the side, Chad rose from the bed and stalked to the bathroom. She gazed at his naked form as the moonlight, coming through the slats in the blinds, cast his magnificent body in shadows. He returned, the front view as amazing as the back, and smiled as he bent over her with a warm washcloth and carefully washed between her legs.

Tossing the cloth to the nightstand, he leaned back over, gazing at her perfect, naked body in the slim light. "You're gorgeous, Dani. Always were from the first time I saw you, but now? Damn, girl, you take my breath away."

She noted his eyes dipped to her stomach. Suddenly nervous, she said, "What about in a couple of months? When my stomach is protruding and stretch marks mar my boobs and ass?" Her voice now unsteady with uncertainty, she said, "What abou—"

He shushed her with his fingers on her lips and shook his head. "I've been in love with you for a long time, Dani. There's nothing about you or this baby or your body that I won't continue to love."

She smiled against the rough pads of his fingers and he slid into the bed next to her, pulling the covers over their bodies as he tucked her safely into his side. With his large, warm body wrapped around hers, one hand of his firmly held against her stomach protectively, they fell asleep.

12

The next morning, Dani rushed into her building from the parking lot, nervously looking at her watch. Waking up to Chad had been amazing—made more amazing by the way he woke her up with his cock nudging her back. Lifting her leg and keeping one hand on her breast, he rocked her world. *More exciting than an alarm clock, but not for getting to work on time!*

As she entered through security, she hustled out of the elevators to her office. A strange sensation of being watched came over her, but as she looked over her shoulder, she saw nothing suspicious.

Jahfar poked his head into her office as soon as she tossed her purse into her drawer. Calling out a *Good morning* to her, she noticed his eyes dropped to the drawer where her purse was located. Locking the drawer, she smiled as she cocked her head. "Can I help you with anything?"

"No, no," he rushed. "I just thought I'd check to see if you wanted to go out with some of us at lunch."

"Thanks, but I've got some work to catch up on, so I'll eat in the cafeteria. It'll be quicker," she replied. Waving as he left, she leaned back in her chair. *Was he checking out my purse drawer? Now, I'm getting paranoid.*

Later in the morning, Ethan stopped by for a short meeting. As he was leaving, she blurted,

"Do you know much about Jahfar?"

Ethan looked at her in question, and she rushed on, "I swear, I hope I'm not stereotyping, but there's something about him that makes me nervous."

"He came on board about the time that you were hired here," Ethan answered, sitting back down in the chair in her office. "Is there something specific?"

Rubbing her forehead, she admitted, "No. Just stupid thoughts, I suppose."

"Well, with the news the way it is each night, it's no wonder we start questioning each other. But as far as I checked, his security clearance had no problems."

She nodded, now embarrassed she had shared her suspicions. *Jesus, that made me seem so prejudiced.*

Glancing down to her desk drawer, she pocketed her keys before turning back to her laptop, forcing her mind to her job.

Jahfar closed his office door, pulling out his secure, private cell phone. Making a call, he waited until the password cleared and he was put through.

"I've got nothing on her yet, but I've got to tread carefully. She's smart. Her former years with ATF have her twitchy."

"Keep looking, but try to win her over. You know…the personal touch."

"You don't have to tell me my job. I'll handle it."

With that, he disconnected, rubbing his hand over his face as his eyes landed on his desk, seeing the picture of his wife and two sons. His family unaware of his double life. *Two months…this job is getting old.*

Chad looked at the other Saints, his gut twisting. "She's gonna hate this."

Jack nodded, but added, "Yeah, but she's in the middle of this investigation and needs to be aware. Better to let her in on the intel now and see if we can have her cooperation."

Chad slid his eyes to his boss before moving them around the table, seeing expressions of sympathy. "We just got together…after almost a year and a half of being apart because we didn't tell each other how we felt. This now? She's gonna think I came back into her life just for this."

Jude leaned in, piercing him with a hard stare. "Haven't known you as long as these other men, but what I do know is that you'd never play a woman you cared about. My guess is that once she gets over the shock, she'll understand that too."

Nodding, Chad heaved a heavy sigh as he pulled out his phone, placing the call. "Dani? Hey, babe. Listen, when you get off work, I really need you to come to Jack's. Do you remember the directions? Good. No, no…we need to go over some things with you and we'll talk to you about them when you're here. Yeah. Okay, see you then."

Looking up, he said, "She gets off in about fifteen minutes and it'll take her about thirty minutes to drive here."

Jack nodded, his taciturn expression firmly on his face. "Then let's get back to work."

Fifty minutes later, Bethany opened the door and welcomed Dani inside. This time, the other women were not around and Dani cocked her head. "I take it from Chad's call, this was business and not pleasure."

Bethany offered her a hug and said, "I'm sorry, sweetie. I honestly don't have a clue what they need to go over with you, but I'll let them know you're here."

Just then Jack and Chad appeared in the hallway. Chad immediately moved to Dani as Jack smiled at his wife and whispered, "Saw her come in on the monitor downstairs."

Chad reached Dani, suddenly nervous, having not seen her since their lovemaking in the early morning. "Hey, baby," he said, his voice sweet and soft.

Rising on her tiptoes, she placed a kiss on his lips, smiling in return. Hearing more noise, she realized the other Saints were coming into the room as well. Glancing from them back to Chad, she steeled herself. "I gather this isn't a social call?"

"Sorry, babe. But we need to go over some things with you."

Nodding, she allowed him to escort her over to the large living room. The evening sun poured through the floor-to-ceiling windows, the Blue Ridge Mountains in the background. It created a peaceful spring dusk. Chad sat down on the end of one of the oversized sofas, gently settling Dani next to him. The other Saints followed suit until they were all comfortable.

Bethany glanced at Jack and said, "Sweetie, I'm heading over to the cabins to meet with Faith." Smiling at Bart, she said, "Don't worry. We'll keep your wedding reception casual." Catching Bart's wink, she left the room.

"Wow," Dani said. "For me to be summoned and then for Bethany to leave, this must be serious." Glancing to Chad and then over to Jack, she said, "Lay it on me."

Jack began, "Ms. Turner—"

"Please," she interrupted, "call me Dani."

He nodded and said, "Dani, I realize this is going to be difficult, but we'd rather you talk to us before you're interviewed by the FBI." Seeing her eyes widen, he continued, "What can you tell us about Adam before he was killed?"

Her body jerked in response to his question and she barely registered Chad's arm tightening across her shoulders.

"Adam?" She was quiet for only a few seconds before she said, "You asked about Adam when checking out my house, but so much was happening that I overlooked it." No one said anything, so she asked, "Why don't you tell me what's going on?"

"Adam's name came up in a joint investigation by the ATF and FBI into terrorist cells, using people's homes to make bombs and computer geeks to detonate them from distances."

Her eyes widened and then narrowed. "Came up? How?"

Jack continued, "It came up twice in correspondence with one of the suspects. There's nothing to link him to the activities, but it has brought up suspicions."

Her lips thinned in irritation. She met each man's gaze as her eyes swept the circle around her. Suddenly her mind took a turn and she twisted around to look into Chad's face. He knew the instant her mind went down the road he was afraid of—so did everyone else.

"Is this what brought you back around, Chad? Your investigation here? Tell me you didn't just waltz back into my life right when your boss needed to dig into Adam." Her voice rose with each question and she shifted out from under his arm and attempted to stand.

"Oh, no you don't," Chad argued. "What we had...what we have...that's got nothing to do with this. I was afraid your mind would lead you to this conclusion and I'm sorry, but our investigation's got nothing to do with my feelings for you. And if you'd calm down and think...really feel, you'll know I'm telling the truth."

She sat, her body perfectly still as her eyes held his. Her breathing was heavy...matching her heart. Her mind swirled with confusion. *Adam, what kind of mess did you leave me with? Did I even know you at all?* Finally heaving a huge sigh, she nodded. "I know, Chad. I know you're telling me the truth."

Letting out a breath he did not realize he was holding, he squeezed her shoulder once more, offering her his strength.

Dani sat for another minute, wondering how on earth she was going to share any part of her life with Adam with these strangers. It was too personal...and agonizing. *Goddammit Adam, does it never end?* Eventually facing Jack, she asked, "What do you want to know?"

"Anything you can think of. Maybe at the time, there were things you didn't notice that now you can look back at and see more clearly."

She chortled loudly. "You're kidding, right?"

"Dani," Chad's soft voice gentled her. "No one here is judging."

Hanging her head for a moment as though lost

in thought, she jerked up and pierced Jack with a glare. "I know what you meant, but I'm sure you've investigated me as well, so you've discovered I was the wronged wife...the proverbial last one to know that my husband was cheating on me. So if you're looking for clear remembrances from when we were together, then you've probably come to the wrong person."

No one said anything and the awkward silence slithered over her. Chad leaned in and whispered, "Baby, no one wants to make this any worse on you than it already is."

"I'll do better with direct questions, Mr. Bryant," she said, leaning back into Chad. "I'm afraid I can't focus right now to just talk about my life with Adam."

"Fair enough, and call me Jack," he directed gently. "Did Adam's schedule change, especially in the last couple of months of his life?"

Hating the discussion, Dani forced herself to answer rotely, pulling herself away from the emotions. "Adam and I worked in different offices of the ATF. I had a little bit further of a commute so I would leave before him in the mornings, although we were up at the same time. Because his hours could be unusual, especially if on an assignment, I would generally get home before him. Even with his extracurricular activities toward the end, his daily schedule did not change much. I suppose this was to keep me from knowing."

"Did you ever read his email or snail mail?"

Her eyes flashed and she said, "Nope. He didn't read my emails and I didn't read his. As far as delivered mail, if I got it first, I sorted it and laid it on the kitchen counter. I dealt with mine and he dealt with his. But before you ask, no, I never saw anything unusual."

"What about his down time? Did he spend more time on the internet? More time out with friends? Was he more depressed or easily upset?"

Barking out another rough laugh, she said, "You had to know Adam to understand him. Adam loved life. He joked, laughed, worked hard and firmly believed in playing hard. Since there's no reason to hold back with you, I'll tell you we got married because of a drunken one-night stand."

"Babe, you don't have—"

Twisting around, she said, "Chad, I've got nothing to hide anymore. Adam's dead and I'm working through that and his personal betrayal, but now you're investigating him as someone who was in contact with terrorists. What the hell would keeping secrets do for any of us?"

She turned back to the others and continued, ignoring their expressions of sympathy. "Adam wanted to get married. We were both hurt at Chad's decision to go overseas, made a drunken mistake one night that resulted in an unplanned pregnancy. I had no intentions of getting married, but Adam felt insistent that his child not grow up fatherless and...well, to be honest, I was overwhelmed and we made the decision to marry. I lost the baby and told

Adam that we could file for divorce. It was Adam who did not want to, saying that I gave him stability. We had a marriage based on friendship…that was all. Not true love. But affection. I was willing to settle for that since the man I loved had moved away from our lives. That part is staying between me and Chad, but as long as I was married, I was married. No cheating…not even in my mind. I thought I shared the same ideals with Adam, but found out his hound-dog days were not over. But never—never—did I see anything that would have indicated he was acting with terrorists. If you only knew him, you'd know that was the last thing he'd do."

Exhausted from her tirade, she leaned back against Chad again, who now circled her body with both his arms as he kissed the top of her head.

"Did you find anything in his personal effects that didn't seem to belong?" Monty asked. "Anything that made you wonder where it came from?"

"I confess that after the wake, I packed up everything and moved closer to my parents. I quit my job with the ATF, no longer wanting to be around people that purported to be our friends… my friends, and kept Adam's infidelities from me. It wasn't until recently that I went through his things. I found nothing that I did not expect to find. Clothes, pictures, some books."

"May I ask what you did with his things?" Jack asked.

"I donated the clothing that was useable and

threw out the socks and underwear. Mementos were given to his parents, but there wasn't a lot. He wasn't very sentimental and didn't save a lot of things. I put everything else back into the boxes to decide later what I want to do with them. There were a few books and some photos." Sighing heavily, she added, "These were the boxes that had been opened by the intruder."

"Dani, I'm truly sorry," Blaise said, regret in his eyes. "I'm sure this whole investigation sucks for you, but can I ask about blackmail?"

Her eyes cut over to the large, handsome blond who looked like he could have stepped off the bow of a Viking ship. "Blackmail? I'm afraid I don't understand."

Blaise's gaze caught Chad's and he hesitated. Chad took over the explanation, saying, "Terrorists, down through history, have sometimes used blackmail to recruit others to work for them. Since at some time while you were still married, Adam had affairs, do you think someone could have blackmailed him to work for them?"

This line of thinking caught Dani off-guard. Biting her bottom lip, she looked back at Chad as she pondered the query. Heaving a ragged breath, Dani said, "Gentlemen, I'm sure it's easy to imagine Adam being caught in an indiscretion and someone blackmailing him to keep either myself or his employers from finding out. I assure you the ATF did not care about his...habits...as long as he did his job, which he was very good at.

And as for me? Adam would never betray his country to keep me from finding out about his affairs."

Licking her dry lips, she noticed Jack stand and move to the kitchen. He returned with a chilled bottle of water, handing it to her. "I appreciate how difficult this is for you, Dani."

Nodding, she gratefully took a long drink. Replacing the twist top, she leaned forward to set it on the coffee table. She lifted her hand to rub her forehead, a slight headache building.

Chad squeezed her shoulder, saying, "Babe, I don't want you to wear yourself out. It's not good for you to have this much stress." His eyes cut to Jack. "She's had enough."

Jack nodded, but Dani shook her head. "No, let me at least answer the rest of the question. I already told you that after I lost the baby, I talked to Adam about a divorce. I was not only willing to have the divorce, but I was all for it. It was Adam who wanted to stay married. He said I made him want to be a better man. Whatever you think of our arrangement, we did have fun together. Talks, walks, good times. We went to ball games, ATF functions, sometimes just hanging at the house. But, while Adam wanted to be married, believe me, we did not share a great love. And if we had divorced, he would have been fine, so if someone was trying to blackmail him about his affairs...he would have laughed in their face."

The room was quiet and Dani stood suddenly.

"Now, if there're no other questions, I'd like to go home. I've had a rather long day."

Chad stood as well but Dani put her hand out to him, palm up. "No, Chad. I drove myself here and want to drive myself home. I really want to be alone right now."

"Not a good plan," he said, moving closer to her as the others surreptitiously slipped away. "I'm not having you go into your house alone."

She hesitated, knowing he was right but angry for the inability to handle things on her own. Standing for a moment in indecision, she finally acquiesced. As she headed toward the door, she halted, then turned back to the assembly. "Jack?"

The Saints all looked up at her as she spoke. "I'd like to think that I'm right about Adam, but it wouldn't be the first time I made a mistake. I don't want my impressions of my deceased husband to cloud my judgment. I'll be glad to have you look at Adam's personal effects that I boxed up. They're in the spare bedroom."

Jack nodded, saying, "We'd appreciate that, Dani. I know this has been difficult and for that, I'm very sorry."

Giving a curt smile to the group, she turned and walked out of the door. Chad gave a tight nod to the other Saints as he followed her.

"Fuck," Marc said, leaning back heavily in his seat. "That was brutal."

Bart nodded, running his hand through his hair making it stand up at odd angles. "It's a helluva lot easier interviewing someone you're not personally involved with. I just hope she doesn't turn this back on Chad."

Jack rubbed his beard and observed, "She won't. With her training with ATF, she knows we have to investigate everything...every lead that was given." He watched the couple out of the front window as they moved to their separate cars after Chad hugged her tightly. "But I don't know if her instincts about Adam Turner are right. I've got a bad feeling she may be in for a difficult surprise."

13

As Chad drove home behind Dani, his frustration was at an all-time high. His mind swirled with Adam—snatches of conversations they had about girls, about Dani, about life, even love.

We sat on a low wall, beers in our hands near the National Harbor, the setting sun creating patterns in the sky that seemed to make both of us unusually mellow.

"You ever think about settling down one day?" Adam asked.

Shocked by his uncharacteristic question, I shot him a long look, but he continued to stare toward the sky. My mind immediately fell to Dani, but before I could speak, Adam continued.

"My dad bolted toward the door when I was real little and never came back. I always figured love was for the stupid and I'm not stupid."

Staying quiet, I let him talk, not sure what to say to this pensive version of Adam.

"Mom got married a couple of years ago to a good guy. Spent the weekend with them and really like him. Kinda surprised me, but," Adam took a pull on his beer and continued, "mom told me that her problem was picking the wrong man to begin with and that the right one makes all the difference." Chuckling, he added, "Said the only thing the first husband gave her was me and that I was the prize."

Noting his embarrassed shrug, I realized he was now self-conscious. Deciding to alleviate the heavy moment, I questioned, "You? A prize?"

We both laughed before I added, "But yeah, one day, with the right woman, I want to settle down. Get married. Have kids."

Adam nodded beside me. "Don't get me wrong," he joked, "I still like variety...love the pussy that comes my way. But some day...with someone like Dani."

My head jerked involuntarily around, staring dumbly at him, his comment ringing in my ears.

"Not Dani, of course. She knows too much about me," he laughed. "But someone like her. Smart. Gorgeous. Sexy. And someone who would make me be a better man...and won't put up with my shit!"

Pulling into the driveway, parking behind Dani's car, Chad's memories only made him more frustrated. Not only did Adam put Dani's life at risk with his inexplicable behavior, but he finally ended up with not only a woman like Dani, but Dani herself...*and still continued his philandering ways. What the hell were you thinking, man?*

Chad had planned on having Dani stay at his house, but here they were, back at her place. He jumped out of his truck, hustling to the door ahead of her. Entering, he secured the house before walking back to her at the front entrance.

Dani kicked off her heels before skirting around him to walk into the small bedroom. Sighing heavily, Chad followed, stopping at the door. Leaning against the door frame, he watched as she unzipped her skirt, noticing how it stretched over her stomach and hips. Pulling her light pink sweater off, she tossed it into the laundry hamper in the corner. She said nothing to him as she continued to dress comfortably. Pulling on stretchy yoga pants and a t-shirt, she finally turned around, lifting her eyes to his.

"You gonna ignore me all night?" Chad asked, his face unreadable.

Her eyes flashed irritation as she crossed her arms over her chest, cocked her hip and began tapping her foot. "I'm not ignoring you! I was just... changing clothes."

"Dani, I get you're in a snit, but the questions had to be asked. Better us than you being called into the local FBI office."

Pursing her lips, she wanted to retort, but it felt empty. Heaving a deep sigh, she uncrossed her arms.

Chad pushed off the doorframe and moved to stand right in front of her. She leaned her head way back to hold his gaze. He placed his hands on her shoulders, giving a slight squeeze before moving into her space. She face-planted into his chest, then mumbled something. He pulled her back slightly, asking, "What?"

"I said I wasn't in a snit. I don't have snits."

Leaning his head back, he laughed. "Babe, you can throw serious attitude when you're in the mood."

"I don't throw attitude," she huffed.

"I remember you'd give Adam shit when he tried sniffing around you when we first met. And then again when he was being an ass."

Her lips curved at the corners as she wrapped her arms around his middle. "Okay, so maybe I do throw a little attitude...but only when warranted!" They continued to stand, offering each other steadiness and warmth for another minute before Dani leaned back again. "I don't know what to think, Chad. I thought I used to be so good at understanding people, but ever since the funeral, my thoughts about Adam are all twisted up in my head...and my heart."

"I know, babe. I feel the same way. I want to staunchly defend him, but feel like I have to be objective or we could miss an important part of the investigation."

Dani nodded, laying her head against his chest again. She reveled in Chad's warm embrace, feeling as though she had found the missing half of her soul when she was in his arms. Just then, her stomach growled, breaking the tension.

"Come on, let's get some food in us and then we'll sort through the mess we've got."

The idea of fixing dinner was daunting right now, even though Dani loved to cook. Just then the doorbell rang and Chad appeared unsurprised as he headed down the short hall. His large body kept her from seeing who was there, but soon the smell of pizza quickly wafted down the hall.

"Ooh, you ordered pizza!" she squealed, running down the hall and jumping on his back.

Grabbing her ass with one hand, holding her in place on his back while the other hand held the pizza box, he made it to the kitchen table. Tossing the box onto the table, he turned and set her down on the counter. Twisting his body around, he stayed between her legs. The extra height had her face closer to his as he leaned down and claimed her mouth.

Capturing her moan, he slid his tongue into her warmth as he held her face gently in his hands. The kiss lasted several minutes and the pleasure had his cock raring to go. Forcing his dick to behave, he slid his mouth from hers with a little kiss at each corner. Then kissing the freckles across her nose elicited a sought after giggle.

She mewled at the loss of contact when he leaned back, but he said, "Gonna feed you, sweetheart. You've had a rough evening and you need to eat."

She nodded her agreement and it did not take long for them to settle at the table, decimating the pizza. After only two pieces, Dani was full but watched in amazement as Chad finished off the other six pieces of the large, meat lovers, extra onions, and cheese pizza.

"Damn, no wonder you're so big," she joked.

"Yeah, in the past hauling around the bomb disposal equipment gave me my workouts. Now I hit the gym about four times a week."

Eyeing him, she smiled. "Well, whatever you're doing, it works." Leaning forward to kiss a dab of pizza sauce off his cheek, she added, "Cause you've got a gorgeous body."

"Hmmm," he said, turning his face so that her lips hit his. "Anything you'd like to do with this body?"

"I can think of one or two things," she grinned. Squeaking, she gasped as he picked her up in one swoop, carefully carrying her down the hall, giving her the chance to show him what she thought of doing with his body. Then he showed her.

In the middle of the night, Dani got out of bed and padded sleepily to the bathroom. As she finished, she flipped off the light and started back but halted at the second bedroom door. Pushing it open softly, she stepped inside and closed the door behind her before turning on the light so as not to wake Chad.

Walking over to the boxes still stored, she flipped open the closest one. She hated the idea that someone had been in this room...in these boxes. Pulling out a few of Adam's books, she flipped through a few pages. Nothing jumped out at her. Nothing appeared misplaced, no secret message, no signs of anything untoward. *Adam, what were you doing? Did you leave something behind? Is there something here that someone would want? Is that why someone is after your things?* Angrily closing the box, she shoved it to the side. *Whatever you were doing, you brought this crap to my door!*

A click behind her sounded and she whirled around in fright. Her hand flew to her chest as she saw Chad standing in the room, dressed in boxers and nothing else.

"Oh, Lordy, you scared me," she said, slumping against the nearest box.

Moving to her in two steps, he held her close, kissing the top of her head. "What are you doing, babe?"

She gave a little shrug, saying, "I just found myself in here, wondering what secrets might be hidden in what little is left of Adam's belongings. I have no idea what Jack was hoping I'd find, cause there's nothing here."

"Come back to bed, Dani," he gently ordered, propelling her into the master bedroom. "Let the Saints do their job searching for answers. You need to take care of you," he said, placing his hand on her stomach. "By the way, when is your next doctor's appointment?"

"Next week. Why?"

"I'm coming," he pronounced, snuggling to her back, curled around her body.

Lying there, in the dark, surrounded by all that Chad was, she smiled. "Okay," she whispered into the night. "I'd like that."

Bart and Cam attempted to stretch their long legs. Even flying first class, as large as they were it was a tight fit. The trip to St. Louis had been fruitful and if the early intel from Jack was correct, the info they retrieved was useful.

The two men had flown in the previous day, taking a cab to a non-descript hotel. Traveling under one of their many assumed names, they had another cab let them out several blocks from their intended location. The suspect they were assigned to, Robbie Carter, rarely left his apartment. The early reconnaissance told them that he had an affinity for take-out food. Luke monitored his phone, just as he was monitoring the other suspects'. As soon as the call to the local pizza place came in, Luke rerouted it to Bart's.

Convincing the suspect that their pizza delivery guy was out sick and he would have to pick it up, they observed as the young man left his apartment.

"Jesus, easiest maneuvering of a suspect I've ever encountered," Cam laughed.

"That's one thing about these loner types," Bart commented. "They order out a lot."

The two men slipped undetected into the apartment. At first glance, it appeared uncluttered. Kitchen unused, living space orderly. Turning the corner, they saw what would be the dining area. Instead of a table and chairs, several desks took up the space, all of them covered in computer equipment. Laptops, PCs, various monitors, external hard drives...all resulting in a multitude of wires coming from the backs and plugging into numerous surge protectors.

"Fuck, man. He's not working a real job and yet has all this computer shit?"

"Remember, Luke said they can work from home for a variety of companies and make serious bucks if they're really talented. Especially talented in the art of covering their tracks and writing programs to help others cover their tracks as well."

The two efficiently inserted the special drives Luke had supplied them with into every computer in the room. Notifying Luke to begin, he was able to start extrapolating the data from the various machines.

"This doesn't usually take long, but with so many we'd better hope it takes him a while to grab his pizza," Bart commented while walking around Robbie's apartment. A quick search found nothing out of the ordinary.

"Done," Cam called out, getting the signal from Luke. Disconnecting his phone, the two carefully removed every thumb drive, pocketing them before slipping unnoticed from the apartment. Back on the street, they noticed the young man going into his building, the pizza box in his hand.

Once they were back in Virginia, driving home, Bart threw his head back against the headrest.

Cam, driving, glanced over, saying, "You've been wound tight ever since we completed the mission."

Sighing, Bart shook his head as though to clear his thoughts for a moment, finally saying, "He looked kind of normal."

"Who?"

"Robbie Carter."

"What'd you expect?" Cam asked. "A sign hanging around his neck saying *I'm a traitor*?"

"Do you think these guys understand what they're doing?"

"You mean who they're actually taking money from?"

"Yeah. I'd like to think that they really don't have a fuckin' clue that they're helping terrorists with bomb detonations."

Cam sighed, "I don't know, man. I don't know."

"As a SEAL, I knew my mission. I fought an enemy overseas so we could try to keep the war from coming into our backyards, and here we've got people undermining everything we did."

The two men drove silently for a while before Cam spoke. "Do you ever wish you were in a completely different business? Like a banker or grocer or...or...hell, I don't know, but someone who goes about their life oblivious to what's in their own city? I used to never have these thoughts, but now with Miriam pregnant, I wonder about the world our child will be born into."

Running his fingers through his hair, Bart knew if Faith was with him she would smile at the way his hair was now standing on end. Thinking about Faith calmed him...gave him purpose...and a place to land when life was coming fast and furious. "Nah," he answered. "As much as I fuckin' hate what we find out sometimes, I'd rather be in the know and keep doing something about it."

Cam nodded, understanding what Bart was saying. Pressing on the accelerator a little more, they churned up the miles heading back to their women...and their own private peace.

Muhammad, Abdul, and Fazan walked into the room occupied by Habib, as he looked up from his computer screen, a smile on his face.

"I've got a good one," he said, handing his written notes to Muhammad. "Took a while, but this one's in."

Looking at the notes, Muhammad said, "Oliver Sands. Atlanta, Georgia. Single. Former student at MIT. Dropped out?" Muhammad lifted his gaze to Habib in question.

"Yeah. He'd been an "A" student but says the money ran out."

"Did you check?"

Habib's irritation showed on his face. "Of course."

Muhammad nodded. "Good. Get him in."

His irritation passing as quickly as it came, Habib nodded. Looking over at Fazan, he said, "I have you scheduled next. The spring is making the selection good. This time of year, more and more are getting online to find the loves of their lives."

The men chuckled as Fazan started to slide into a seat. He was halted as Muhammad placed a hand on his shoulder, saying, "No, not now."

Fazan looked up in surprise but said nothing, waiting for their leader to speak. Muhammad continued, "I've got a new assignment for you. We've got a new site for you to supervise. We have a man nearby that will offer assistance. This will be different—our explosives will still be easily made but our detonators will be more sophisticated...and with our computer recruits, we will be able to program them to detonate from greater distances. The man works for a company where he can obtain what we need to make a bigger...statement."

The others laughed and Fazan nodded his agreement as he stood, following Muhammad out of the door as Abdul took his place at the laptop.

Luke eagerly began collating and analyzing the data from Robbie Carter's computers that Bart and Cam had delivered. He could have worked from home, knowing his security was absolute, but there was something about being in the compound. It was quiet—when the other Saints were gone. Perhaps it was the professional surroundings that were stimulating—as opposed to his house which was lonely. *Funny, I've never thought of my house as boring. I like boring. I like predictable. I like—*

The sound of an incoming email rang through the silent night. Jerking his gaze to his computer, he smiled as he recognized the sender. His mystery assistant.

I see you have a new project.

Chuckling to himself, he typed, **Yes. I'm not sure how you can see what I'm working on. But yes, new mission. National security.**

The reply came back after a minute. **I'm just special, I guess. You will find that you need to extrapolate the intel from the garbage they encrypt it with. I will send you coding.**

Luke sat for a moment waiting to see what they were sending, but he already knew it would be invaluable. He would be able to figure it out alone, but having his mystery assistant help would make the job go quicker. Finally, his email alerted again and he downloaded the program sent.

Thank you, he typed. **I wish I could repay you.**

No need. Just keep me a secret. Until next time.

Luke immediately let the program begin to do its work, watching as lines and lines of code ran across his screen. Several months ago, he had been contacted by this person who could see what he was working on, even though his system was equipped with the best encryption available. But they needed to be anonymous, saying it was too dangerous for them to be discovered.

When the other Saints inquired about his mystery helper, he told them that there were leagues of brilliant computer geniuses and the ones not snapped up by the big companies would sometimes work independently. For the most part, legally. But there were some employed by the criminal underground, and the money was good. Some had no idea what their genius was being used for, thus entrapping them when they wanted to leave. He often wondered if this was not the scenario of his mystery assistant. *At least, I hope so. I'd hate to think they were willingly involved in criminal acts!*

He stood to leave, knowing the programs would run all night. As he made his way up the back stairs to Jack's garage, he slipped out to his jeep. Driving home, he felt the loneliness seep in. He thought of his fellow Saints, whom he loved like brothers. Many of them were now involved with someone special. Like them, he was a tall man, physically fit, and sure of intelligence...if a little rusty in the social graces. Allowing himself a moment of pity, he wondered who would go for a man like him—one who preferred the quiet life.

14

Feet up in the stirrups, Dani decided she had to be in the most vulnerable position for any woman to be in. Her shirt was pulled up to under her breasts and a sheet covered her bottom half. Glancing nervously to the side, she met Chad's grinning face and pretended to glare.

He leaned forward, taking her hand in his, lifting it to his lips and placing a kiss on her palm. His lips were warm and comforting. They both jumped as the doctor came in.

"Mrs. Turner, how are you?" the friendly doctor asked, her eyes moving between Dani and Chad.

"I'm doing well," she replied. "Um...this is a good friend of mine, Chad Fornelli."

Chad stood and shook the doctor's hand.

Smiling, the doctor nodded and proceeded with the examination. We'll move to the sonogram in a few minutes, but everything looks good now. You're approximately fourteen weeks along so we won't be able to determine the sex at this appointment, but we should be able to by the next one."

The doctor left after answering Dani's few questions and the sonogram technician came in. Lowering the sheet, exposing Dani's small baby bump, she squirted the cool jelly on her stomach and began moving the sonogram transducer around.

Swush, swush, swush immediately sounded throughout the room.

"Baby's heartbeat sounds good," the sonographer said, as she continued her work.

Dani's eyes filled with tears as she turned her head, capturing Chad's gaze. His eyes were riveted to the screen before dropping down to hers. Linking their fingers, they peered in awe as the sonographer completed her measurements.

The machine printed out a length of pictures, showing the tiny baby against the black background of the amniotic fluid. Tiny legs and arms stood out and its head was clearly visible.

"Oh, my God!" Dani cried as the pictures were handed to her. Chad stood and leaned over, seeing the images. He kissed her forehead and whispered, "Congratulations, little mama."

Lifting her eyes from the picture of her baby, she turned to Chad, her anxiety replaced by gratefulness at the smile on his face.

As the sonographer left them, he assisted her from the table before handing her pants to her. She dressed quickly and then turned nervously back to Chad, her eyes at chest level.

He lifted her chin with his fingers, saying, "What's wrong? And don't tell me *nothing*, because I can always tell when something's wrong."

"This is a lot...I mean, the pregnancy is a lot for me to take in so I can only imagine this is a lot for you. I don't want you to feel...trapped."

"Trapped?" he said, his voice dropping an octave.

Sucking in her lips, she nodded. "You said you wanted to be here, but Chad...I'm afraid of...of..."

"Of what? That I'll turn tail and run? That I'll wake up tomorrow and feel trapped? Don't you know me better than that?"

Her nervousness was now replaced by irritation. She grabbed her purse off the chair and tried to move around him.

"You do that, you know? When you're pissed," he commented, his feet apart and his hands on his hips.

"Do what?" she glared.

"Try to maneuver around me without actually looking at me."

Stopping, she grumbled, "Well, if you weren't the size of a barn, maybe I'd have an easier time getting around you!"

"Babe," he said, his voice now gentle. He waited until she looked up at him, her gaze uncertain. Stepping closer, he cupped her cheek. "I'm here because I want to be. Not out of guilt. Not out of a misplaced sense of duty. I'm here because you're the woman I want to be with. You're everything to me. And this baby," he said, placing his hand on her slightly rounded stomach, "will be mine to love as well."

Her eyes filled with tears as she looked up into his beauty. He pulled her in, and as her cheek rested on his chest, his steady heartbeat comforted her. "My life is so crazy right now," she whispered, her voice catching on the words. "And this," she held up the fetal pictures, "just makes it all so real. Chad, I can't screw up again."

"I know. And I'm here to be with you every step of the way. I promise." He leaned down, placing a soft kiss on her warm lips, feeling them curve into a smile underneath his. "Now how about we go feed this baby?"

A week later the Saints were meeting, this time with Roscoe and Mitch on video-conferencing, now that Luke's programing analysis was complete. He had sent the results to both ATF and FBI the day before.

"We appreciate the information you sent to us. Of course," Roscoe added, "we don't want to have any knowledge about how the intel was discovered."

The Saints grinned as Bart and Cam fist bumped each other.

"Our analysisists are using it to pinpoint where we think more cells will be located and to see if we can interpret what their next moves are. Good work. We have a couple more for you to do the same with and then that should complete the original contract with the Saints," Roscoe finished.

Jack looked up quickly. "Original? You have more?"

Mitch nodded, saying, "We've got intelligence telling us that another local location may be created for the purpose of bomb making."

"Damn!" Chad cursed, the memory of Adam fresh in his mind. Ever since he took Dani to the doctor and heard the heartbeat, he had Adam in his thoughts—wondering what he had gotten mixed up with and how the situation was now carrying over to Dani and the baby.

"We've got no location and no specifics at this time, but are hoping to gather more intel from what we got from the computer links that we now have access to," Mitch added.

"So what do you need from the Saints?" Jack queried.

"Right now, just the same mission as with Robbie Carter. I'm sending you two more. One in Dallas and a new one in Atlanta. Once we obtain their computer information, we hope to know more about the local cell."

After Mitch and Roscoe signed off, the Saints continued to process their cases. As the others reported on what they were working on, what had been completed, and new missions assigned, Chad continued to turn his mind over and over to Adam.

We were heading to a call in a Metro station outside of D.C. and as usual, Adam was driving while I was coordinating with the other team members.

Tamping down the adrenaline that always ratcheted up before a mission, I was shocked when out of the blue, Adam said, "This never gets old, does it?"

Shooting him a curious look, he continued, "This. You know, heading into the unknown. Someone reports a strange bag and we get called."

Still not knowing where he was going with his thoughts, I waited, aware that Adam would keep talking.

"We always hope it's nothing, but in this day and age...that bag represents all the possible evils in the terrorists' arsenal."

I nodded, understanding dawning. He was right. The old days of an unidentified object in a public place would not signify anything. But now...we went in with full protection, robots, and a desire to keep others safe.

Not finished, Adam kept going as we drew nearer to our destination. "Every single time we head to one of these, I always wonder if it'll be my last. And swear to God, Chad...when it's my time to go, I'll be damned if it's at the hands of a fuckin' terrorist."

Nodding my agreement, we pull up to the blockade at the Metro station and show our identification. My mind flashes to Dani—it always does nowadays.

Glancing over to Adam as we hop out of our SUV to begin suiting up, I wonder who he's thinking of.

Suddenly realizing all eyes were on him, Chad looked over at Jack. "Sorry, boss. My mind's on Adam. And Dani. And the baby."

The others gave him their attention as he heaved a sigh. Taking a deep breath, he continued, "I'm committed to Dani. I've loved her for almost two years and I'm not fuckin' things up again. I want her...and I want the baby. Adam was a good friend, at one time, and I'm determined to care for the child as my own, but always let it know who Adam was."

Looking around at his friends, he added, "At least, as long as I find out he wasn't a traitor."

"That's maybe why Dani is so defensive about Adam," Blaise observed. "She's under a lot of stress and the thought that her husband was in the deep pockets of terrorists, may be more than she can deal with."

"Jack, I realize you're handing out new assignments, but I'd like to focus for a few days, continuing to find out what Adam may have become involved with. If for no other reason than to protect Dani. If someone at MES is involved, then this may be bigger than what we think."

Jack nodded his agreement. "I think you're right. Take time to see if you can dig up anything on what Adam was doing." Pinning Chad with a hard stare, he added, "But Chad? Be prepared to accept whatever you learn...even if it's not what you want to."

Accepting that piece of tough advice, he offered a head jerk before leaving the compound.

Dani looked at the time on her computer and realized she needed to prepare for the afternoon meeting. Before she left her office, her phone rang. Seeing Adam's mother's phone number on the display, she answered. "Janice?"

"Hello, Dani," Mrs. Turner greeted. "I know you're at work and don't want to bother you, but Terry and I wanted to thank you for giving us some of Adam's things."

"Oh, Janice, you don't have to thank me. I'm still going through some of the pictures and will make sure to send copies to you as well."

"That would be lovely, dear. I also wanted you to know that we found a key in the things you gave us. It was somewhat buried in the box, but it looks like a bank's safety deposit box key. We thought you included it by mistake or maybe didn't see it, so I'd like to get it to you."

A key? We didn't have a safety-deposit box. "Um... okay. I don't really know what it goes to, but I'll certainly come pick it up."

Dani settled on a time she would come by before they disconnected. Glancing back at the clock, she hustled down the hall to the conference room, her mind whirling. *Key? Oh, Adam, what now?*

Dani sat in the meeting, looking over the latest project she had been assigned. The military was interested in the newest explosives, especially the C-4, along with the CH-6, as well as the HMX line. They were also interested in the newer detonators being developed, which was her specialty. As the meeting droned on, her eyes shifted from Jahfar to Ethan. Now that she had discussed her reticence about Jahfar to Ethan, she noticed Ethan observed him closely.

She never observed Jahfar doing anything untoward, but the way he always seemed to be interested in anything she did, made her nervous. As the meeting concluded, she noted he left quickly, leaving a few papers behind. About to follow him she was halted by a committee member needing her input. As she finally walked down the hall toward her office, she saw Jahfar's door open, with his computer on, but he was nowhere to be found.

"Looking for Jahfar?" one of the secretaries asked. "He said he was grabbing an early lunch."

"Thanks," she responded. "I'll just lay these papers on his desk." Walking in, she moved to his desk, taking a look at his laptop. Leaning over, she tried to see what he had open.

"Can I help you?" his voice called from the doorway.

"Oh, Jahfar. Sorry. You left these papers at the meeting. I thought you might need them."

He walked around her to the desk, closing his laptop with a click while smiling at her. "Thank you, Dani. It's nice to know you are looking out for me."

His dark eyes pierced her gaze and she blinked, determined not to look away. "Sure thing, Jahfar. I'll see you later."

As she left his office, his door closed firmly behind her. *Damn, that was unproductive.* She stood for a moment in indecision of what she wanted to do next, when she heard his voice—soft, but discernable.

"Yeah, I think she was snooping."

Dani's heart pounded as she moved quickly away from his door and hustled back to her office. Grabbing her purse and briefcase, she made her way to the secretary. "I'm taking half a sick day," she said. "I think a migraine is coming on."

With wishes for feeling better ringing in her ears, she made her way out of the building and into her car. Sitting there for a moment, she let the pieces of the puzzle swirl around her. Adam. Jahfar. Chad and the Saints' mission. All unrelated...and yet, her stomach seized in apprehension. Glancing down at her baby bump, she placed her hand carefully on it. *Oh, Sweet Pea, what a mess your mom is in.*

Arriving home after a visit with Adam's mom and stepdad, Dani dropped her purse beside her on the sofa. She was pleased, but not surprised, they had taken the news about Chad in her life so well. They always liked Chad and she secretly thought they wish Adam had been as steady as his friend. She smiled as she remembered his mother hugging her tightly, whispering in her ear how happy she was that Dani had a man like Chad in her life now.

Kicking her shoes off, she curled her legs up under her as she reached into her bag and pulled out the key. No doubt about it...it was a bank's safety deposit box key.

Twirling it around in her fingers, she tried to remain calm, but her heart pounded. *What bank is it from? And what's there?* The realization slammed into her once again that the man she married had more secrets...and they kept coming out.

She spied a picture of Adam on the mantle. Her legs moved of their own accord taking her closer, and she scrutinized his face. *Smiling...always smiling...as though he didn't have a care in the world.* Rage began to build, coloring her vision red.

"What the hell were you doing, Adam?" she screamed at the photograph, holding the key in her uplifted hand.

A noise from the front of the house sounded, but the roar of fury in her ears kept her from responding. A few seconds later she looked up as Chad walked into the room.

Seeing Dani's car outside but hearing her scream, he had charged into the house only to find her standing at the mantle, yelling at a picture of

Adam. Rushing forward, he cried out, "What's wrong?"

As he held her body, ready to crush it to his, he saw she was holding an object in her fingers. A key. *A key to a bank's safety deposit box?*

15

Staring at the key in her hand, he reached out and gently put his hands on her shoulders. "Okay, Dani. Talk to me, baby."

"I came home early. I'm not even sure why...just overwhelmed with everything going on." She halted and he led her to her room to sit on the bed, brushing her hair from her face. "I got a call from Adam's parents. They had found a key with the things I gave them and wanted me to have it." Her eyes implored his to understand. "Chad, I keep seeing conspiracy theories all around me. With Adam...at work. I just want to know what's going on. Now, I'm wondering if Adam hid something and that's why someone was searching my things."

"Do you recognize the key?"

"No, not at all."

"What bank does it belong to?" Chad asked.

"I don't know. We had a joint banking account but very little in it." Shoulders lifting in a slight shrug, she confessed, "We both put money in the account to cover our bills, but we still kept our separate savings accounts."

Chad took the key from her cold fingers and moved it around in his hand, hoping an answer would pop up clearly. *Of course not. Come on, Adam, what were you trying to do?*

The thick, flat key only had a number engraved on it, indicating the bank box number. "Do you have a magnifying glass?"

Her brow knit as she thought. "Um, maybe in the junk drawer. I'll go take a look." In a minute, she came back with one in her hand. "I found one," she exclaimed as she handed it to him. "Did you find any marks on it?"

Chad held the key where the thin edge was facing up and looked through the magnifying glass carefully. "There're scratches on the edge that look like just indiscriminate scratches. But maybe they mean something." The marks were tiny and he wasn't able to discern what they were. Looking up in frustration, he said, "We need a microscope. Something with strong magnification."

"Where can we find one?"

Chad paced the room for a moment before pulling out his phone. "Blaise? Got a strange request. Do you happen to have a microscope at your house? Perfect. Dani and I need to come over now. Gotcha. Thanks, man."

Dani looked up in confusion. "Blaise has a microscope?"

"He's a veterinarian. Doesn't practice in private. He worked for DEA." Seeing her questioning expression, he said, "Yeah, DEA hires veterinarians, mostly for work with their dogs and also biological warfare. He's trained as a vet, but also drug enforcement, and has one of the most analytical minds we have with the Saints."

Grabbing her hand as they quickly alarmed the house and headed toward his truck, he settled her in. "He also has a menagerie of rescue animals so I'm sure he has vet equipment at his place."

Shaking her head, Dani confessed, "I have no idea how Jack managed to recruit such a diverse group of men, but it works!"

About twenty minutes later, Chad turned off the road onto a long, gravel driveway. "This kind of looks like Jack's driveway, without the security gate," she observed.

Laughing, he warned, "Don't get your hopes up, babe. Blaise's place is more of an animal shelter than a luxury cabin."

As they came around a curve in the drive and into a clearing, she saw what he meant. A modest house sat in the middle, with numerous outbuildings to the side. As they approached, she viewed kennels with fenced dog-runs to the side. Parking, Chad assisted her down from the truck and they were immediately surrounded by barking dogs.

A loud whistle cut through the cacophony and the dogs stopped barking, each sitting. Blaise came from the house. "Sorry, guys. They're excited to see visitors."

"They're all gorgeous," Dani exuded, bending to pet one.

"Thanks," Blaise said, smiling as he rubbed the ears of the closest dog. Looking at Chad, he said, "Follow me and I'll show you the microscope."

They walked into the house and Dani noticed the room was exceptionally clean and neat for so many animals running around. They bypassed the living room and kitchen, heading to a large room built onto the back, equipped just like the inside of any veterinarian's office. "Wow," Dani said. "This is amazing."

Blaise shrugged. "I examine all of the animals that I find, making sure they are well and inoculated before I try to adopt them out."

They moved over to the counter with the microscope and Chad pulled out the key. As he examined at it under the scope, Blaise turned to Dani with a questioning expression.

"Adam's parents came across this when they went through his things, but we have no way of knowing what bank it goes to. Chad noticed scratches on the thin edge of the key."

Nodding, Blaise leaned over Chad, adjusting the light to its maximum potential.

"Got it," Chad said. "It's barely visible, but the scratches make up CNB."

"Charlestown National Bank. That's not where

we banked, of course, since we lived about forty miles north of Charlestown."

As the three walked out of the house, Blaise pulled Chad to the side as Dani walked ahead to pet the friendly dogs. "Man, do you think she's ready for whatever may be in that box?"

Chad watched Dani as she laughed at the dogs' antics. "I don't know, Blaise. Hell, I'm not sure I'm ready." Clapping Blaise on the shoulder, he added, "But we've got to find out what he was doing for either of us to have any peace."

Dani nervously stood in the Charlestown National Bank lobby as a man approached, introducing himself, and asked if he could assist.

"Yes, I have an unusual request," she said. "My deceased husband left this safety-deposit key for me, but I haven't been in this bank before. I brought his death certificate and my identification, as well as our marriage license, if that helps."

Mr. Sedwick looked at her paperwork and then went back to the safety deposit box vault. He motioned for her to follow him. Chad walked with her, his hand resting on the small of her back.

"According to our records, Adam Turner rented the box a month before his death certificate was issued. Normally, anyone obtaining access to the box has to sign the signature card ahead of time, but he wrote on the application that his wife was to have full access if he were deceased. Since you have all your documentation, there's no problem. May I have the key?"

Chad felt her quiver underneath his fingertips and hoped whatever was in the box would supply them with answers. Bracing himself, he watched as the box was pulled from its vault and handed to Dani. The banker left the room and she looked up at Chad, her heart pounding.

"I'm terrified," she confessed.

"Babe, I'm right here."

Nodding, she lifted the lid and peered inside. A single piece of paper, folded in half was the only contents. With shaking fingers, she lifted it out, but said, "Chad, I can't do this here. Please take me out of here."

Leaving immediately, with the paper still clutched in her hand, he helped her to his truck. Sliding to the middle of the front seat so that they were side by side, she opened the missive so they could both read it at the same time.

Dani, if you are reading this then I'm gone. I'm so sorry. I became involved in something and I'm trying to not have it blow back on you. Please find Chad and trust him to know how to take care of you now. I need you to understand that not everything is as it seems. Even this note needed to be hidden and I took a chance that you might never find it. Just know that, for the time we were together...I was happy. I did care for you, even if I didn't always show it. Honest Dani, I'd hoped to see you rock our child in that old rocking chair of yours, but maybe in the future, you'll still be able to. I know I wasn't the husband you wanted and, honestly, if anyone were to take my place, I hope it would be Chad. He's a good man...the only one I can think deserving of you. With love, Adam

The note dropped into her lap as shaking overtook her. Chad pulled her into his lap, holding her body as tightly as he could, letting her tears flow. "Let it out, babe," he murmured into her hair as her body bucked with sobs. He tried to give her his strength, but his mind ran over and over the words of the note. *Damnit, Adam. What the hell were you involved with? And what were you trying to tell us?*

Slowly Dani's sobs lessened and she lifted her tear-swollen eyes to his. "I was so happy earlier after talking to Adams's parents and now...now, I don't know what I think about everything!"

Chad wiped tears from her cheeks and tentatively asked, "So, Adam's mom was okay about us?"

Nodding, she sniffed loudly, then answered with a watery smile. "She always liked you, Chad. She told me she was glad I had a man like you in my life."

Letting his breath out in a whoosh, Chad felt relief flood his body. *Well, at least that's one less thing hanging over her head.*

"Take me home, please," she begged. Nodding, he shifted her to the middle of the seat and buckled her in. The drive was silent except for the hitching of her breath. Pulling onto his road, she became aware of her surroundings.

"I want you here tonight, Dani," Chad explained. "Here. In my place. Surrounded by everything that is me...and only me."

Looking over at his strong profile, she nodded. "I'd like that. I need that."

Unlike with Blaise's property, Dani barely registered when Chad pulled off the road and drove down a long drive. As the fog in her mind slowly cleared, she saw the wooded property and the old two-story farmhouse at the end of the drive. The white painted house with dark green shutters stood out starkly with the pine and cedar trees surrounding it. The front porch held a porch swing as well as several rocking chairs.

"It's lovely," she said, truthfully. Chad pulled her gently from the truck cab and easily lifted her down to the ground. Linking fingers, he led her up the steps and into the house, not stopping until he made it to the master bathroom upstairs.

The modern space, finished with blue, white, and grey tile, sported a huge, jetted tub along with a separate shower. Looking around wide-eyed, she said, "Chad, I hardly know what to say. Did you do all the work on the house?"

"Most of it," he admitted, smiling at her pleasure. "I work on projects during weekends and down time."

"You hustled me up here so fast, I didn't have a chance to see the rest of it."

Laughing, he said, "Well, I started in the bathroom and kitchen first. So a lot of the house still has projects to complete." Leaning over, he turned on the faucet to the tub, saying, "Take a hot bath and try to let some of the stress drift away."

He left the room and she turned back to the tub filling with steaming water. Walking over to the small window, she looked out onto the green yard flanked by woods. Stripping, she settled into the water, sliding down until her head leaned comfortably back on the tub edge and closed her eyes.

Blissfully relaxed, unaware of anything other than the warm water, a knock on the door startled her. "Yes?" she called out.

"I've got a clean shirt for you, babe."

"Come on in," she invited.

Chad opened the door, surprised to see Dani still in the tub. "Isn't the water cool by now?"

"I added more hot water so I could stay longer." She smiled up at him. "Why don't you join me?"

Moving over, he looked down at her beauty, rosy with the heat, and his cock swelled painfully. "Join you? You need to rest and that's not what'll happen if I get in there with you."

She leaned to the side of the tub, her arms hanging over as she looked up at him squatting next to her. "Chad, I need you. I want you. I want to forget this case...forget what's happening all around us. I just want to feel you."

He reached behind and jerked his t-shirt over his head. Standing, he shucked his jeans and boxers off in record time, stepping over into the tub. "Well, I aim to please."

Dani scooted forward and allowed him to slid in behind her. As big as he was, the water rose to a dangerous level. She let some out then replaced the stopper. Leaning back, she rested her back against his chest with his knees on either side.

Chad soaped his hands and then moved them over her slippery body. Her shoulders, then down to her breasts. Giving each one attention, she arched her back, pressing them into his palms even more. Her moans filled his ears as his cock pressed against her lower back.

Lowering his hands, he moved them over her slightly rounded belly. The sensuous feeling was heady, knowing there was new life beneath his hands.

Suddenly, Dani twisted around, facing him. She placed her legs on the outside of his, bringing her aching core right to his cock. Lifting herself she settled just to his tip. His large hands spanned her waist as he assisted her. Wanting her to set the pace, he allowed her to settle a bit at a time down his shaft until she was fully seated.

Chad groaned, repressing the desire to fuck her hard and fast. With her hands on his shoulders for support and his hands on her waist, she began to move up and down. The friction was sending sparks throughout her body. Throwing her head back, she picked up the pace.

He viewed her beautiful body as it moved over his. Her breasts bounced in front of him and he leaned forward, pulling a nipple deep into his mouth. Nipping it lightly, he felt his cock swell even more. "Come on, baby, give it to me," he called out.

Her body, muscles coiled tightly, was so close as she rode up and down, his cock filling her, rasping against the raw nerve endings.

Moving one hand lower between them, he pressed against her clit, sliding his thumb around the swollen nub. He felt her body jerk as her tight sex grabbed his dick. His balls tightened and he lunged upward, thrusting over and over as they both came.

She fell forward, her head landing on his shoulder as her ragged breathing matched his. Chad lay boneless for a moment, his energy sapped once his orgasm poured himself into her. He took her weight gladly as his arms managed to pull her closer. Slowly, consciousness brought awareness to him. Shifting her in his arms, he hefted his large body from the tub, settling her feet onto the thick bathmat. She stepped back, smiling up at him. *My gentle giant.*

She watched as he let the water out of the tub after wrapping her in a thick towel. He turned back to her, grinning as he toweled off rapidly. Moving over to her, he pulled her in possessively, his lips latching onto hers.

Placing his large hand on her stomach, he asked, "Are you okay, little mama?"

Smiling up at him, she nodded. "Yeah. Thank you."

Rearing back, he looked at her in surprise. "You never have to thank me for loving you, babe. Being with you...is my life. My dream. The one I thought I gave up. So every minute with you is a miracle to me."

"I was overwhelmed earlier," she explained. "We still don't know what Adam was into, but he was right. I was always meant to be with you."

Kissing her once more, he pulled one of his large t-shirts over her head, settling it over her baby bump. "We'll go back and get your clothes tomorrow. If..." he peered into her eyes, "you want to stay here."

"There's nowhere else I'd rather be," she answered honestly, cupping his stubbled jaw. Raising on her tiptoes, she kissed his lips. Soft. Sweet. With the promise of many tomorrows.

16

"Did the shipment come in on schedule?" Muhammad asked, walking into the house with Abdul.

"Got it here," Fazan answered, pointing to the unmarked boxes on the table.

Muhammad's eyes roamed around the room, seeing Habib coming in from a back room with several more men and two women with him. He pinned the newcomers with a hard stare. "Do you understand your instructions?"

They nodded hurriedly, eager to agree to whatever he asked. Scowling, Muhammad looked at Habib, mollified when he nodded as well.

"They have the materials now and understand what they are to construct," Habib answered. "They've also been informed how to conduct themselves to keep a low profile."

Muhammad looked at them again, saying, "Your assignment here is important to the cause...if your actions draw unwanted attention, our work is all for nothing. This," he pointed to the box on the table, "is what we need for setting off the explosives." Leaning in for emphasis, he said, "We do not want anyone to suspect we are here until we are ready to show them."

Again the men and women nodded their understanding, fear in their eyes. "Your work here," Muhammad said, "is part of the grand jihad in eliminating this civilization from within." Pride replaced fear from the group as they gazed upon the man they knew was in charge.

Muhammad left Habib to work with the newcomers and walked into another room with Fazan and Abdul. "I want more of the detonators from our contact. We will need time for the new recruits to learn how best to use them from a distance. How soon can we expect the shipment from him?"

"It will be a while," Fazan confirmed. "He is exceedingly cautious. We can go slow and get what we need or possibly lose everything if we rush."

Muhammad agreed, shaking his head slowly. "We know what it is to go slow. This country always wants things fast...in a hurry for everything. It will be their downfall." Turning to Fazan, he said, "Stay in close communication with our contact so we know when we can expect our next shipment." To Abdul, he added, "And find out where that Turner woman is. I want to know what she knows about her husband's activities."

He and Abdul walked out of the house and Fazan placed a call. "He understands there is no guarantee of another shipment soon, but wants to know when you think it will take place. I know, I know. Fine, stay in touch."

Jahfar hung up the phone, wiping the perspiration from his brow. He had walked out of his home to take the call and as he came back in, he observed his wife in the kitchen and heard his two sons playing in the den. His wife turned from the stove, smiling until she glanced at his face. Laying the spoon down, she walked over to him. "Are you all right?"

Forcing a smile on his face, he returned her hug. "Of course. I'm fine." She moved back to her dinner preparations.

"Tell the boys dinner will be soon."

Jahfar nodded as he walked to the den, hoping to hold everything together until all could go as planned.

Chad reported to the Saints and Mitch what the note from Adam said. No one spoke for a moment, their shock evident on their faces.

Finally, Blaise asked, "Did Adam say anything else? Just that not everything is as it seems?"

"What the hell did he mean?" Jude asked. "That he was working with terrorists and was sorry about it or that he wasn't even though he appears guilty?"

Shaking his head, Chad threw his hands up. "I've got no idea."

"There's got to be more than that," Marc added. Gaining the attention of the others, he continued. "He went to the trouble of putting a note in a safety deposit box and hiding the key. That makes no fuckin' sense."

"Do you have the note?" Mitch asked, from the video conference.

"No, Dani has it. Other than that, the words are mostly personal and I think she put it in her purse." Seeing the looks from the others, he added, "She's moved in with me. We went to her place yesterday and packed up everything we could and brought the haul to my place. We're getting movers this weekend to bring the rest."

"She's had a lot of changes," Luke commented. "That's gotta be a lot of stress on her."

"Yeah, well this one will be the last," Chad vowed.

"If she'll let me, I'd like to look at the note," Luke said. "I could run it through some decoding programs to discern if there was something else."

Nodding, Chad agreed. Pulling out his phone, he called her. "Hey, baby. Do you have the note with you? Can you scan it to me? Luke would like to run the message through some programs to see if he can discover a code. We don't know. We're grasping at straws right now. Okay, thanks. See you, tonight." Looking at Luke, he confirmed, "She's sending it to my email."

Jack, turning back to Mitch, said, "So where are we on the sleeper cells?"

Mitch grimaced, "Fuckers are coming in faster than we can keep up with them. Got a group in Fairfax and Richmond, plus about three others in smaller communities. We're keeping an eye on them. Here's the part that bites us in the ass—the Mexican drug cartels are sneaking in terrorists from the Middle East, through the Texas border."

Cam's eyes jumped up to the screen, a curse escaping from his lips. He spent time in Mexico on a mission to rescue a nurse from a drug cartel. The mission was successful and he was now married to Miriam, the nurse he rescued, but he had seen up close the long arm of the Mexican drug cartels.

"Can you use us?" Bart asked.

"I wish I could, Bart, but with the homemade and professional explosives these people have, I can't trust that even your skills would not trigger whatever the fuck they've got set up."

The group's frustration ran high, not used to spinning their wheels and getting nowhere.

Dani sat at her desk, finishing up the latest proposal for the new explosive devices MES produced to sell to the military. She glanced at her watch and was surprised to realize it was almost time to go home. Sending her files to a secure drop box, she forwarded them to Ethan for final approval before digging the note from Adam out of her purse. Standing, she walked to the printer/scanner on the credenza beside her desk. She held the note for a moment in her hands, rubbing her fingers over the words. The fierce anger she felt toward Adam after he was killed had slowly morphed into resignation. And with that came the remembrances of good times. Now, her emotions moved toward complete frustration.

Aaron popped his head around the corner of her door. "Hey, Dani, Melissa's here and wanted to confirm if you were coming to the company picnic this weekend?"

"I hadn't really made up my mind," she confessed. "Does she need to know now?" She watched as his eyes dropped to her hand holding the note.

"She's in my office, do you have a minute to talk to her before you leave?"

"Uh...yeah, sure." Placing the note on the scanner, she quickly closed the lid before he had a chance to observe what was in her hand, unwilling to share any of her crazy life with someone from work.

She followed him out and made her way to his office, greeting his wife warmly. The two women chatted for a few minutes, before Dani headed back to her office. As she turned the corner of the hall, she saw Jahfar leaving her office. His eyes met hers and she swore she imagined guilt piercing his gaze.

Aaron came from the other direction with Ethan and met them at the entrance to her office. "Hey, did you and Melissa get things straightened out?" Aaron asked.

Her lips pressed into a tight smile, she forced a pleasant expression on her face. "Yes, thank you." Turning back to Jahfar, she cocked her head to the side. "Find what you were looking for?"

Smoothly, he replied, "I was looking for you, so now I have."

Lifting an eyebrow, she waited for him to explain, but he only looked at his watch and said he would talk to her tomorrow. She stared at his back as he walked down the hall.

"You okay?" Ethan asked, studying her carefully.

Sucking in a deep breath, she replied, "I may be wrong, but I just don't trust him."

Neither man spoke as she moved back into her office. She finished scanning the note and then sent it to Chad's email. *Luke, if you can find anything from this, good on you!*

"You're right," Marc said, looking at the note. "There's not much to go on, is there?"

Even Luke gazed at it dubiously. "I'll run the words through some decoding programs I've got, but you said Adam wasn't much of a computer techie."

"At least not the Adam I knew." The idea that for over a year he did not truly know Adam gnawed at Chad. *If I'd stayed with the ATF, would I have been able to keep Adam from going off the reservation? If he actually did?* Heaving a sigh, he rubbed his hand over his face and stood, stretching his large frame.

"I'm going to take a run, guys," he announced. "Maybe that'll clear the cobwebs from my brain."

"Want any company?" Bart asked.

"Sure," he replied. The two men changed in the locker room and headed out. Chad was grateful that Bart kept the run challenging, but also stayed quiet so he could process the myriad of thoughts zinging through his mind. *Adam's note to Dani sounded like the note a man would give to his wife, knowing his life could end at any time. Was that just because of his dangerous job? If so, why leave it in a safety deposit box? Why not with a family member...or stuck in a book...or... No, Adam wanted to make sure that not just anyone could get to it. Therefore, there has to be some meaning behind the words. But what? And since the note was in a safety box, why did Adam have to be so cryptic?*

His feet pounded the trail, sweat poured off him, his muscles worked hard...but no clue came to mind. *Was it because Adam was afraid that someone might find the key besides Dani, so he didn't want to speak plainly?* Finishing the run, Chad decided he did not think that Adam had the ability to plan something so intricate. *Not the good-time Adam that I knew!*

Dani drove down the driveway to Chad's house sitting in the woods. She sat for a minute in her car, looking around. *How many moves have I made in the past year? Ugh!* Noting the few blooming dogwood trees dotting the woods amongst the cedars and pines, she had to admit she appreciated the view. She knew Chad had been working on house projects and she loved the results. The house was beautiful...*a good place to raise a child?* She waited to see if the ensuing panic would set in, but it did not. With her hand on her belly, she said, "All right, little one. I'm trying to do the best thing here for all of us. Honest, your mommy's never been so flighty in her life. I was always the calm and steady one. Rational to a fault." Sucking in a deep breath, she stepped out of her vehicle and walked to the front door.

"Well, for now, this is home, baby, and I pray it's the last move we have to make!" Stepping inside, her eyes landed on her cherished rocker sitting in the living room, where Chad had placed it. She had been avoiding it—the memories too painful after her miscarriage and then Adam's death. Now, the time seemed right to enjoy the comfortable chair. Grabbing a bottle of water from the fridge, she walked to the rocker and settled down in its comfort.

Leaning her head back after taking a long swig, she closed her eyes. "Even your daddy wanted me to be right here in this rocker." Her mind roamed over Adam's note once more, but soon she rocked herself to sleep.

Chad came in an hour later, smiling as he pulled up and saw Dani's jeep sitting in his driveway. This was where he wanted her...where he had always wanted her. Stepping inside, he viewed her sitting in her rocking chair, head leaning slightly to the side, sound asleep. Thinking of the note, he realized Adam may have come home from work and seen her in the same position. Instead of feeling envy, he felt a kinship with his former friend who had tried to do the right thing for Dani when he insisted they marry. *Your motives were good as always, buddy, but sometimes your actions were completely fucked up.*

Seeing Dani stir, he pushed all thoughts of Adam from his mind and moved over so when she awoke, he would be the first thing she saw. Kneeling in front of her, he yearned to reach out to touch her thick auburn tresses. Her hair was what had captured his attention when they first met, until getting closer and having her green eyes focus on him. He had been lost ever since.

Her eyes fluttered open, a second of confusion on her face that blended into a beautiful smile when she looked at him kneeling in front of her.

"Oh, I must have fallen asleep." She reached her arms above her head in a long stretch. "I keep wanting to take naps, but can't at work."

Finally able to allow his fingers to move through her silky hair, he bent forward, kissing her lips. "I've read where that's common in pregnancies. So you nap whenever you want, babe."

Standing, they walked into the kitchen together. Dani looked around and asked, "Do you mind if I make supper?"

Chuckling, he replied, "I don't know a man alive who wouldn't love to have a meal cooked for him." Sobering, he added, "But I don't want you to wear yourself out."

"Nah, the nap did me good." Opening a few cabinets and the refrigerator, she was surprised to see them well stocked. Looking over her shoulder, she asked, "Do you always have this much stuff?"

"I went shopping when I hoped you were coming and made sure to buy everything I could. I mean, I do eat well...and a lot, but I tried to get anything you might want."

Smiling, she pondered for a moment, then pulled out a package of chicken breasts and pasta. "How about chicken parmesan? I'll go light on the garlic. I find it kills me with indigestion since I've been pregnant."

Kissing the top of her head, he said, "Sounds great. I'll shower and be out to help you."

Her eyes followed him as he walked out of the room, admiring his body. Giggling as she shook her head, she turned back to the dinner preparations.

Sitting at the table an hour later, she said hesitantly, "I guess I need to let my parents know where I am."

Chad halted his fork halfway to his mouth. "Uh yeah, babe. Is there a problem with that?"

"I just didn't want to worry them."

"About...?"

"Everything. My place being searched, Adam's note, staying here for protection—"

Interrupting, he asked, "Is that the only reason you're staying here?"

She caught the expression on his face, a cross between irritability and vulnerability. Laying her hand on his muscular forearm, she felt the muscles tense underneath her fingers. "No, that's not the only reason. It's just that we were going to go slow and then everything crazy happened, and here I am. My parents know we're together, but not about me being out of my house. They trust me, but..." she leaned back in her chair, "I must look like a complete ditz to someone on the outside. First widow, then pregnant, three moves in as many months..."

Placing his hand on hers, he replied, "Dani, anyone who knows you, knows you're not a ditz." He caught her eye roll and added, "Tell you what. Why don't we go visit them together? Let them know where we stand. They need to know I'm committed to you...and to the baby."

"Really?"

"Babe, I'd do anything for you. But the trip will be as much for me as for you." Seeing her look at him, a question in her expression, he said, "I need to talk to them. About me...about who we were and who we are now. They need to hear that from me."

Leaning forward, he kissed her lips...softly... with promise.

17

Oliver Sands, a recruit in Atlanta, was proving to be more difficult to extricate out of his apartment than Robbie Carter had been. Bart, with Jude this time, grew frustrated.

"We've got to figure out how to draw the little shit out of there," he growled.

Jude, new to breaking and entering for the Saints, had nonetheless worked in stealth when he had been a SEAL. Looking around, he said, "If we can't get him out alone, then let's empty the building."

Bart smiled, looking up at the eleven-story apartment building near the campus. The two slipped from the alley into the maintenance area on the first floor. A quick recon told them there were no security cameras. Moving quietly, they made their way to one of the fire alarms. Bart said, "You go up and let me know when you are in place.

Make sure he comes out; then you know what to do. I'll be up as soon as I can."

Following Bart's lead, Jude jogged up the stairs to the fourth floor and alerted Bart. He pulled the alarm, then slipped into the stairwell nearest the alley.

As the alarm sounded, the rooms began to empty. It appeared most of the residents were in class, but Jude saw Oliver coming out, grumbling while locking his door behind him. As soon as Oliver disappeared down the front staircase, Jude quickly picked his door lock and entered.

Fuckin' hell! The room was filled with computer equipment. Absolutely filled. Not knowing how many minutes they would have, Jude immediately contacted Luke and began inserting the thumb drives into as many computers as he could find.

Bart entered the apartment, looked around, and shook his head. "Shit!"

Jude barked, "I've got the ones on this table and along this wall." He swung his arm, indicating the direction. Bart immediately began inserting the special thumb drives. Glancing at his watch, he said, "We should have about fifteen minutes before Oliver makes his way back up here."

"Is there any way he can tell his machines were hacked?"

"Nah, Luke's programs are better than this guy's." While the drives did their job, the two men did a quick search of the apartment. Dirty dishes and old pizza boxes piled on the kitchen counter.

Bed covers thrown back, sheets in a tangle. And dirty.

"Jesus, the guy in St. Louis was a helluva lot neater than this dude. He might as well do his dating online, 'cause no woman would want to be involved with him."

The alarm stopped sounding and Jude groaned. "How close are you man?" he asked Luke, getting him on the phone.

"I need one more minute, then yank them out," Luke replied.

Jude looked at Bart and said, "One more minute."

"Fuck!" Bart ran out of the apartment and down the hall. He returned about twenty seconds later, explaining, I barred the stairwell door. Hopefully, he'll think it's a locked fire door."

At the end of the minute, the two moved stealthily around the room, removing the drives, counting them as they went. Once they were all accounted for, they slipped out of the apartment, locking it behind them. Hearing someone pounding on the front stairwell door, they moved to the one at the back. Within another minute, the two moved out into the alley, undetected.

Cam and Blaise flew to Dallas at the same time Jude and Bart were in Atlanta. Their mission was Lester Wyant, a new recruit. Cam got off the phone with Bart, hearing about their experience with Oliver's apartment.

"Ours will be easier," Cam commented, relating Bart and Jude's story. "At least this person goes out."

Their recon showed that Lester was not at home. Quickly entering, they noticed the bank of computers on an L-shaped desk, papers neatly stacked, and an apartment that was orderly. It seemed rather more like an office than an apartment.

The two men went to work, immediately contacting Luke and plugging in the drives. Cam's suspicions were high and he stalked into the bedroom. In a moment he came back, glaring. "There's no clothes in the closet, nor anything personal in the bathroom."

"Maybe he just rents this place for computer work," Blaise surmised. Walking to the kitchen, he threw open the refrigerator door, finding it empty. "Fuck, get Luke on the phone. Find out how much time he needs."

Cam made the call on their secure line, telling him what they were finding...or rather not finding. "You done?"

Disconnecting, he began to retrieve the drives, nodding to alert Blaise to do the same. They left the apartment as they found it, leaving the building and walking down the street to hail a cab.

Eyes followed them from another window in the building. The real owner of the equipment, Charlie, walked down the hall to the door, stepping into the apartment. Looking around carefully, noting everything. Moving over to the bank of computers, Charlie began to unplug everything. *Time to get out. That's okay. Dallas was getting old.* Within an hour, Charlie had boxes loaded onto a cart and rolled it to the elevator after one last look around.

Getting to the outside door, hailing a cab, Charlie managed to pack all the boxes in. Giving the driver an address and cash, eyes watched the skyline fade away.

And a smile escaped.

Luke processed the drives from Bart and Jude first. He viewed as line after line of code was searched, hoping somewhere his program would allow them to see where the contacts were located, what they wanted the recruits to do. The emails were encrypted, but Luke was confident his program would be able to ferret out the information.

After hours of working on the drives from Oliver, he moved to the drives from Lester Wyant's apartment. His preliminary searches told him that Lester was a false name. *Okay, let's see who you really are Lester...and what the hell the recruiter is asking you to do.*

Nothing. Not one line of code appeared. *What the hell?* Luke quickly began checking the drives. Nothing. He refused to panic—work the problem.

Thirty minutes later, he threw up his hands in defeat. Something was wrong.

His incoming email sounded. Checking, he recognized it was from his mystery programmer.

Left my last residence. Too many visitors. Had 2 today.

Luke stared at the cryptic message. His mind, swirling with the problem of Lester Wyant's computers searches, left little room for focusing on anything else.

I'm sorry, I don't understand, he answered.

In a few in minutes, another message came in. **I think they were friends of yours.**

His breath caught in his throat as the realization of their words sunk in. *Fuckin' hell...Lester Wyant is my mystery programmer. And Cam and Blaise were in his apartment?* Before he could respond, another message came.

But no matter where I live, I can keep up with you. If you want, that is.

Luke replied, **Absolutely. I know your name isn't what it appears.**

Yes, but that is still my secret. Danger lurks all around. Be careful.

Luke waited, but no more messages came. Leaning back in his chair, he pulled the useless drives out. He was sorry that he had not gone with Cam, just to have been in the apartment of such a computer genius. Getting up, he poured another cup of coffee, then looked back at the information coming in from

Oliver Sands using the programming from his mystery helper. *I may not know what my friend is doing or where they live now...but at least they're still helping.*

As he thought about their warning, he was filled with the realization that this person was also in danger. *I hope you take your own advice and are careful.*

Pushing them from his mind, he sat back down to work.

Dani waited nervously outside the doctor's office, alternating between checking her watch and the parking lot. Hearing a noise, she grinned as Chad's old truck rumbled down the street. Letting out a huge sigh of relief, she smiled as he alighted from the vehicle and jogged to her. She watched his natural grace—despite his size. His dark hair brushed to the side, clean-shaven jaw, white teeth showing with his huge smile. Her head tilted back as he approached. Not stopping until he was directly in front of her, his arms wide as he enveloped her in his embrace. She rested her ear against his chest, hearing his steady heartbeat.

"You okay, little mama?" he asked, kissing the top of her head.

She nodded against his chest, so he lifted her chin with two fingers, wanting to look into her eyes. "Babe?"

"I'm fine. Really. I was afraid you weren't going to make it."

"Not make it?" he said, with mock indignation. Hugging her tighter, he added, "I wouldn't have missed this for the world. Now, are you ready to find out what we're having?"

She heard him use the possessive word *we're* and smiled. It seemed right. At first, when she found out she was pregnant and her husband was newly deceased, the idea of being a single mother was daunting. *It's still unnerving, but now...*heaving a sigh...*it's nice to share this with someone else.* Linking her fingers with his, they walked into the doctor's office together.

Twenty minutes later, after the blood pressure check, weigh in, and physical exam, all proving her healthy, they waited impatiently as the sonographer rolled the probe over Dani's stomach.

"Measurements are good. Everything looks great," she reported, her eyes on the monitor. Glancing over at the couple she said, "Well, are you ready to find out what you're having?"

Dani sought Chad's eyes, catching his nervous expression. He nodded, squeezing her hand. She turned back and confirmed, "As ready as we'll ever be."

The sonographer continued to roll the probe around. "Ooh, the little one has their legs open and in a good position, so I've got a good shot."

Dani felt her hand being squeezed harder—*or is that me squeezing?* Either way, she felt her heart pounding, wondering if it sounded out in the room instead of the baby's heartbeat.

Clicking a few more buttons, the sonograph spit out a strand of pictures. Handing them to Dani, the sonographer smiled and exclaimed, "Okay, here's some pictures of your little girl."

Girl. *Girl? Oh, my God, girl? I'm having a little girl!* Gasping, she burst into tears as Chad bolted out of his seat.

He scooped her into his arms, picking her off the table, cradling her in his embrace. "A girl. We're having a baby girl." His chest was tight as he thought of what all Adam was missing. Continuing to rock Dani in his arms, celebrating the news with her, he silently vowed, *I'll do you proud, man. I'll do you proud.*

Later, that evening, after a celebratory meal complete with non-alcoholic sparkling cider and dessert, they drove back to Chad's house. Walking in, the elation of earlier still at an all-time high, Dani walked to the rocking chair in the living room and sat on it, rubbing her tummy.

Watching her, Chad followed, kneeling at her feet. "You look good there, little mama."

She smiled, saying, "This chair is practically an antique. It's been reupholstered twice. My grandmother rocked my mom here when she was a baby. Then I was rocked here." She rubbed her hands along the material on the arms and said, "I can't believe that I'll be rocking my baby girl here also."

Chad reached out, tucking her hair behind her ear. "You look perfectly natural there, babe."

The smile left her face as she appeared lost in thought. He cupped her face and asked, "What're you thinking?"

Her eyes searched his and she said, "I need to make a couple of visits. I know you said we'd go to my parents together to talk about where you and I are in our relationship and we can do that this weekend. But, Chad? I've got to talk to Adam's parents as well. I didn't want to say anything to them earlier about the pregnancy, until I was sure I was going to make it to the second trimester."

Nodding, he rubbed her silken cheek. "I know you do, babe. I'd like to go with you for that, as well, unless you think it would be awkward."

Her eyes brightened, a burden being lifted from her shoulders. "Oh, no. I think they'd love to see you and know that you're involved." Heaving a sigh, she said, "Thank you. It means so much to me."

"I'm in this, Dani. I'm in this for the long haul."

She cocked her head to the side, holding his gaze.

"Babe, I'll be here for her birth. But so much more than that." Deciding to make sure she understood the extent of his devotion, he continued. "I'll watch her take her first step and say her first word. I'll take pictures when she starts school and teach her to ride a bike." Seeing Dani's smile, he kept going. "I'll scrutinize her prom date and, when the time comes, I'll walk her down the aisle."

She leaned forward, clutching his jaw in her hands, pulling him in for a kiss. Without pulling back, she whispered against his lips, "I love you."

He immediately took over the kiss, owning her mouth, drinking from her as a thirst-starved man. Tasting her essence, he thrust his tongue inside her warmth.

Without giving up his mouth, she shifted forward so she could reach the buttons on his shirt. Undoing them as quickly as she could, she pushed the material off his shoulders. He grabbed the bottom of her shirt, pulling it over her head, their mouths separating only long enough for the material to pass between them.

Chad slid his hands down her sides to her waist, lifting her as he stood. Her hands went to his zipper at the same time his moved to her skirt. Laughing, she pulled away.

"I can do it faster," she said, quickly unzipping her skirt and stepping out of it. Lacy topped, thigh stockings ending in her modest, strappy heels, plus a pale pink lacy bra and panty set captured his lust-filled gaze. Her breasts were barely contained in the bra, their luscious mounds pouring over the top.

Chad's gaze roamed from the top of her deep auburn hair to her toes peeking out of her shoes. "Damn, girl." His cock, already raring to play, strained at his zipper, demanding to be free.

Glancing down at his impressive erection, she lifted her eyebrow saying, "Looks like someone is eager."

Bending down to undo her shoes, he growled, "No way. Panties and bra off only." Smiling, she obliged, unfastening her bra and letting it drop to the floor. Shimmying out of her panties, they landed on the floor as well. Shifting her hips toward the back of the sofa, he pressed gently on her upper back.

Grinning, she bent over the sofa, her hands holding onto the soft cushions on the back. Automatically spreading her legs, she moved her ass back, rubbing it along his crotch, loving the groan from his lips.

He jerked his jeans and boxers off, then leaned over her body. He massaged her shoulders before sliding his hands down the smooth expanse of skin on her back. Palming her ass cheeks, he chuckled as he heard the sounds coming from her lips. "Now who's moaning?"

As his hands then roamed around to her heavy breasts hanging, he tweaked her sensitive nipples. No longer moaning but full out begging, she pleaded for him to take her as she pushed her ass back further.

Wanting to make sure she was ready, he kept one hand working her nipple and the other sliding through her wet folds. After a minute of blissful torture, she cried out, her body shaking with the ripples of her orgasm. As the quivers subsided, she slumped over the back of the sofa, unsure her legs would support her. "Damn, Chad," she groaned, her body pliant.

Chad smoothed his hands along her back as she recovered and grinned when she finally cast a glance over her shoulder at him. "I'm just making sure you're okay first, babe." Her smile was his answer.

He looked at her perfect body, but realized his height was going to make his amorous intentions difficult even with her heels. Grabbing a couple of pillows off the sofa, he tossed them to the floor. "Step up," he ordered gently and watched as her perfect ass rose to the perfect level. *There's no way a woman can understand what it does to a man to have that gorgeous ass presented to him!*

"Chad," Dani said. "I need you now! Stop looking and get moving!"

Laughing, he slid the tip of his cock to her entrance, saying, "I live to serve."

Plunging in, they both gasped—her, at the delicious sensation of fullness and him, at the exquisite torture of tightness. Thrusting in and out, slowly at first and then with more vigor, he closed his eyes in awe of the beauty that was all her. His fingers dug into the flesh at her hips, careful not to bruise but desiring to crush her to him.

Her slick channel grabbed him, causing her entire body to tingle. The electric jolts shot from her core outward as the friction increased. Her fingers clutched the sofa cushions in an attempt to hold her body in place as his thrusts pushed her forward. Digging her heels into the pillows on the floor, she was grateful for his hands on her hips holding her steady.

The movements were hard, but not harsh, tying celebratory and sensual all into one package. There was no one in her mind but Chad...no other thought but their two bodies coming together. Adam had been a gentle, even playful lover, but nothing prepared her for the perfection of she and Chad. As she felt one of his hands slide to hold her tummy with his fingers splayed she knew without a doubt, he loved this baby.

His balls tightening, he was close to coming. This woman...this baby...it all tied together for him to love. If it made him a bastard to be glad to have this chance with them, then so be it. With a final thrust, he powered through his orgasm as his thumb pressed on her clit, pulling her along with him.

Coming together, they both screamed out their torturous pleasure. Collapsing onto her back, he held her with one hand to keep from crushing her against the sofa. His legs threatened to give out and he began to question the wisdom of not taking her to the bed. Prying his eyes open, he saw her standing in lacy-topped stockings, heels, her hair tousled, and his come sliding down her legs with a well-fucked expression on her face. *Hell yeah!*

Forcing his body to move, he scooped her up in his massive arms and she threw her arms around his neck as he stalked up the stairs to the master bathroom. Setting her feet gently down on the floor, he wet a warm cloth and washed between her legs. Tossing the cloth to the tub, he turned her body to face the mirror, plastering her back with his naked frame.

His eyes once more moved from the top of her head down to her rosy-tipped, full breasts, to her rounded tummy. Then he caught her eyes in the reflection.

"What do you see, Chad?" she asked softly.

"I see perfection, little mama." Placing his hand on her tummy with the other arm wrapped around her chest pulling her back against his body, he repeated. "I look at both of us and I see perfection."

18

Chad pulled into the parking lot of the active living community apartments. The neat grounds and early spring flowers gave an indication of the care given to the outside appearance. He was always pleased that when he visited his grandmother, he found the buildings to show just as much care. He walked up the pathway to her unit and entered the warmly decorated interior. Making his way down the hall, he raised his hand but the door flung open before he had a chance to knock.

"Chad," his grandmother called out, enthusiastically grabbing him in a hug, "I've been watching for you." Her small, but strong body gave him a squeeze. "Your parents called to check on me this morning. I told them to stop worrying and enjoy their vacation."

Grinning as he kissed the top of her head, he returned her embrace. Her long, grey hair was pulled back with a headband and the soft silver layers fell down her back. "Hey, gramma," he greeted, as she reluctantly turned him loose.

"Come on in, boy," she said, ushering him into the apartment. The inside was as warm as the rest of the building and she had decorated with many of the paintings she had finished over the years.

"The place looks good," he commented, eyeing her walls. "Looks like you've got some new paintings up."

Bobbing her head, she grinned in reply. "I've been spending time at the new studio that is near here. Not as good as the one I used to have, but a good one nonetheless."

Lorna Casinella, born in Italy, had come to the United States as a college student studying art fifty years ago and never left after falling in love with a dock worker from New Jersey. After retiring, they moved to Virginia to be nearer to their son and his family. Chad's grandfather died several years ago and Lorna decided to give up the stress of a home and move to the apartments specifically for older adults.

"You still like it here?" he asked, more out of politeness since he already knew the answer.

"What's not to like?" she laughed. "No yard to care for, someone else grows the flowers, I have bus transportation to wherever I need to go when I don't feel like driving, no shoveling snow, lots of time to work on my paintings...it's fabulous!"

Patting the sofa next to her, she said, "But enough about me! Tell me what's new with you."

She peered at him astutely as he sat down. "And I can tell something's on your mind!"

Grinning again, he nodded, certain there was no way he would ever be able to keep anything from her. Leaning forward, his forearms on his knees, he wondered where to start.

"Chad, don't worry about me," Lorna said softly. "Just start talking, boy, and I'll catch up."

With that, he began telling the story of he and Dani, going back to when they first were together with Adam. As the story unfolded, he watched his grandmother's expression waver with the different emotions the story brought out. But finally her smile grew as he related where he and Dani were at this time.

Leaning back, she said, "That's quite a tale, my boy. This woman has been through a lot."

Shaking his head ruefully, he added, "Yeah, that's what drives me crazy. Looking back, we could have saved ourselves so much heartache."

Patting his leg, Lorna stood up as the teakettle whistled and moved to the kitchen. A few minutes later she came back in with two steaming mugs. Setting them on the coffee table, she sat down in the chair facing the sofa.

Chad smiled at her lovingly. Her floral broomstick skirt hung to her ankles, her purple top flowing over the waistband. A large, turquoise necklace around her neck. And a twinkle in her dark brown eyes. She settled her gaze on him and he waited, knowing she had been pondering what to say to him.

"Your grandfather loved working on the docks, the wind in his face, and the hard work honing his muscles. Your namesake was a big man...his blood was Welsh as well as Italian," she reminded, although Chad had no doubts about where his stature came from. "One day, I got a call from his boss. My Chad was injured and they had taken him to the hospital." Shaking her head as the memories came back, she said, "When I got to him, he was so angry. The injury would keep him from going back to his old job. The company gave him a desk job, but at the time, he was like living with a hornet."

Chad smiled, watching his grandmother reminisce.

"After a couple of years, he was able to be in a position in the company to make a difference in the safety of the other dock workers. They used to stop by his office just to thank him after new safety regulations had been passed that he started and forced through. As it turned out, he ended up in a position to help. The sacrifice of one career for another became a good thing. No more looking back...no more wondering *what if*."

"So what you're saying is..."

"Your grandfather was named for St. Chad, the Saint of sacrifice. Your parents and we were always so proud of you, both in the Army and when you worked for the ATF, but we were so afraid. Your willingness to sacrifice yourself...walking toward a bomb…" a shudder ran through her before she continued. "We recognized it was just who you were on the inside, but we were not sad to see you leave that job." She cocked her head to the side, saying, "In a roundabout way, the situation with Danielle was what made you leave that profession."

He nodded slowly, having never thought of how his career choices affected his family. He looked up as she leaned over, patting his leg again.

"Don't make yourself crazy thinking about the past. What you didn't do or didn't say. The circumstances around Danielle's widowhood are tragic, but you two are back together now. No looking back. Just look forward. No more *what if*!"

He stood, embracing her once more, and then turned to walk to the door.

"Chad," she called, fiddling with a chain around her neck as she pulled out a diamond ring dangling on the end. Holding her arthritic knuckles up, she said, "I can't wear my diamond anymore, but would be so proud if you wanted to take the diamond and have it reset."

Stunned as he looked at the diamond solitaire, he remembered so well as a child seeing it on her hand. "Are you sure?"

"Oh, yes," she exclaimed. "Your grandfather would be so proud to see the diamond he gave me so many years ago on the hand of his only grandson's wife. And you need to hurry up before that baby comes!"

"I'd be honored, gramma," he said, a lump forming in his throat.

Smiling widely, eyes twinkling even more, Lorna clapped her hands in delight. "The baby will have lots of love...from her biological grandparents, your parents, and goodness...for me, a great granddaughter after all these years of sons in the family! God be praised!"

Dani left the Human Resources office, having informed them about the pregnancy and her approximate due date. She could not keep the smile off her face as she walked to the elevators. Entering, she saw Jahfar was the only occupant there. Still smiling, she stepped to the side as they made their way to the fourth floor.

"You and I were hired about the same time," Jahfar said. "I was so busy learning the business I did not learn much about my co-workers."

His statement did not seem to indicate a comment was warranted, so she just nodded politely and looked up at the elevator numbers again.

"I understand you came from the Alcohol, Tobacco, and Firearms Department. That must have been interesting."

Once more, a polite nod seemed to be the only required response, but she wished the elevator would hurry.

"I did not realize you were a widow," his smooth voice said.

Immediately, her eyes jumped from the floor of the elevator to his. Cocking her head to the side, she stared at him, dumbfounded.

"I wanted to offer my condolences," he continued. "The circumstances of his death must have been...devastating."

Heart pounding, Dani heard a roar rushing through her ears. Throwing her hand out, she balanced herself against the wall. Just then, the doors opened, and she hustled down the hall to her office. Inside, she sat heavily in her chair. *Why does he give me the creeps? Am I just paranoid? Stereotyping? Is he just trying to be polite? Or is there something going on with him?*

She hated that she allowed his presence to mar her feelings of excitement about the baby. Sucking in a deep breath, she pulled those feelings back to the surface. Her computer calendar alarm buzzed and she grabbed her notes and headed back down the hall to the conference room.

Inside, she avoided Jahfar's eyes and took a seat at the farther end of the conference table. Sitting next to Ethan, she noticed he shot her a questioning look. Shaking her head slightly, she mouthed *Tell you later.* Todd and Cybil Marsden walked in and the meeting began.

Two hours later, Dani squirmed in her chair. Uncomfortable, and needing to pee, the conference was almost unbearable. Unable to last any longer, she slipped out to the ladies' room and then hurried back to her seat.

Ethan leaned over and whispered, "What's going on?"

"Too much to even begin to describe," she whispered back.

Just as she thought the meeting was over, Cybil stood up and started her presentation on a new project that would be culminating in the fall. As assignments were discussed, Dani realized she would be on maternity leave at the crucial time of the project. She planned on waiting to let others know about the pregnancy, but realized she needed to let her co-workers know for assignment purposes.

Clearing her throat, she said, "I need to inform you of something that will affect the timeline from the military sales division. Next fall, about the time the project is finalizing, I will be on maternity leave."

The room was silent for a second before *Congratulations* were heard all around. Cybil hustled over to offer her a hug. Todd lifted his cup of coffee in a toast.

"It was a surprise, I admit. I did not realize it until right after Adam's death." As soon as she said the words, she realized what a pall it created over the assembly. Looking around, she said quickly, "I was stunned at first, but it'll be fine."

The others smiled once more, continuing to offer their congratulations. Looking to the side, she was surprised to see Ethan's face a mask of doubt. Cocking her head to the side, he caught her expression and his face cleared.

"Sorry, Dani. I was just selfishly thinking about the project and how to make it all work while you're gone."

Patting his hand, she said, "Well, I'm not gone yet. We'll have the summer to plan."

"Unfortunately, we won't—"

"Since this seems to be the time for announcements," Todd declared, "I'd like to announce that Ethan has been promoted to Head of manufacturing production security. It'll be his job to make sure our shipments get where they're going...on time...and intact."

Another round of congratulations followed. Leaning forward to look at Cybil, Dani got a glimpse of Jahfar...looking angrily toward Ethan.

The meeting broke up at that point and Dani found herself having difficulty getting out of the room with all the well-wishers. She saw Jahfar leaving immediately and wondered what he really felt about Ethan being over production.

The rest of the day flew by as her news had she and Cybil re-working the timeline for the new project. As they finished their work, Dani said, "I just have to ask about Ethan's promotion."

Cybil nodded but stood and walked to Dani's office door to close it before speaking. Sitting back down, she smoothed her shiny, black hair away from her face and said, "We've gotten some warnings from your former employer—the ATF—that there are terrorists hoping to infiltrate into munition plants. Dad and I talked it over and decided we needed to increase our security before something becomes a problem."

"Do you have any suspicions?"

"No, we've never been lax in security, but you never know."

"Was this a job Ethan wanted?"

Cybil's face scrunched in distaste as her sharp gaze sought Dani's. "Actually, Aaron wanted the job. It would be a promotion and I know he felt as though he should have gotten it. I'm hoping it does not create a problem between egos."

Dani turned that information over in her head, but found it was hard to imagine laid-back Aaron involved with security. The two women finished their meeting, but thoughts of Jahfar continued to weasel their way into her thoughts. By the end of the day, she was exhausted. Leaving, she was startled when Jahfar stepped into her office.

"I wanted to congratulate you personally on your news," he said. "Children are a blessing from God."

"Yes, they are," she answered, her eyes sharply watching him. As he nodded and turned to walk out of her office, she quickly stopped him. "Jahfar? What did you think of Ethan's promotion?"

His dark eyes held her gaze for a moment. "I understand the need for ultimate security in this business. I have some concerns though."

Cocking her head to the side, she waited to see what else he would say. *Concerns about a lack of security or MES increasing their security?* He did not offer anything more and she was surprised when he stepped closer. She did not have to lean her head back as he moved in; she was determined he would not intimidate her in her own office.

He stopped a foot away, his face cold and hard. "There are those here, I am not sure I trust." He leaned in further toward her, lowering his voice. "Have a care. Snakes can hide in the grass." He then turned and stalked out of her office.

Dani was glad her desk was directly behind her, as her ass landed on it when she leaned back heavily. *What the hell was that? A threat? A warning? About what?*

The Saints gathered for their meeting and before Jack could begin, Luke said, "Sorry, boss. But something came up from the Dallas location that I've got to go over with you all."

Gaining Jack's nod and curious look, Luke turned to Cam and Blaise, asking, "Did you guys see anything personal at all in the apartment? I know you said it looked like it was not lived in."

"That's right," Cam answered, "At first I thought the recruit was just neat, unlike the slob Bart and Jude had. But then I checked out the bedroom, bathroom, and kitchen. Nothing. Not even a bottle of water."

"What's going on?" Blaise asked, his eyes pinning Luke.

Shaking his head while chuckling, Luke projected his messages from his mystery assistant onto the white board. It only took a few seconds for the Saints to read, understand, and then quickly break out into *What the fucks* all at once.

"So what does that mean?" Cam asked, irritated at being played. "Are they a recruit? Or...or...hell, I've got no idea what to think."

Luke, looking at Jack, said, "All along, I've figured that the person helping me must be one of the brilliant computer techies who works solo. I've wondered if they worked for an underground criminal organization...or for the government on a contractual basis. They mentioned that it wasn't safe for them to communicate too often or too clearly, and at first that had me concerned. Thinking about it though, that could really mean anything. Techies, the really good ones, and this person certainly is, like to stay under the radar and anonymous—wouldn't want to give me any clues on how to track them. Whatever the answer is... they discovered me working on our last assignment and helped out. Now, they contact me occasionally and continue to help. I'm wondering if they haven't figured out what some terrorists are doing and are working against them. Lester Wyant doesn't exist, but whoever this is was in contact with Habib."

"I wondered why it was so easy to get him out of the apartment," Cam grumbled.

"Yep, I'd say that he knew all along that you were coming…when you were there…what you were going to do…and probably smiled at you as you left."

"Fuckin' hell," Marc cursed. "Do we ever really know who the good guys and who the bad guys are anymore?"

The group fell silent, each pondering his question. Finally, Chad spoke up, asking, "So other than him, did we get any intel from the others?"

Nodding, Luke said, "Yeah, we did. We've got a list of a few more people they were in contact with, which of course has been turned over to the FBI. That helps expand their list and it also gives them IP addresses to follow the trail to others."

Monty took over. "According to Mitch, they've identified two more sleeper cells in rural Virginia, so it's not just near D.C."

"And we can't check them out," Bart groused.

"No fuckin' way," Chad answered. "Even ATF now have to go in so carefully, especially with the explosion that killed Adam."

"How do they do that?" Jude asked. "How do they enter a house with known explosives?"

Shaking his head, Chad just responded, "With a fuck load of training and the right equipment. If possible, we'd identify the explosive device, either ourselves or with the robot. The world's getting crazier, though. With the newer explosives, especially if someone gets their hands on manufacturer's grade detonators along with the easily-made, but highly unstable explosives, a small amount can do a tremendous amount of damage. Even in purposeful detonation, to get rid of the risk is difficult. We'd let the robots do as much as they can."

The other Saints looked at Chad, knowing he used to suit up and walk toward explosives the way most others ran from them.

"Damn, man. I knew what you did, but fuckin' hell, you have to be about as selfless a person possible to volunteer to walk toward a bomb."

Shrugging, he looked at the others and chuckled. "Yeah, so say the SEALs, Special Forces, CIA, FBI, DEA, and undercover police that're sitting at this table with me. We've all been to the cave and seen the critter. I'm no different than you."

"And found the Saints," Jack added drolly. The others laughed before turning their attention back to the agenda.

"So here's where we are with our contract," Jack continued. "We were given three locations to acquire computer information for the FBI, and that has also been shared with Roscoe at ATF. Luke has done the preliminary analysis since his equipment...and friend...is far superior to what they have. Essentially that concludes our initial contract. Now..." he looked over at Chad. "Chad has asked to look into the death of Adam Turner. I've given him the go ahead. But there's a new twist to everything and it may involve Chad directly."

This announcement gained Chad's full attention as he looked around the table, seeing that none of the Saints seemed to know what Jack was about to say.

"I was contacted by Todd Marsden, from Marsden Energy Systems, one of the nation's largest producers of explosives. His company supplies the U.S. military as well as civilian and government contracts...mines...road building...that kind of thing. He got my business name from the FBI, who will also be looking into his concerns. It appears he has some security concerns and wanted to discuss what the Saints might be able to assist him with."

"What is he looking at?" Chad asked, his thoughts immediately on Dani.

"Right now, he has no crime that he knows of, so the FBI has nothing to investigate. I also told him that a *feeling* of possible security issues doesn't give us much to work with either. But Chad, with Dani working there, I wanted you to know of his concerns. We do not have a contract with MES at this time but be aware that something could come in. Other than that, you all can check your new assignments on your tablets."

The meeting ended and as Chad left Jack's compound, his mind rolled over Dani, the note from Adam, MES security issues, Adam's death, the terrorist cells...the strange puzzle pieces that were not fitting. *Hell, I don't even know it they're from the same puzzle.*

19

Dani reached into her large, leather purse, grabbing her sunglasses as the clouds separated allowing the sun to pierce through the windshield of her car. She glanced over, seeing Chad pull his out of his shirt pocket and, with a one-handed flip, open and slide them onto his face as well. She agreed to let him drive, knowing as chauvinistic as it was, he wanted to be behind the steering wheel. It only took about thirty minutes to drive to her parents' house and soon they pulled into the driveway.

As he turned off the engine, she sighed loudly. Reaching over, he took her hand, lifting it to his mouth, placing a sweet kiss on the back of her fingers.

"You okay, babe?"

Smiling, she said, "Actually yes. I'm excited about telling mom and dad...I just had a flashback to when I was here last. I'm not sure I've ever been so alone in my life."

He nodded and pulled her hand over as he leaned toward her, meeting in the middle of the console. Kissing her lips, he murmured, "I'm here for you now and I vow to never have you feel that alone ever again."

"I know," she replied, returning his kiss. Tucking her hair behind her ear, she said, "Okay, let's get this show on the road."

Assisting her from the passenger side, he threw his arm around her shoulders, tucking her protectively in his side. "Lead on, little mama."

Before they made it to the porch, Dani's parents came out smiling and waving at the couple. Dani's mother was an older, mirror image of Dani. Chad noticed their eyes darted between their daughter and him. He realized that, just like Dani, they had gone through a lot of changes in the last few months. Suddenly nervous, he wondered how they felt about everything.

He watched as her parents swooped her into a huge hug then turned their attention to him, as Dani made the introductions. Her father stepped over, his hand outstretched. Chad shook it, surprised when the much smaller man pulled him in for a hug as well.

"Thank you, son, for everything you're doing for our Dani," he said.

Barely stepping back, he was immediately

hugged by her mom as well. "Come in, come in," she offered.

The two women moved into the house, but Chad stopped her father on the way inside. "Just to be clear, Mr. Houston. You don't have to thank me. I'd sacrifice anything for her and the baby."

The older man's eyes teared, but he nodded as he cleared his throat. "Come on in, son. And call me Paul."

They made it into the living room, where Mrs. Houston had a spread of food out for them. Small sandwiches, cookies, and drinks sat on the coffee table. She looked up at Chad and said, "Don't worry, this is just a snack. We'll have a full lunch in a little bit."

"Mrs. Houston, it looks lovely," he said, sitting next to Dani on the comfortable sofa.

"Please call me Tammie," she said. Her eyes sought Dani's and she threw her hands up to the side and said, "Well?"

Laughing, Dani said, "I guess you're a little anxious to see what I'm having."

Bouncing in her chair, Tammie threatened her daughter lovingly if she did not hurry. She reached over and clutched her husband's hand.

Dani smiled at Chad and then bent over to pull something from her large purse. A newborn baby's outfit was in her hand, still on the hanger to show it off to perfection. And it was a little pink dress.

It took her parents a second to process the outfit before her mother screamed, jumping up from her chair in a hurry to hug Dani again. Her mom rushed her and would have pushed her back into the sofa if Chad's arms had not been tucked around her. The two women began immediately gushing about baby girl clothes while Paul sat quietly, a silent tear sliding down his cheek.

Looking over at Chad, he said, "Son, let's go fire up the grill."

As they moved onto the deck, Paul cleared his throat again, gave his eyes a quick swipe and said, "You have no idea how good it is to see Dani smiling again. Chad, I've got to tell you that about four months ago, I didn't know when I'd ever see my girl happy."

Nodding, Chad assisted with the grill and said, "Sir...uh, Paul, I understand. I have to tell you, I take a lot of responsibility for her unhappiness." Seeing Paul's look of confusion, Chad explained what he and Dani discovered about their feelings two years earlier and the mistakes they made.

Her father listened patiently but as Chad finished, Paul said, "I've lived a lot of years, made my share of mistakes, goofs, and some just plain dumb decisions. But they were mine. I owned them. I worked to redeem myself when I did them and then learned from them." He pierced Chad with a hard look and continued. "Now my Dani... she's done the same as you. She could have told you how she felt about you before you left. She and Adam made a decision that cost them. I'll be honest, I never thought Adam was a good match for her and I know they got married because of her pregnancy, but..." he shook his head, staring out into his yard, "her mom and me thought it was rushed and not well thought out."

Chad listened respectively as Paul reminisced, respecting the man's views.

"Now, Adam was a lot of fun, and Tammie and I never doubted that he was fond of Dani and seemed happy about the pregnancy. But..." breathing out a heavy sigh, he said, "we wanted more for our daughter. We wanted someone who would put their life on the line for her. The kind of marriage her mother and I've had. Adam just wasn't that man."

Holding Chad's gaze, he said, "You've confessed to me what you thought your mistakes were and essentially they were just not expressing your feelings before going to a war zone, which I don't necessarily think is a mistake. And separating yourself from them when you got back. Don't know about that, Chad. But what I do recognize is that you accept what you think you did that wasn't good and you're taking care of your business now."

Chad took Paul's words in, churning them over in his mind as he flipped the steaks. *Own my mistakes, redeem myself, and learn from them.*

"Now enough about all that heavy stuff. Tell me what's going on with my daughter and that little baby girl she's gonna have," Paul said, handing him a beer.

Inside the kitchen, Dani stood at the sink overlooking the porch, seeing her dad and Chad talking. Or rather, her dad was talking and Chad appeared to be listening intently. Startled when her mom walked up, wrapping her arms around her daughter to watch the men, she asked, “Mom, what do you think they’re talking about?”

Her mother placed her arm around Dani’s shoulders, pulling her in for another hug. “If I know your father, he’s letting Chad understand how glad he is about the two of you.”

“Really?” Dani asked, smiling at the thought.

“Honey, it’s no secret to you that neither your dad nor I were all that enamored of Adam. We respected your choice and we respected Adam’s willingness to get married. But we knew he was not the love of your life. But this young man,” she said, nodding toward Chad, “he makes you sparkle.”

Laughing, Dani replied, “Sparkle?”

“Absolutely!” her mom insisted with a grin.

Later that night, Dani got to show Chad her sparkle when he had her in the shower. Her ass in his hand, her back against the tile, the water pelting Chad, his other hand next to her head on the tile, and his cock in her as he thrust.

He’d started out with her on the bathroom counter, on his knees between her legs with her feet around his back, licking and sucking until she screamed out his name. Then he turned on the shower, waiting until the water was warm before helping her in. Washing her hair and then her body, paying close attention to her enlarged breasts and stomach now protruding more, before hefting her in his arms. Now, he felt his balls tighten and he wanted her to come with him.

Dani threw her head back, her body molten as every nerve tingled. *This man, right here with me... this is it. What I wanted almost two years ago—*

Before she finished the thought, her orgasm slammed into her, the electricity jolting from her sex out to her fingers and toes. Screaming his name, she felt him swell even more as she clutched his shoulders and tightened her legs around his waist.

Her fingernails dug into his shoulders, creating small crescent divots he would wear proudly. Hearing her cry out his name, Chad poured himself into her, his legs almost giving out with the intensity of his orgasm. The thrusts, first fast and furious, gradually slowed to an easy cadence until every drop was wrung from his body. As he slowly came back to full awareness, he felt her body pressed against his with such clarity. Her distended stomach against his rock hard abs. Her legs wrapped around his hips and her delectable ass in his hands. *Mine. Finally, irrevocably mine. I need to do something about that.* But after what she had been through with Adam, he was not sure how she'd respond to another proposal. *I need to—*

"Chad?"

He heard her voice call his name as her fingers found his face. Looking down, he saw her concern.

"Honey, where'd you go? I was calling your name but you looked as though you were completely lost in thought."

"I'm sorry, babe. My dick may be out, but my mind was still firmly planted inside of you."

Turning off the water, he wrapped her in a fluffy towel and began to dry her off. Quickly drying himself, they walked into the bedroom, sliding under the covers. Chad drew them back up over their bodies, tucking her into him in his favorite position. She was on her side, where she was more comfortable with her growing womb, and he spooned around her. His body was so large, he engulfed her in his protectiveness.

For once, sleep came quickly to him, but Dani found herself lying in his embrace for a while, thoughts rolling through her mind. *What was he really thinking? Is this too much for him? It's one thing to say you want a baby...even another man's baby. But as it gets closer, does he truly want this? He told me he talked to his parents about us reconnecting and they were pleased. But he needs to tell them about the baby. What will they think?* Squeezing her eyes tighter in an attempt to purge her rushing thoughts, she knew he had been right when he said being pregnant means they can't go as slow as she originally thought they could. Unable to find the answers, she drifted off to an unsteady sleep.

Jahfar, almost home from work, glanced down at his phone as it buzzed an incoming call. Seeing the caller, he detoured, needing to continue to drive as he took the call.

"Yes?"

"Can you talk?"

"Yes, I'm alone in my car. What is going on?"

"It seems some of our new recruits have been compromised," Fazan answered. "Muhammad is finding out now, but we've got to move carefully."

Jahfar sucked in a breath. "What does this mean for us and the cause?"

"Tread lightly. Pieces are coming together, but they seem to revolve around Ms. Turner."

"How can that possibly be?" he asked.

Fazan replied, "I have no idea. She did not know what her husband was up to...at least that is what we supposed. When he was out of the picture, we thought that would end the involvement. Muhammad has his eye on her and wants no problems."

"I'm on it...I'm working it," Jahfar promised. "She's going to be contained."

"She'd better. If it looks like she going to be a problem, he'll want her neutralized. You know what that means."

"She's getting curious...I can tell. But she announced that she's with child." Silence met this statement, so he continued, "A woman bearing a child will not be a problem. She'll focus on her condition and not on us."

"You'd better hope she does," Fazan noted. "If not, things will become messy."

Another silence and then Jahfar asked, "Did the shipment get through?"

"Yes, it's in place. A new group is in the home working on it."

"Does anyone suspect?"

"Not on my end, but are you sure about yours?"

"I'll take care of MES...you take care of yours."

With a final goodbye, Jahfar disconnected the call, tossing his cell phone onto the seat next to him. Wiping the sweat from his brow, he glanced around not recognizing where he had driven. Seeing a familiar shopping center ahead, he pulled through the fast-food restaurant ordering dinner for his family. *A surprise...the children will like that.* Sucking in a deep breath, he knew his wife would wonder. Closing his eyes for a second while waiting for the take-out to be handed to him by the pimpled-faced teenager working the cash register, he prayed. *Keep my family safe. Let this endeavor be over soon. And let the right side win.*

Getting home from work, Dani saw that Chad was not home yet. Making a cup of herbal tea and a piece of toast, she settled in the rocking chair to watch the birds at the feeders in his yard.

Her back ached and she shifted in her seat, unable to find a comfortable position. For some reason, the cushioned padding of the rocker bottom felt lumpy on one side near the back. She smiled, thinking of the chair being re-upholstered several times by her family. Glancing down, she realized the sky-blue material did not match Chad's living room décor. *I'll be sitting in it every day so I could re-do it in a more neutral color. Maybe tan. Or a dark burgundy.* Curious as to how difficult it might be to re-upholster it by herself, she stood and eased the rocker over on its side to see the underside.

The rocker was old, unlike any she had seen in recent years. The underside was a combination of heavy, zig-zag springs that were exposed with the padding and material covering the rest. The material appeared torn in one area and she realized the chair would need to be re-finished soon anyway. As she squatted down on the floor, she noticed the tear was quite long—at least six inches. Knowing her parents' propensity for completing projects almost perfectly, she was surprised at the large tear in the material. *Did the movers damage it during the move?*

And then she saw it—the corner of something tucked inside the tear. Her fingers felt the object and with a jerk she could see the bottom half of a notebook poking through. Pulling it the rest of the way out, she looked at the small, spiral bound notebook. Her heart pounded, not knowing what she had found. Instinctively though, she knew it had something to do with Adam. *His letter! He mentioned the old rocker in his note! Had that been a clue I was supposed to figure out?*

With shaking fingers, she opened to the first page and recognized his chicken-scratch writing. Almost indecipherable, it was filled with jibberish. Letters, numbers. Nothing made sense. *Oh, my God, Adam? What now?*

"Babe?" Chad's voice broke through her revelations as he wandered into the room. Seeing the rocking chair on its side and her sitting on the floor, he assumed she had fallen. Rushing over, he knelt next to her, about to crush her body to his, when he saw what was in her shaking hands. "What have you got?"

"It's Adam's. Adam's notebook. He must have left it for me to find."

20

Chad took the notebook from Dani's shaking hand, sliding down onto the floor next to her, his legs on either side of her body. His eyes moved over the writing on the pages, a grimace of frustration on his face.

"Fuck, man, I don't know what this means." He looked at Dani's face to see if she expressed any understanding at what he was holding but her confusion mirrored his own.

"Chad," she began shakily. "If he wasn't doing something wrong, why would he have hidden this? And why would he want me to find it?"

Leaning back against the sofa, Chad rubbed his hand over his face. He placed his large hand on her leg, giving her thigh a slight squeeze. "I've got no fuckin' idea, babe. But, if it's some kind of code, Luke'll break it. I need to get it to Jack's."

She nodded, heaving a sigh. "We can't seem to catch a break can we?"

He looked at her, not answering, but allowed her to finish her thought.

Placing her hand over his, she linked her fingers in his, her expression pensive. "I thought we'd be able to take things slow. Focus on us. The new us. A chance to make sure we wanted the same things. A chance to get to know each other again. Focus on the baby." She captured his gaze, holding it for a long minute. "But here I am, living in your house. Giving up the last of my independence. And still dealing with Adam and whatever mess he was involved in."

Wrapping his arm around her shoulders, he pulled her in, nuzzling her sweet smelling hair. Neither said anything for a moment, both lost in their own thoughts as his hand smoothed up her arm, tangling in her hair and then back down before traveling that path again. Kissing the top of her head, he said, "I'll call Jack and see if he wants this now or in the morning."

A few minutes later he walked back into the room, seeing her sitting in the rocking chair, her hands on her stomach. Eyes closed, her pale face in the setting sun coming through the window. She had kicked off her heels and had her feet propped on the coffee table. Her silk blouse was partially pulled out of the elastic waistband of her skirt. He had noticed she was no longer able to zip her non-maternity clothes. His heart skipped a beat as he stood watching her.

Slowly, Dani opened her eyes, watching Chad

as he stood in the entryway to the living room, leaning against the doorframe, arms crossed over his impressive chest and one thick leg crossed over the other. Her green eyes scanned him from his dark, short hair down to his booted feet, loving everything she perused. Offering him a small smile, she asked, "What'd Jack say?"

Pushing off the doorframe, he walked into the room keeping his eyes on hers and said, "Jack said we can get it to Luke tomorrow." He watched her nod before leaning her head back on the padded back of the rocker. "You rest, babe. I'll fix dinner."

As he turned to move into the kitchen, she rose from the chair and caught up to him. Linking fingers again, she said, "Let's make it together."

An hour later, they pushed their empty plates back having consumed the grilled pork chops, corn, and fresh salad. They cleaned the kitchen together, making quick work of the dishes and pans before settling on the sofa to watch TV. She thought it would be difficult to keep her mind off the notebook, but found that snuggled in Chad's embrace, his steady heartbeat underneath her fingers as her hand rested on his chest, he was the only thing on her mind.

He felt her fingers moving slowly, setting his blood on fire. *Down boy, she's gotta be tired.* Trying to steady his breathing, he chanced a glance at her upturned face. The look in her eyes turned his blood from fire...to molten. He watched her lips moving toward his and that was the only invitation he needed. Bending down, he latched onto hers. Soft...yielding. Sliding his tongue inside her warmth, he tasted her own blend of intoxicating.

With his arms wrapped around her securely, he rolled gently so her back was on the sofa and his body was slightly covering hers without letting loose of the kiss. His hand splayed over her stomach, thinking of the life below his fingers. The kiss continued languorously as his fingers slipped underneath her blouse on a slow trail toward her breasts.

Dani clutched his shoulders, fearful of digging her fingernails too deeply into him but unable to let go. His mouth sent all rational thoughts from her head. Losing herself in his methodical onslaught, she felt his fingers stop at the bottom of her breasts, but yearned to have them move higher.

He teased the underside of her bra before slipping his hand over the lace. Tracing the tops of her mounds at the lacy edge, he continued the assault on her mouth. She arched her back, pushing her breasts upward, whimpering in his mouth as he finally pulled a bra cup down, palming the fullness. His thumb swept over her taut nipple, feeling it harden even more.

The zing from her breast to her core bolted through her as her nipples responded to his touch. Sliding her hands up to cup his face, she sucked his tongue into her mouth, pushing her hips toward his heavy leg as it lay between hers.

Trying to rub her core on his jeans, he chuckled

into her mouth as his thumb and forefinger lightly pinched her nipple. Finally lifting his lips from hers, he gazed into her lust-hazy eyes and said, "Babe, I want you but I want you comfortable. No way my body fits on this sofa the way I want without possibly hurting you."

Her response was to mewl at the loss of his lips, but before she had a chance to protest, his body knifed off the sofa and she was lifted into his arms as he stalked toward the bedroom.

Once there, he lowered her slowly, allowing her full frontal to glide down his body, stopping her before her feet quite reached the floor. Her full breasts pressed into his chest. Her protruding belly pressed against his. And his prominent erection pressed into her hips as he held her tightly with one hand on her ass and the other around her middle. Their lips, still exploring, became more urgent. Thrusting his tongue into her warm mouth, he swallowed her moans as he explored each crevice, dueling with her tongue for dominance.

Bending slightly, he set her feet on the floor, hands moving to her shoulders. He reluctantly lifted his head, separating their lips but capturing her eyes. "Want to take care of you, baby. What do you need?"

Dani heard his words, soft and caring. She knew he would do whatever she wanted...a hot bath, going to sleep...but all she needed was standing right in front of her. The corners of her lips curved into a slow smile as she slipped her hands around his neck. One gave him a little squeeze as the other moved up to cup the back of his head, her fingers threading through his dark hair, pulling him toward her. "I just need you," she whispered. "All of you...in all of me."

Grinning, he stared at the promise in front of him. The realization that he had the woman he loved in arms washed over him. "You got it, babe." His hands went to her blouse, his fingers nimbly undoing each button until the silky material slid over her shoulders and down her back, allowing it to drop to the floor in a puddle behind her.

The creamy skin of her breasts spilled out of the top of her lacy bra and he lowered his head. Trailing his lips down her neck, he sucked at her pulse before kissing his way tortuously into her cleavage.

Dani's head fell back as her skin tingled from his lips—not just from his kisses, but from the promise of what was to come. With a flip of his fingers, her bra was unsnapped and she shifted her body so that the scrap of material could join her shirt on the floor.

Her hands slipped under his shirt, moving torturously upward over the hard ridges of his stomach and chest. The material bunched as she gathered it and stood on her tiptoes to pull it over his head. Slowly, her fingers splayed over his chest and down to his waist, her nails slightly digging in as they trailed the muscles.

Her hands at his belt, she easily unbuckled it

before unzipping his pants, feeling his cock straining at the impending freedom. His hands moved to her skirt, slipping into the wide elastic waistband. Catching her panties, he slid them off as well, allowing the clothing to puddle on the floor.

She moved back, sitting on the edge of the bed before shifting her legs up and scooting backward. Lying on the comforter, her auburn hair displayed across his pillows, she held his blue eyes with her green ones before lifting her arms to him.

Stepping back as he toed off his shoes and shucked his jeans and boxers, he perused the naked woman in front of him. Her body was a perfect picture of desire. He crawled over her, resting his weight on one hand as he admired her perfection.

Her rosy-tipped nipples beckoned and he moved his hand over her breasts, teasing the underside before circling her nipples with his forefinger, watching them pucker with need. Sucking one deeply into his mouth, he halted when she jumped. "Was I too hard, doll?" he murmured.

"No," she grinned. "No, they're just sensitive. More so than usual."

Realizing that her pregnant body was already responding differently, he moved back to her breasts, this time licking her nipples before sucking gently on them. She writhed underneath his ministration, each pull on her breasts sending a jolt to her womb.

She watched as he laid a trail of open-mouth,

wet kisses from her breasts down her stomach, ending at the sought after prize. Her legs spread wide, he feasted on her wet folds, sliding his tongue deep inside. Holding her head up, she continued to watch as the sensations swept across her body, threatening to drown her in their intensity. Her sex throbbed as his tongue continued its thrusts. She began to rock her hips up seeking more contact, more pressure, more...anything.

He chuckled, placing his large hands under her ass to pull her up even closer. He continued to lick her folds, pressing his tongue inside her sex, then moved up slightly to pull her clit into his mouth. Over and over, he nipped, sucked, licked until she was crying out for her release. His hand slipped up towards her breasts, lightly pinching a nipple at the same time.

Screaming his name as her world exploded in a shower of sensations, sparks flew out from her core in all directions. Boneless, not sure she could move, she floated on her cloud until she felt the mattress shift as he sat up next to her. Lifting her head, she admired the physique towering over her. She would never get tired of seeing him naked, his muscular body proudly on display. Over six feet of sinew honed from years of hauling equipment. Equipment that took him to the brink of disaster—willing to give the ultimate sacrifice to save others.

Chad observed the flush of satisfaction move over her chest and face. Staring into her green eyes, he saw her languorously lift her arms to him once more, this time wanting all of him, not just the pleasure he gave her.

Crawling up her body, with the scent of her sex filling the air, he lowered his hips between her legs, his dick straining to enter her as though it had a mind of its own. Eyes on hers, he held her gaze, marveling that such a perfect creature wanted him. Her pale complexion was reflected in the moonlight shining through the windows. Her shiny mass of thick hair lying on the pillow.

"I love you, Dani," he whispered. "I think I've loved you from the moment I first saw you."

"I feel the same," she replied. "You know...this isn't new. So going slow doesn't make a lot of sense."

He silently listened, not knowing where she was going, but cocked his head in question.

Licking her bottom lip as she continued, she said, "You're right, Chad. We both fell for each other over a year ago. We got to know each other. Spent a lot of time together. We...lost our way, but have found it again."

"What are you saying, babe?"

"To hell with going slow. I want you, in my life. In my baby's life. I want to make a life with you. Having you back has only brought that to the forefront. I want all of you with all of me."

Instead of moving toward her, he rolled over and reached into the drawer of his nightstand, pulling out a jeweler's box, hearing Dani gasp beside him. Her eyes were wide as he rolled back toward her and popped open the lid, showing off the exquisite engagement ring nestled inside. *I never planned on doing this now when we're both naked in bed...but maybe the timing is perfect after all.*

"The middle diamond was my grandmother's. She gave it to me, with her blessing. I had it reset with the other smaller diamonds around." His voice shook with nerves as he held her gaze. Taking the ring out of the box, he reached for her hand and slid it on. "Danielle, will you do me the honor of becoming my wife? Allowing me to love you for the rest of your life? Allowing me to become the father of your baby?"

Her breath caught as the moonlight glistened off the ring and the shaking fingers of the man holding her hand. Her chin quivered as she sucked in her lips to keep the tears at bay.

"Don't leave me hanging here, babe," he commanded in a whisper.

Swallowing deeply, she smiled. "Yes, yes, and yes!" she said, jerking her hand out of his so that she could cup his face and pull him in for a kiss.

Grinning, he kissed her, plunging his tongue in once more while also sending his straining cock deep inside her, fully seating himself in one thrust. Her hips moved upwards to meet his as his thrusts became more forceful. With wild abandon, he pumped furiously as though reaching for a secret place inside of her that he wanted to touch. With that intensity, it did not take long until she was screaming his name as her climax roared through her.

He thrust until her channel had stopped milking him, then he quickly pulled out, much to her dismay. Before she could question him, he said, "Babe, want to take you from behind. Are you okay with that?"

Her brilliant smile was his answer and he moved her over onto her stomach gently before grasping her hips to pull them up and back. He shifted to place a pillow under her hips, seeing to her comfort.

"You sure you're okay?" he checked.

She cried out, "Yes, now hurry!" desperate for his cock again.

He chuckled again as he thrust his engorged dick into her waiting core, hearing the moan escape from her lips.

This angle brought new sensations as her world tipped on its axis. His fingers gripped her hips, digging in to hold her as he thrust faster. She rocked back and forth as his body drove into hers, over and over. She loved the friction inside but wanted to feel the sensations on her clit. Slowly moving her hand down between her legs, she fingered herself.

"Oh, babe. Seeing you touch yourself is gonna make me harder," he panted between thrusts.

Sliding her fingers back to her clit, she rubbed and pulled on the swollen nub, the tingling indicating her orgasm was near.

Wanting her to come again before he did, he reached around tugging gently on her sensitive nipple, sending her moaning.

"Are you close, babe?" he asked roughly.

"Yes," she panted. "Yes, yes." The gripping sensations from her core were sending sparks outward as the pressure began to build. Her hands went back to the bed as his hard thrusts pushed her forward.

Her sex convulsed around his cock and with a few more thrusts he gave over to his own release. Head thrown back, thick neck muscles straining, he pulsated into her waiting body, experiencing a release unlike any he had ever felt in his life.

They both fell forward onto the bed, his large body moving to the side protectively, pulling her back to his front. Sweating and breathing heavily, Chad never felt so sated in his life. Pulling her hair back, exposing her neck, he nuzzled her soft skin.

She twisted in his arms, facing him as his arms snaked around her body, holding her closely. He peered into her green eyes, searching their depths and finding...love.

Reaching up her small hand to cup his strong jaw, she gently rubbed the stubble. "When we're here, like this...when I'm in your arms...I can pretend nothing else is swirling around us. Nothing can touch us."

"Nothing will ever touch you, babe. I promise."

She held his gaze for a moment, hiding her thoughts about Adam, not wanting them to intrude on what she and Chad experienced. But she knew, as much as she cared for Adam, she did not love him. And he never promised her more than just taking care of her.

"I love you," she whispered. "Like I've never loved anyone else before in my life."

Chad understood what she was giving him. True love. Not based on need...or circumstances... or feeling trapped. But true love.

He closed his eyes momentarily, realizing once again how lucky he was. "Love you back, Dani. Forever."

The moon moved across the sky, blanketing the couple in shadows as they lay tangled in the sheets. Her body half draped over his, he pushed her hair back from her face. With her head on his shoulder, he smoothed his hand over her body, ending at her protruding stomach. His long fingers splayed out over the area that nestled their baby.

21

Mitch waited impatiently for the video-conference to begin as all of the Saints gathered. It did not take long for Luke to decipher Adam's coded notebook. To save time, Chad took pictures of the pages from the notebook and sent them to Luke early that morning to give him a chance to begin his intel as soon as he arrived at the compound.

"He used a very elementary system of exchanging letters and numbers, which would not fool anyone for long but would have the effect of appearing like jibberish to anyone just happening upon the book."

"So, do we know what he was into?" Chad asked, tension rolling off him. *I thought I knew him. He had my back when we went into danger. How the hell could I not have known him?*

"Basically, it's a type of diary he seemed to

keep." Luke stopped and stared at Chad for a long moment. "Man, I don't think it's good news."

Chad's face, set in stone, was indecipherable to the casual observer, but his friends saw the flash of anger in his eyes.

"It seems he entered a dating site and was contacted by some people he kept track of."

The air in the room chilled to sub-zero. No one spoke. No one moved.

"He entered a dating site while married to Dani?" Chad asked, each word slowly punched out, his heart pounding as his chest hurt. Actually hurt. *Jesus, I can never let her know this.*

"Here's what's crazy," Luke said. "He entered under a false name. He used his first and middle name only. Adam Jackson. The account has been deleted but I'm working to see if I can get my hands on the substance of his encounters."

"What site?" Mitch asked.

Luke sucked in a breath before letting it out slowly. "Geeks2gether."

Once more, the silence in the room was deafening as the Saints looked at each other in surprise.

"Why the hell would he do that?" Blaise asked. "It makes no fuckin' sense."

Shaking his head, as it felt ready to explode, Chad replied, "Damnit! Adam was such a jokester. Always trying to be the center of attention." Rubbing his hand over his face, he said, "How he could have gotten involved in this..." His mind reeled at the implications.

"Dani?" Jack prompted.

"No fuckin' way. Jesus, I've got to keep this from her. They might not have had a marriage of love, but it was built on mutual respect and friendship. She trusted him." Leaning back heavily in his seat, his heart was heavy as his rage began to build. "Whatever he was doing, he put her at risk and that is fuckin' unforgivable."

Luke, catching Jack's eyes, nodded and proceeded carefully. "The best I can tell from the few pages is that he met a woman online named Sabah Masrah—"

"Fuck!" Mitch cursed. "That's a name that's come across our desk as a local recruiter. Or at least she's being used that way. Hell, she might not even be a real person or a real woman."

The expletives resounded around the table as each man felt the punch of Chad's friend being in contact with a known ISIS recruiter.

Luke responded quickly, "He never mentioned meeting her personally." He sent Chad a glance but, seeing his friend's lips pressed tightly in anger, he continued. "Adam noted when he had online chats with her. He doesn't say what the chats were about...so, uh...maybe they were...uh...just chatting."

"You think that fuckin' matters? He was on a dating chat-line while married! While I can't see Adam looking for a date on a geek site, he was either being recruited or cheating on Dani. Either one sucks."

"Look, maybe he was getting in over his head and that's why he kept notes. I mean, he left a trail for Dani to find," Jude argued.

"Uh...there's more," Luke added, his expression a mixture of hard...and despondent.

"Oh, Jesus, I don't know how much more I can take," Chad said, putting his elbows on the table and resting his head in his hands. After a moment, he sat up and pierced Luke with a stare. Nodding, he gave his approval to continue.

Luke flashed new information onto the screen on the wall. "A bank account. With only Adam Jackson's name on it."

The Saints turned their questioning gazes back to Luke. "He set this up about six weeks before he died. The money's still there. He opened the account at a different bank than what he and Dani used. She would have no idea it's there."

The men visually scanned the cash deposits; a thousand dollars each week. For six weeks. Stopping the week he died.

"What does this mean?" Bart asked, his eyes turned toward Chad.

Chad shook his head, saying nothing...feeling everything.

"Until that piece of evidence," Jack said, nodding his head toward the wall screen, "I thought Adam got in this as a joke, got caught up in something and it went too far."

"And now?" Mitch prodded.

"Man, I'm sorry, Chad," Jack continued, "But if

that account means what I'm afraid it does...if he took money from them...he's guilty."

Heart pounding, Chad felt his throat closing up. "Why would he keep written notes? Why the fuck would he leave them there for Dani to find?"

"It leads her to the bank account. He has her listed as the beneficiary. Since she never knew about it, then she'd have no reason to go to close it out," Mitch surmised.

"What about the rest of the notebook?" Jude pressed.

"He'd already told her to go to Chad. Maybe he realized his days were numbered if they found out he wasn't who he said he was. Maybe the explosion he walked into was aimed at him. Maybe it was called in, on his watch...just for him to respond. And if he thought things might happen, he wanted someone to know."

Once more, silence reigned in the compound. Luke's fingers were stilled over his keyboard. Chad's mind raced, thinking of the man he knew. The man he called a friend. *Please, Adam, let us find something that lets us know what you were doing. You couldn't have been a traitor, so what the fuck were you up to?*

Finally looking up at Jack, he asked, "So what now, boss? Where does this leave us?"

"Chad, we understand you weren't in close contact with Adam at that time, but do you have any idea who he might have talked to? Another ATF agent?"

He thought a moment and said, "Dani

mentioned a couple of our former friends he would hang out with, go drinking with. I saw two of them at the funeral."

"Talk to them," Jack said. "Find out if they knew anything to give us an idea of what he was doing."

"Damn, this is still fucked up!" Marc cursed. "I don't see what kept him in with this...the money wasn't that good."

"Blackmail," Mitch said, gaining everyone's attention. "Same as what they use for the recruits who work on their computer programs. If they discovered he was an ATF agent, they could have blackmailed him into giving them information...or turning a blind eye. Otherwise, they could release his name in documents, obliterating his career and security clearance."

"Right," Jack said, pulling the meeting back to order. "Marc, you go with Chad. I want two of you on Adam's friends. Luke, get the names from Adam's book and send everything to Mitch. We're not investigating them, just turning them over to the FBI."

"There appears to be only one other name mentioned. Adam noted having an online chat with someone named Fazan."

"Fazan?" Mitch asked, his voice strident and eyes wide. "Fuckin' hell, If this is the same Fazan, he is one of the leaders of the ISIS cells recruiting in Virginia. Luke, get me everything you've got. The FBI is putting this on our highest priority."

Mitch disconnected, leaving the Saints unusually quiet as they processed the latest information. Chad soaked in the appreciated silence, wondering what he was going to tell Dani. *Fuck you, Adam. What the hell were you thinking?*

22

The inside of the bar was just as Chad remembered from his years with the ATF. A regular haunt, he was reminded of nights when Dani would come up from her office and meet he and Adam for beer and wings.

She would arrive, parting the crowd as she moved over to us, never realizing how many men stared at her as she walked straight to our table. Long, auburn hair swinging from her ponytail. Her body, unable to be hidden underneath the basic uniform of black pants and white blouse. Her smile widened as soon as she laid eyes on us.

Lost in memories, Chad startled as Marc nudged his arm, nodding to a man walking toward them. The first friend of Adam's that they spoke to had no idea what Adam was doing near the end, but Jon Stahl agreed to meet Chad at the old stomping ground.

Man hugging, Chad greeted Jon and introduced

Marc. Jon, a small man with a friendly smile, settled in with the other two, making easy conversation for a few minutes.

"So you want to know about Adam?" Jon finally asked. "Anything in particular?"

"Yeah, we're interested in anything...uh... different he may have been doing." Chad knew his request sounded stupid but became instantly alert at Jon's demeanor.

Hanging his head, his lips in a grimace, Jon bit out, "Damn, I knew he was being a dumbass. But swear to god, until you called, I didn't have a clue he'd kept up with anything after the first little bit."

Chad and Marc shared a confused look, but Marc smoothly said, "Why don't you just tell us what you do know."

Taking a deep pull on his beer, Jon set it back on the table a little too hard, jumping at the sound. Sighing, he nodded his acquiescence. "Hell, it happened right here. We'd been at some god-awful, boring training my division was presenting and the ATF bomb squad agents had to come to it. Adam complained the whole time and when we got here and he got some beers in him, he began to laugh about the geeks in my division who'd presented. Gotta say, he was right and it was pretty funny. He wondered how anyone could get laid when they were such geeks and I swear he googled it on his phone."

"Googled what?" Marc asked, dumbfounded by the turn of the conversation.

"How a geek gets laid," Jon replied. "Honest to god, he came up with some dating sites for geeks." Shaking his head again, he said, "He sat right here and created some fake account to one of the sites." Looking up to Chad, he said, "Never thought he'd follow through with anything."

"Follow through with what?" Chad asked.

"I didn't see Adam for a couple of weeks and the next time we met here he told me he'd gotten some hits on the geek dating site. Said he wasn't going to meet any of them, but he was having a blast pretending to be a real nerd and seeing who he could fool." Jon looked nervously at them, pushing his glasses up on his nose. "He contacted me a couple of times to ask me technical questions. Since he was pretending to be a tech geek, he needed my help to keep up the ruse."

"Anything else?" Chad asked.

Confused, Jon said, "No, but I heard through the grapevine in the office that you and Dani have gotten together. I...well, I...uh...figured that was why you were asking."

"So, other than at the beginning, he didn't tell you anything else about the dating site?"

"No," Jon said, shaking his head. "I felt bad for Dani. Even if Adam was being his usual joking self, I still thought it was a dumbass move."

Leaning back in his seat, Chad nodded. "Yeah, that seems to be what he excelled in—dumbass moves."

Driving home thirty minutes later, Chad said, "I

keep playing this whole fucking thing over in my mind. I've got a former ATF buddy being a jokester and, on a whim, got involved in a site that terrorists happen to use to recruit computer loners for their skills."

Marc clarified, "So, he starts a chat, pretending to be someone he's not, gets Jon's help to sound more like a computer nerd, and then what? Gets in over his head? Actually takes money, still thinking it's a joke? Or maybe, he does something stupid and they threaten blackmail and so he takes their money and he's hooked?"

"I've got no idea, but whatever it was, he must have known it could blow back on Dani. That's what fuckin' kills me."

"His clues?"

"What did he think he was? Some super sleuth? Goddamn, he left Dani the key, that stupid note and then the book in the rocking chair. What a fuckin' moron! That's like some bad movie script!"

Marc shook his head. "I know, right, man? Playing around with a dating site, just to be a dumbass. Then continuing the charade. Then not knowing how to get out...or not wanting to get out."

The two friends were quiet for a few minutes as the dark road passed underneath them. "Maybe he really got in over his head," Chad said. "Maybe, by the time he figured out he was dealing with some shit, he was already found out. Then he had to take their hush money and hope that if something happened, he could let someone know."

"Have you decided what you're going to tell Dani?"

"No...I mean, sort of. I have to tell her what's going on because she already knows a lot. And I need her to be vigilant."

Pulling into Chad's driveway, Marc said, "I don't envy you, man. But for what it's worth, you're exactly what she needs. Just hang onto that and ride it out."

"It's no sacrifice to be with Dani. I'd do anything for her and the baby. They've become my life...a life I'd lay down just to keep them safe."

Saying goodbye, Chad got out of Marc's truck and jogged up his front steps. Letting himself in, he set his alarm and was greeted by a sleepy Dani walking down the stairs as he turned around. Her sleep-tousled hair fell around her shoulders. One of his old, faded ATF t-shirts hung to her mid-thighs. She blinked in the light, her green eyes focusing on him.

He watched, his heart pounding, heavy with handing more to her. *I should be fuckin' keeping anything bad from happening to her.* Seeing her standing at the bottom of his stairs, in his house, in his t-shirt...he watched as her face lit with her beautiful smile. She stumbled forward, face-planting into his chest, her sleepy arms around his middle. Kissing the top of her head, he breathed her in as he wrapped his arms around her.

"You find out anything?" she mumbled, her

words muffled since she did not lift her head from his chest.

"Not much," he said, giving her a squeeze. "We'll talk in the morning, okay?"

She lifted her head back and peered into his eyes. Whatever he had learned, it did not set well with him and she could see the emotions behind his gaze. She wanted to know. But she wanted to give him a chance to process...and sleep. "Yeah, sweetie. Let's go to bed."

Chad looked down at her, knowing she was curious but giving him the time to work through what needed to be done. *Easy...you make things so easy, babe.* He smiled in return, moving her toward the stairs. "Yeah, let's go to bed."

Sleep did not come readily, but when it did, it came with them wrapped around each other.

Dani sat at her desk, knowing she was not very productive. She flipped through emails, deleting the unnecessary ones, answering the easy ones, and holding off on the others that required more thought than she had in her at the moment.

Her mind wandered back to the conversation she had with Chad before they left for work. Hearing that Adam had played around with a dating site as a joke actually did not upset her—or surprise her. *Geez, Adam. Looking back, you were always goofing off...well, except with your job—then you were the consummate professional.* As her eyes wandered to her stomach, she remembered that when she was pregnant, he was completely into it. *Okay, so I guess with impending fatherhood you got serious about something else also.*

So it was not what Chad told her about Adam's stupid fake nerd dating site—it was what she heard about that was happening the two months leading up to his death. Chad had asked her about what she saw in Adam's behavior, but she told him she did not notice anything unusual.

Now, hours later, she twirled her pen around in her fingers, forcing her mind to go back to the months before Adam died. *Maybe he was a little more distracted. Maybe he...no that's not right! He'd actually become a little more loving...that's why it hurt so bad when his bimbo showed up at the wake.*

"Augghh!" she groaned loudly.

"Are you all right?"

She jumped as she saw Jahfar at the door, staring at her. *How long has he been spying on me?* Forcing a smile on her face, she replied, "Yes, I'm fine. I was just working on a difficult email."

He walked in, hesitantly at first, his eyes never leaving hers. "Anything I can assist with?"

"No, thank you," she replied, more sharply than she intended. "Sorry, I seem to be having a trying day."

He glanced behind her desk to the pictures sitting on the windowsill. "Your husband was a handsome man. And working with a bomb squad...

a very brave man. A man willing to sacrifice. I'm sure your child will be blessed. He was in the D.C. office wasn't he?"

"I don't believe I ever mentioned that," she said, the hair on the back of her neck prickling.

"Oh, I must have heard it from someone else," he said smoothly.

She cocked her head to the side, not knowing what to say to that. Before she had to come up with a response, Ethan knocked on her door.

"Oh, I didn't realize you were busy," he said.

"No, no," Jahfar interrupted. "I was just leaving." He walked out with a nod to both of them.

Ethan walked in, sitting in the chair in front of Dani's desk. "You okay?"

"I swear he gets creepier every day. I don't know what it is, but he seems to want to talk about my former husband. He's mentioned him several times."

At that, Ethan's attention perked. "What kind of questions?"

Rubbing her head as a headache loomed, she said, "Oh, I don't know. It's probably nothing, but I can't figure out why he'd be so fixated on my deceased husband."

"Was there anything in particular Adam was working on that would have made anyone curious?"

"Not that I know of. I mean his death was public; I think every paper in the nation carried the story of the brave ATF bomb squad member that triggered an explosion in a house that had held an ISIS bomb-making group." She leaned back in her seat, resting her head on the padded back. "I don't know, Ethan. Maybe I just have an active imagination."

Ethan looked speculative for a moment, then leaned forward in his seat, putting his forearms on her desk. "Look, Dani, stay vigilant when it comes to Jahfar."

Capturing her attention, she leaned forward as well. "What's going on?" she asked in a whisper.

He signed heavily as though weighing whether or not to speak before finally admitting, "Todd's brought me on board with the security because he's got concerns. I'm trying to figure out if we have a problem or not."

"What kind of problem?"

Looking behind him, Ethan then turned back, an expression of indecision on his face. "Let's just say that we're keeping a close eye on all our shipments now. We don't want any to go missing. Or should I say...any *more* to go missing."

Eyes wide, Dani understood what he was implying. "Oh, shit."

"Look, I've said too much already, but just keep your eyes on Jahfar. Let me know if you see or hear anything suspicious."

"I doubt that will happen," she admitted. "I avoid him when possible."

Nodding, he agreed. "Not a bad plan." Looking

at her carefully, he asked, "How are you doing...um, feeling?"

She smiled, her hand automatically going to her stomach. "I'm fine. A little sick at the beginning, but now, I'm fine."

"I'm sure this must be a difficult time to be a widow," he commented, concern in his expression.

Dani had not talked about her personal life to anyone at work, not having had time to build close friendships. She hesitated, then added, "I'm seeing an old friend...someone that I knew from my days with the ATF. He works in investigations now."

"Good," he replied, a smile on his face. "You deserve that." He stood, moving toward the door, stopping just inside as he turned back and said, "Make sure you let me know of anything suspicious you hear, okay?"

"Absolutely," she agreed.

Watching him walk out, she rubbed her aching head again. *Thank God, time to go home.* Grabbing her purse and laptop case, she made her way out of the building, never noticing the sharp eyes of Jahfar as they watched her get in her car.

She had barely walked into Chad's house when her phone rang. Looking at the display, she grinned seeing Bethany's name.

"Hey, what's up, Bethany?" she called out.

"The girls want a night out. Are you up for that?"

"Oh, my God, you have no idea," Dani replied. "I'd love to."

"Well, I know you and Miriam can't drink, but Elixer has some great non-alcoholic drinks."

"I've never been there, but I know where it is."

"Perfect. Meet us there about seven okay?"

Disconnecting, Dani felt a bounce in her step that had been missing all day. She could not remember the last time she went out with a group of girlfriends. Smiling to herself as she headed to the master bathroom, she knew this was just what she needed.

23

The girls sat at a high-topped table, ordering appetizers and fruity-flirty drinks. As the waitress took everyone's drink orders, Bethany stunned the group when she ordered a non-alcoholic daiquiri.

The silence lasted only a second before the *Are you pregnant* questions rang out. Grinning while nodding, Bethany said, "Yes! We just found out! I'm six weeks along."

Hugs, screams, and laughter filled the air as the women celebrated. The lively conversations jumped from one topic to another as the women relished their girls' night out. As the food was delivered the women pounced on the appetizers.

"God, I needed this," Dani exclaimed, popping another nacho in her mouth.

"Seriously," Angel agreed. "I had a wedding order to get ready, plus two little girl birthday parties."

Dani touched her stomach thoughtfully and said, "Will you do parties for my little girl when she's old enough?"

"Hell, yeah," Angel nodded, her head bobbing enthusiastically. She was already on her second Lemon Drop and was smiling even more widely than normal. Her long blonde hair, with its pink, purple, and teal stripes caught the lights in the bar, creating a colorful halo.

"I knew you'd be good for my business," Bethany grinned at Angel, throwing back the rest of her drink. The natural beauty had her blonde hair plaited in a long braid, hanging over one shoulder. "Now that the best, kick-ass cabin wedding venue in the area has partnered with the best, kick-ass cupcake bakery, we're unstoppable!"

"Which reminds me," Sabrina interrupted, tapping a perfectly manicured nail on the table. "I have the new designs for your reception hall. I left them in my bag but can bring them by tomorrow."

"How's your job going?" Faith asked Miriam, going after the popcorn shrimp.

"Good, I really love it. I have to admit that it's a pain to keep buying maternity nursing scrubs, but then that's a lot cheaper than what Dani's going to have to do," Miriam laughed. Her dark hair, tucked behind her ears, hung down her back in a thick sheet.

"Don't remind me!" Dani replied. "For a while I've been pinning my skirts and pants and leaving the shirts hanging out, but recently bought a couple of maternity outfits. Geez, they're expensive!"

"My sister still has some and she's about your size," Miriam added. "She gave them to me, but since I wear nursing scrubs most days, you can definitely have whatever you want."

The appetizers were refilled, as were their drinks, before the conversation turned around to Dani.

"So, how's it going with your Saint, Dani?" Sabrina asked.

Dani looked askance for a second, then laughed. "Things are great with Chad." She sobered for a moment and said, "Look, I realize from the outside, it must look incredibly crazy for me to be living with a man so soon after losing my husband."

The other women quickly shook their heads in denial.

"Honey, when it comes to a Saint that has found the one, you usually end up at their house within a few weeks!" Miriam said.

"Yep, once they make up their minds, well, the alpha side comes out and nothing's going to stop them from doing just that," Sabrina added.

Faith, sitting next to Dani, placed her hand on Dani's arm. "What really matters is, how you're feeling."

Dani turned to look at the soft-spoken beauty and smiled. "Honestly? I'm...truly happy." Looking at the faces of the women around the table, she smiled, a little sadly. "I was always such a careful person...holding myself back. I did that with Chad the first time and then began to make a series of mistakes. It's harsh, but my marriage was both right and wrong. Right...because of the pregnancy. Wrong...because we didn't love each other."

"And now?" Bethany asked.

The sadness left her face as Dani replied, "Now? I love Chad. I don't spend any time thinking of all of the *what-ifs*."

"No life can be spent happily with the *what-ifs*," Faith agreed. "You have to take life as it's handed to you. What you do with the here and now."

Lifting their glasses together, the women toasted to their *here and nows*, laying their pasts to rest.

An hour later, not wanting the evening to end but with half of them pregnant, they decided to take the party to Angel's Cupcake Heaven.

"I've got some that didn't make the cut for the wedding, so they were going to go in the case tomorrow anyway," Angel explained as she set a dozen gorgeously decorated cupcakes on their table. Each woman grabbed one and dove in, not caring about the colorful frosting now coating their lips, tongues, and even cheeks. Orgasmic moans ensued from all, followed by peals of laughter.

Dani had never been in Angel's shop and her gaze wandered the colorful bakery before landing on the back wall. A painted mural graced the space —a medieval monk taking bread from a stone oven.

Cocking her head to the side, she commented, "I love your wall painting."

"That's my Saint," she grinned.

Dani shifted her eyes from the wall to the other women, noticing their smiles as well. "Your Saint?"

"Jack was named for Jacques, the Patron Saint of Soldiers," Bethany said. "His mother told him about his name when he was a boy and it meant so much to him, he named his business after Saints."

"I had no idea," Dani confessed.

"Monty used to feel a little odd that he did not have a Saint's name, but his parents gave him the family names of Montgomery Honor Lytton. He had no idea that St. Honorius was the patron Saint of bakers," Angel added.

Before Dani could ask, the others chimed in as well.

"St. Camillus was the founder of the Red Cross. That's who I was working for when he rescued me," Miriam said proudly. "Cam says he was meant for me."

Sabrina smiled, "St. Jude was the Patron Saint of lost causes, something Jude had thought about himself, after his SEAL injury, before he started working for Jack."

Turning her eyes to Faith, she waited to see what the quiet, dark-haired beauty would say.

"Bart is obviously for St. Bartholomew, seeker of truth. I confess that it made for a rocky beginning for us, but once he discovered the real me, well, he found truth...and Faith."

Shoving in a bite of her cupcake, Dani grinned at her new-found friends. “Hmmm, so is Chad a saint’s name? I confess, I have no idea.”

Shrugging, Bethany said, “I don’t know. The names mean different things to each of the men. You’ll have to ask Chad about that.”

Thoughtful as she shoved more cupcake into her mouth, letting the moist goodness melt on her tongue, Dani thought about how to ask Chad what the Saints meant to him.

Lying in bed later that night, legs tangled, slick bodies pressed together, coming down from their post-orgasmic bliss, Dani traced her finger over Chad’s chest. A tattoo over his heart found her fingers moving over the letters. **EOD Sacrifice**

Never having asked about the significance, she leaned up on her elbow, resting her head in her hand as she stared down at him. Holding his gaze, she smiled as she leaned forward, touching her lips to his in a whisper soft kiss.

“Can I ask you something?” she said, her voice soft and with a hint of uncertainty.

“Babe, you can ask me anything,” he responded. “With you, I’m an open book.”

Moistening her lips, she said, “Can you tell me about this tattoo?”

He had wondered when she might ask about the tattoo, having noticed her tracing it at times, like now, when they laid tangled after sex. He was silent for a moment, considering how to explain what it meant to him. Sucking in a deep breath through his nose before letting it out slowly, he rolled over to face her. Her hand continued to splay over the letters as their bodies shifted.

"It means just what you think it does, Dani. You were an ATF investigator, so even if you weren't diffusing and disposing bombs, you understood what it took to walk that walk. When I was in the Army, EOD was the patch we wore for those of us who worked with ordnance disposal. It was…a strange club…those of us who wore that patch. Didn't matter which branch of service we served in. We saw that patch on someone else…we knew. Knew what they were…who they were."

Dani's fingers stilled, but continued to feel his strong heartbeat underneath them.

"Sacrifice was the word that others used for us. The word that defined us. Not that we were better than others, just…different."

The dark night enveloped them as the silence floated between them.

"You walked toward the ultimate known danger," she said softly, her heart overflowing for this man in her arms. "Not many can do that. I can see where the word sacrifice comes from."

He slid his hand up her back to tangle in her hair, pulling her head forward so it rested on his chest, right over the words tattooed on his soul. His mind raced for a few minutes, and then he gently moved her head back slightly so he was able to hold her gaze and slid his hand to her stomach.

"Babe, a lot's going down with us, but I want to lay something out. As a man, I'm not real big on talking about any other man while were here, in our bed. But Adam's going to be a part of our future, just like he's part of our past. He's the father of our daughter, while I'll be her dad. And I'm good with that. But with all the shit that's been swirling around about him, stepping out on you, what he was doing and what he might have been involved in before he died...that's tainted him. In your eyes...in mine. But one thing to remember, that we'll want to let our daughter know...at one time, he had the EOD patch as well. Respected. Dedicated. Sacrificing. So when all this shit-storm is swirling, we need to remember that's who he was."

A silent tear slid across Dani's nose and onto the pillow. Chad's rough thumb soothed away the next one that followed.

Swallowing deeply, she nodded. "Thank you for that reminder, sweetie. I really needed to remember the friend I married. I've spent so much time in the past months since his death being angry with him and wondering why the hell I ever became involved with him to begin with. And that made me doubt myself." Sucking in a ragged breath, a watery smile escaped. "And now...we have to find out what all he was doing and then accept the Adam that he became. But thank you for reminding me that he was a sacrificing hero at one time."

Continuing to hold his gaze, she fingered the St. Chad pendant resting on his chest, and asked, "The other ladies tonight were talking about Jack's decision to name his company the Saints. They said the other men discovered their own meaning for their names. I wondered about you...if that's not too personal."

"Nothing too personal between us, babe," he assured. His mind roamed back to when he first learned of the meaning of his name. Not raised in a faith that studied the Saints, it meant nothing to him at the time. But now...

His voice slid into the quiet once more as he continued, "I was named after my grandfather. Sacrifice is also a word used for St. Chad. I didn't even know this as a child. I learned it when I was speaking to a priest after the death of one of my teammates in the service."

Tucking her head back under his chin, he kissed the top of her hair, breathing her in. Together they found sleep...peaceful sleep.

24

TGIF Dani thought as she left work at the end of the long workweek. Now into the second trimester, she felt healthier, breathed easier about carrying her daughter to term, and smiled thinking about the coming weekend. The Saints were having a cookout at Jack and Bethany's place. With their huge deck, kick-ass massive grill, and a view to kill for she could not wait.

Driving to the grocery store to buy the ingredients for her world-famous potato salad—*well unofficially world-famous*—she ran the ingredients needed through her mind. Glancing into her rear-view mirror, she noticed a car behind her with dark-tinted windows. Including the front. *I thought it was illegal to have a dark-tinted windshield. Wasn't that so the police would be able to observe who they were approaching if pulled over?*

Trying not to focus on who was behind her, she

realized the light ahead just turned yellow. *Damn,* she sped up slightly to rush through, irritated that she had not paid closer attention. Glancing into the rearview mirror again, she noticed the dark car had followed her through the light.

Stop looking, she chastised herself. *Stop being paranoid.* To get to the store she wanted to shop at, she needed to go through Charlestown, making several turns along the way. The car stayed with her. Every lane change. Every turn.

The fear grew until she was no longer paranoid—she was certain she was being followed. Grabbing her phone, she called Chad on speed dial. Before he had a chance to speak, she began as soon as she heard the call connect.

"I'm being followed. Black sedan, license plate has dark covering and I can't get a good read on it. Front windshield is dark. Can't see who's driving. They've been with me for at least twenty minutes."

"Fuck, babe. Don't go to my house, I'm not there yet. Go somewhere public. Park as close to the front as you can and run inside the store. Stay on the line while I call Jack."

She heard him fire off the information to Jack as she kept her eyes peeled to her rear view mirror.

"Where are you now?" he asked, his voice sharp with command.

"I'm near the ShopMart in the Southside Shopping Center," she replied. "He's still with me."

"Go there. Park near the front. Stay on the line

with me and tell me exactly what's happening." Switching between phones, he told Jack where she was. In a moment, he added, "Jude is close by. He's going to be watching for you. Tell me everything that's happening."

Dani's investigative training kicked in and she reported succinctly, staying as calm as she could. "I'm pulling into the shopping center parking lot now, but on the far end from ShopMart. I'm driving on the road directly in front of the stores."

"Dani? Jude's got you in his sights. Don't worry about him, just keep driving until you find a close parking space. Then wait for my instructions."

A tense moment passed and then she said, "Found one. It's just three spaces from the front, near the double doors leading to the lawn care section."

"Jude's got you. He says he sees the black car following closely...now they're circling around. Go! Now! Get out of the car and head inside as quickly as you can!" he ordered.

Without question, she grabbed her purse and jumped out of her car, hustling into the store with her phone still at her ear.

"Jude's parked and has your car in close sight. You stay inside the store and keep your phone on, babe. Whatever you do, do not go back to your car until I've gotten there and cleared it."

"Chad?" she whispered breathlessly, standing in the front court of the store.

"Yeah?"

"I love you," she said, still whispering, but her voice now stronger.

Only a heartbeat of silence fell before she heard the words in return. "I love you too, little mama."

Closing her eyes, a deep breath escaping, she moved back inside the store, her phone gripped in her hand.

Thirty minutes later, her nerves taut, she was ready to explode if her phone did not ring soon. She had grabbed the items needed in record time and now was pacing as she waited for word of what was happening in the parking lot. Every minute that dragged by was agonizing. *What's happening? Is the black car still there? Did Jude do something? Is he all right? Where is Chad? Did he—*

The long awaited vibration of her phone startled her, causing her to jump. Connecting quickly, she said, "What's going on?"

"Where are you?" Chad asked.

"Inside the store where you told me to be."

"No, babe, I mean where are you in the store?"

"I'm near the front, where the lawn equipment is. I'm at the deck chairs and umbrellas. Can I come out now?"

"Stay," he barked, before disconnecting.

Staring at the phone, her eyes widened in frustration. *Stay? Did he just tell me to stay? I can't belie—*

"Babe." Chad's voice reached her and she whirled to see him standing there. One look at his concerned face and all irritation fell away. Rushing the three steps it took to reach his arms, she flung herself into his embrace.

"What's going on? I hated being in here and not being able to tell what was happening. What did Jude see—"

"Shhh," he gently admonished. "Just let me hold you for a second."

At those words, she melted into his arms, her legs fighting to hold her up. His arms tightened around her middle protectively...and possessively, feeling her pregnant stomach pressing into his.

"Okay, baby, let's get out of here." He started to lead her out, but she jerked back, grabbing two shopping bags from one of the display deck tables.

"Wait, these are mine." Seeing the look on his face, she said, "I told the girls I was bringing my potato salad, so when I first got in here, I ran to buy what I needed and then ran back over to the door to wait."

Laughing, Chad said, "That's my girl. Smart, brave, and always thinking ahead, even in dire circumstances."

They reached the outside, making their way over to her car, seeing Jude and Bart standing next to it. Both men appeared almost identical as they stood with their blond hair, arms crossed over their muscular chests, legs apart, and reflector sunglasses on making it impossible to see their eyes. But if their matching scowls were anything to go by, their moods were as identical as their stances.

Dani approached with Chad's arm still protectively around her. "What's going on?"

Not answering her, Bart looked at Chad and said, "Jack wants us at his place. Jude'll drive her car."

"Uh, hello? I'm here," she said, waving her hand in front of their faces, surprised that the men were ignoring her.

"Babe," came Chad's soft reply, carrying more of a command than an endearment.

Jerking her head up to look into his face, she opened her mouth to retort, when she felt his arm squeeze her shoulders slightly. Pressing her lips together, she handed her keys to Jude and then turned with Chad as he directed her to his truck. Climbing inside, she counted to ten as he rounded the front and got in the driver's seat.

Before she could speak, he immediately said, "I know you're pissed, babe, but the middle of a parking lot with people around was not the time to go into what all happened."

Sucking in a deep breath, she nodded. "You're right. I'm just wound up tight...I...oh, hell, I'm furious at everyone right now. I'm sorry."

"Understandable. Okay, here's what happened after you went inside the store. Jude had you in his sights and parked where he had a clear view of your vehicle. By the time the black car came around again, you had made it inside. The license tags on both the front and back were indistinguishable as you said. He watched as a man got out of the passenger side and walked toward your car. Jude got photos of him but wanted to make sure that no device was being planted on it. So he got out and began wandering close to your car as though he had come out of the store and was looking for his own."

"Genius," Dani admitted. "What happened then?"

"As soon as Jude was approaching the car next to yours, the man got back in the black car quickly and they took off."

"So what now?"

"He sent the parts of the license number that he could ascertain and the pictures to Luke. He'll process them and send them to Mitch at the FBI."

Dani leaned back, resting her head against the leather seat. Chad reached over and took her cold hand in his, linking their fingers together.

"You did good, baby. I know you were with the ATF and you can handle situations, but it's different when it happens to yourself."

Still leaning against the headrest, she rolled her head to the side to face him and gifted him with a small smile. "I was more angry than scared."

Chuckling, he said, "I think I could tell that."

"So, I guess the picnic is off?"

"No way! We're still heading to Jack's. The

Saints will have a quick meeting, but then Jack's got steaks to grill and good food to eat."

"I'm really glad," she said. "First of all, I would hate for any drama going on with me to interrupt everyone's pleasure."

"And what's the second reason?"

"Um...Bethany's cobbler, Angel's cupcakes, and my world-famous potato salad!"

"Hell yeah!" Chad agreed as they turned into Jack's drive.

Hours later, after the sun had presented the gathering with an exquisite sunset over the Blue Ridge Mountains, the food consumed, and the desserts now decimated, the group settled in chairs around a fire pit on the compound.

Dani was pleased her earlier incident had not marred the event, and even relaxed as she leaned back against Chad. Once they had arrived, the women swooped in, making sure she was all right, before she met with the Saints to explain exactly what happened. Then she jumped in to prepare her potato salad and hung around the kitchen talking as the Saints finished their impromptu meeting. It might seem sexist, she thought of the idea of the men meeting while she was in the kitchen, but she had to admit she felt safe.

Now the dark of night was chased away with torches lit on the parameter of the huge deck, as well as the flames casting dancing light over their faces.

Feeling a little shoulder squeeze, she turned to look at Chad expectantly. Seeing the concern on his face, she smiled. “I’m fine,” she assured. “But I’d really like to understand what’s going on.”

Jack, overhearing, said, “Right now, Dani, we don’t have any more than what you already know. I expect our FBI contact to get back with us tomorrow with an ID of the man who was out of his car and looking at yours.”

She nodded, grateful for the explanation, and burrowed deeper in Chad’s embrace.

“You okay, babe?” he asked.

Grinning, she replied, “I’ve got great food in my belly, am surrounded by friends, and snuggling with you…what could be better?”

The chuckles around the deck let her know the others agreed.

The next morning dawned bright as Dani padded her way to the kitchen, following tantalizing smells. Hearing noises from the room, she turned the corner to see Chad standing at the stove. Bare chested with jeans hung low on his hips, the view made her mouth water. Then she glanced down to the pan and realized he had bacon sizzling and fluffy scrambled eggs and her stomach growled loudly. Now she was not sure which made her more hungry.

Turning with the spatula in his hand, Chad grinned. "Sounds like baby girl is hungry this morning."

Patting her stomach, Dani returned his smile, saying, "She's starving."

"Good," he said, plating the food and setting it on the table. "Come sit down and I'll get you a glass of milk."

An hour later, as she walked from the bedroom into the living room, her hair still wet from the shower, she heard the sound of trucks pulling into the driveway. Her face scrunched in confusion as she looked over at Chad. "Were you expecting company?"

He jumped up, blushing. "I have a surprise, babe. I hope it's a good one, but if you don't like it then I can tell everyone to leave."

"Well, you'd better tell me before our friends start pounding on the door," she said, peeking out the front window and observing several of the Saints and their women.

Stalking over, Chad said, "The group asked what they could do to help us and I thought maybe you'd like them to help create a nursery out of the spare bedroom."

Her gaze jumped to his face, seeing his hesitant expression. "Oh, Chad! That would be wonderful... but I haven't ordered anything yet."

A huge grin replaced his look of uncertainty

and he replied, "No worries. The guys are going to help move the old furniture in there to either the Re-Sale store or into the storage space in the back of the garage. A couple of the women wanted to clean the room to have it ready to paint." He hesitated once more as he continued. "Uh...and I saw the crib you had marked on your wish list and well...I...uh...sort of went ahead and bought it."

Dani's eyebrows raised as her heart leapt and her green eyes sparkled with glee. Before she had a chance to speak, a knock on the door interrupted.

"Babe, is this okay?" Chad asked, his hands on her shoulders. Peering into her eyes, he vowed, "If not, just say the word and I'll have everyone leave."

"No, no, this is perfect!" she effused. "I can't believe you got the crib I wanted!" Standing on her tiptoes, she gave him a quick kiss before turning to rush to the front door. Opening it, she grinned as she welcomed their friends inside.

By lunchtime, Bart, Jack, Jude, and Monty had easily moved the excess furniture out of the room across from the master bedroom, while Cam and Chad tackled assembling the new crib.

Faith, Bethany, and Angel had scrubbed the room clean while Sabrina sat with Dani, poring over paint color swatches. Miriam prepared sandwiches in the kitchen and the group moved to Chad's back patio to enjoy lunch. The sun was high in the sky, but with the mature trees in his yard, the group was lounging comfortably in the shade.

That evening, while Chad checked the doors,

Dani stepped inside the room, now designated as the nursery. With her hand on her stomach, she looked around. The spotless space held the beautiful crib and matching dresser as well as her beloved rocking chair. She and Sabrina had chosen the colors for the nursery and as a baby gift, Sabrina was having someone from her interior design company come to paint and decorate, as well as reupholster the chair.

Lost in pleasant thoughts, she jumped as Chad's arms encircled her. "Is the room beginning to look the way you envisioned?" he asked.

"Absolutely," she assured. "The crib must have been difficult to assemble."

"What makes you say that?"

"Well," she began, leaning her head back against his chest. "I seem to remember hearing some cussing coming from this room earlier when you and Cam were in here."

Chuckling, he agreed. "Yeah. I thought Cam would be an expert, since he'd already had to take care of their nursery. But damn, that thing," he said, nodding toward the beautiful crib, "had more parts, nuts and bolts. And I swear, it had fifteen pages of instructions, written in six different languages!"

Laughing, the couple stood for a few more minutes soaking in the realization that this room would be holding a baby. Finally, nuzzling her neck, he murmured against her warm skin, "Happy, Dani?"

Turning in his arms, she reached up to cup his

jaw. "With you...and this baby...I have everything I could ever want."

Leaning down, he captured her lips in a warm kiss, full of promise. "Let's go to bed," he said, picking her up and carrying her across the hall. Worshiping her body, he showed her that he felt the same. *This woman and this baby are all I need.*

25

Looking at the sleeping woman in his bed, Chad smiled as the sun peeked through the blinds illuminating the brilliant red highlights in her auburn hair. She appeared to still be deep in sleep, so he slipped out from beneath the warm covers. Pulling on his jeans, he walked to the kitchen to fix a cup of coffee. Walking to his deck, he felt his phone vibrate.

"Yeah, boss?"

"Sorry to call so early...and to mess up your Saturday," Jack apologized. "We've heard from Mitch and need to have you bring in Dani this morning to go over some things."

"She's still sleeping right now. When do you need us in?"

"I haven't called anyone else yet, so why don't we make it eleven."

"Perfect, thanks." Disconnecting, he sipped his hot coffee. He thought of the events of yesterday with the men following Dani. Sighing deeply, he pulled in the fresh morning air into his lungs, slowly letting it out. *We've got to get this case figured out...and soon. I want this done so she can peacefully enjoy this pregnancy. And I want the baby safe.* Protective emotion for the baby rushed through him, causing him to grab the deck rail for support. *Adam, I don't know what the fuck you were up to, but Dani and the baby are now mine to care for and I'll be damned before letting anything happen to either of them!*

"Hey, sweetie," came the gentle voice from behind as small arms encircled his waist. "You were so deep in thought, you didn't even hear me come out."

Dropping his chin to his chest, he felt her warmth hit his back as she laid her cheek against him. Squeezing her hands on his stomach, he turned and wrapped his arms around her as well, resting his chin now upon her head.

"You sleep good?" he asked.

"Mmmmmm," was her reply.

Chuckling, he lifted her chin with his fingers so that he could look directly into her face. Seeing clear eyes smiling at him, he leaned down to settle a gentle kiss on her lips.

She looked up, the dreamy expression morphing into a questioning one. "You look like a man who's talked to his boss this morning. What's up?"

Laughing, he said, "It's going to be hard to keep

you from finding out about the cases I'm working on, isn't it?"

"Hey, I was an investigator. Granted, I spent most of my time investigating the explosive devices, but I had enough field time to be able to read people."

Kissing her forehead, he nodded. "Okay, here's the deal. Jack wants us to meet at about eleven with the others. Seems our FBI contact has some information for us and you'll need to be in on some of it."

"What time is it now?"

"A little after nine. We slept late, but then, after last night's activities, I'm not surprised."

Grinning, she said, "Well, I've got to shower, but how about I fix a super-duper breakfast for you?"

"Super-duper?" he teased.

"Yeah, and if you liked my world-famous potato salad, you'll love my super-duper breakfast!"

"Then, by all means, dazzle me, baby!"

Arm in arm, the two walked into the house, enjoying the moment of levity before having to face whatever was coming.

Dani sat at the table in Jack's dining room, surrounded by the other Saints. Her heart pounded but she willed it under control. Watching the screen on the tablet given to her, she saw as Mitch Evans appeared and was introduced.

"Nice to meet you, Mrs. Turner—"

"Dani, please."

"Alright, Dani, and you may call me Mitch. Okay, here's what we know so far about yesterday. I want to congratulate you on your quick thinking, by the way, but you were a trained agent, so I'm sure you don't need me to tell you that you did a great job. It'll be no surprise that the license plate was fake – the number did not register to anyone and the DMV does not have that number in their system. The dark-tinted windows made it impossible to see who was driving, even when we followed it in the traffic light camera system. By the time the police were following, they had gotten the car out of the city and out of our camera range."

"Why the hell didn't the police follow immediately? I called that shit in as soon as I tagged its partial number and description," groused Jude.

Mitch, his lips tight with irritation, said, "I was pissed about that also. Found out there was a new dispatcher on the job and they did not understand your relationship with the police...nor recognize my authority as an FBI agent. I assure you that won't be happening again."

Rubbing his hand over his face, the fatigue showing, Mitch continued, "The good news is that we got a match on the man who stupidly stepped out of the vehicle. The bad news is...their identity."

This gained the attention of the group, including Dani, who felt her heart pounding wildly again. Chad, recognizing her change in breathing, linked his fingers with hers, giving her a reassuring squeeze while working to tamp down his own rage.

"The man identified was Abdul Nagi, the right-hand man of Muhammad Hakim. Right now, he appears to be the leader of what we consider to be the biggest ISIS cell in Virginia."

"Can't you just arrest him?" blurted Dani, indignant that this Muhammad was known yet he wasn't taken out of commission.

"Sorry, Dani, but right now, we have no proof. He's a person of interest and we're on it, I promise. He's being watched by a joint task force of ATF, CIA, Homeland Security, and FBI. I have contact with them, but I'm not on that task force, so my information is somewhat limited. But I will say, they have been informed of the events of yesterday."

Dani noticed her irritation was mirrored on the other Saints' faces, but had to admit that even when she was with the ATF, not every agent knew everything that was going on. Most of the time, the agencies worked on a need-to-know basis...and sometimes the left hand definitely did not know what the right hand was doing.

"Why do I have the feeling there is more bad news?" Monty asked. As Mitch's friend, he could tell when the agent was not happy about something even when his face appeared professionally impassive.

All eyes jumped back to the screen, their attention once more riveted to Mitch's face.

Nodding slowly, Mitch added, "Yeah, there's more." He pointed to a board behind him, and said, "Here are some of the ones we're keeping an eye on. Muhammad is at the top, with Abdul. Also in their leadership group is Habib El-Amin and Fazan Darzi. They usually use burner phones and we can't get a line of who they talk to, but occasionally someone screws up. We have one phone contact that links Fazan Darzi with Jahfar Khouri, who happens to work at Marsden Energy Systems and you—"

"Oh my God!" Dani burst out, sitting up straight, her expression openly distressed. She did not feel the squeeze of Chad's arm until he repeated the action. Jerking her head toward Chad, she explained, "I work with him. Closely with him. Oh, Jesus," she leaned back, "I thought something was off there but wondered if I was being biased. I even talked to Ethan about him." The words came rushing out; the dam broke as she no longer held back.

"Okay, Dani," Mitch began, "let's go back over this. Marsden is a huge company and I had no idea you might work with this guy. Start at the beginning and talk me through what you know."

Blowing out a deep breath to clear her mind, Dani placed her hand on Chad's thigh, grateful when he clutched it in his own. "I don't know much, but he mentioned the other day that we were hired about the same time, so he's only been there a few months. He works in the military sales division, as do I. My work is more about ordinance safety and his is in the actual sales department. His office is across the hall and about two doors down. He's punctual, efficient, mannerly, asks appropriate questions in meetings...I...uh..."

"Dani, that's good," Monty said, knowing he was saying what Mitch was thinking, having been a former FBI agent himself. "What can you tell us that we won't find on a dossier?"

Sucking her lips in, Dani was suddenly self-conscious. "I...maybe I'm just...I..." she looked around the table at the other Saints before her eyes landed on Chad.

He leaned over, touching his lips to her forehead. Murmuring on her skin, he said, "Just talk from your heart, babe. Anything you've thought."

"I don't want to be wrong," she said, her voice agonizing. "I mean, he gives me the creeps, but that doesn't make him a terrorist. I don't want to be ethnically profiling in a way that could ruin someone's life."

"Okay, Dani, I'm getting that this is uncomfortable for you personally. Here's what I want you to understand. He's already a subject of interest because of the contact he had with Fazan. You're not putting him on our profile list...you're providing background information. That's all. I promise."

Nodding her understanding, she said, "Now, this all may seem silly, but he's given me reason to be suspicious. He seems to be outside my office door at times when I'm speaking with others. They'll walk out and say, 'Oh hi, Jahfar', which lets me know he must have been lurking right there. Or I'll hang up the phone and as soon as I do, he'll walk in as though he's been out in the hall listening. Maybe he's just being polite and waiting his turn, but it makes me feel weird to think that someone... anyone...is right outside my office door listening."

"Good, this is good," Mitch encouraged. "Keep going."

"He left a meeting earlier than I did one day and I thought I saw him coming out of my office when I went back, but I couldn't be sure. Then as I opened my file drawer to get my purse for lunch, my purse had been rifled through."

Chad squeezed her arm, wanting to be supportive...and wanting to find this guy and confront him immediately. *To hell with him being a possible FBI suspect...he's fucking with the wrong girl if he thinks Dani is going to be a target.*

"Honey?"

Dani's voice broke through Chad's thoughts. "Yeah, babe?"

"You're squeezing too tight," she said, with a small smile.

Loosening his grip instantly, he said, "Oh, shit, babe. Sorry."

"Is that it?" Mitch asked.

Thinking for a moment, Dani said, "No. A couple of weeks ago, we had a new person promoted to Head of Production Security. He beat out a couple of others who wanted the position." Her mind roamed to Aaron for a moment, but dismissed him as she had seen no professional jealousy from him at all. "Ethan Petit is his name. He's good. Been there for a while, easy to work with. In fact, I've shared a few of my concerns about Jahfar with Ethan. Anyway, after Ethan was promoted, Jahfar gave me a warning."

"A warning?" Chad growled.

"Yeah, he told me to watch out, there were snakes in the grass."

"What the fuck?" Bart asked, leaning back in his seat. His sentiments were echoed around the table.

"Okay, settle," Jack ordered, seeing Chad's, as well as the others', faces masked in anger. "Monty, Mitch, what do we need to do now?"

"Jack, I'm going to need to process this information and get back with you. Dani, you did real good. For now, I can tell you that the best thing you can do is just keep a low profile at work and keep your eyes open."

Monty disconnected the conference with Mitch and turned back to the group. Looking at Jack, he said, "You've already had contact with the head of MES. Do you want us to focus on Jahfar?"

Dani had grown quiet as the men discussed their options. Chad noticed her sitting still, but could tell her mind was racing. Just as he was going to ask how she was, she suddenly looked up and spoke.

"You can focus on Jahfar outside of MES, but you can't see what's going on inside. I can. I can get to him. His office. His computer. I can do that."

Chad's body involuntarily jerked as her words punched him. "Oh, hell no!" he said. He scooted her chair around so that it faced him, but her hand came up before he said a word.

"I'm not talking about doing something dumb," she explained. "But who better than me to keep an eye on him? That's really nothing more than what I'd be doing anyway."

Before Chad could protest further, Monty interjected, "That's not a bad idea." Seeing the fury building in Chad's face, he continued quickly, "I'm not saying she needs to investigate actively or do anything to tip him off. No subterfuge. Just watch. Keep a closer eye on him. Let us know anything that he's doing out of the ordinary...or even what his ordinary is."

"I can pull up everything about him," Luke said, his fingers flying. "Even more than what the FBI can get." He looked up and said, "I should be able to get inside his computer...maybe."

"Maybe? Just maybe?" Cam joked. "Thought *maybe* wasn't in your vocabulary."

"Yeah, well, not usually, but occasionally even I have trouble getting something." After a pause, he looked around the table sheepishly, "Um, of course, if I had the direct info into his work computer, then

I wouldn't have to work around Marsden's security."

"Like the drives we used when getting the access to the recruit's computers?" asked Bart.

"Oh, hell no," Chad bit out, his eyes pinned on Luke. "The only way you could obtain that was if Dani did it herself. You've got balls asking—"

"Chad, he didn't ask me to do anything. He's just throwing it out there." Dani lifted her hand and cupped his tense jaw. "Honey, I'm not some wilting flower. If there's something going on at MES... if one of my co-workers is a terrorist...or working with terrorists, then I want to know. If there's anything I can do...active or passive...then I want to help."

Turning back to Luke, she asked, "What would this entail?"

Luke, his eyes moving between Chad's hard gaze and her focused one, said, "I would need you to insert a special thumb drive into Jahfar's computer. Contact me by cell and let me know you have done it. It takes about five minutes and then I'll tell you when to remove it."

"That's all?" she asked, incredulously.

"That's it. It installs encryption that will keep him or anyone else from knowing the computer was compromised. It will allow me to see anything that has been on his computer, as well as give me a secure link to see what's going on."

"Is it legal?" It only took a brief pause for her to

immediately say, "Never mind, I don't want to know."

Jack spoke up quickly. "Dani, no one here is asking you to do anything. Chad, you need to understand that. Not one of us would ask our woman to do anything that could cause her harm and we are not encouraging Dani to be the first."

The silence in the room settled over the occupants, blanketing them in battling emotions. After a moment, Dani said, "How about this. Luke, you give me the drive and your number. If I think I'll have an opportunity to use it, I'll contact you first just to make sure the time is right for you. If not, I do nothing. If so, I'll see what I can do. If I'm fearful or uncertain, I won't do anything. If I can, I'll get the information."

Nodding, Luke replied, "That's fine with me if everyone is in agreement. I'll continue to work on hacking in from here."

"What about his personal computer?" Cam asked. "I can get inside his house and take care of his personal one as well."

Jack saw acceptance from everyone except Chad. Piercing him with his steely gaze, he asked, "Chad?"

Chad was still battling but knew that if anyone could pull it off, it would be Dani. *Hell, she's smart, resourceful, quick on her feet...and fuckin' pregnant.* "I know she can do it. I'm scared about the stress on the pregnancy," he admitted.

This reminder sent doubt across the faces of the others, but Dani responded to his concerns.

"Right now, with the idea of Adam consorting with known terrorists, and a co-worker potentially doing the same, I'm about as stressed as I can be. If I can actually do something...I think it will get better."

Chad finally agreed, after obtaining her promise that she would do nothing unless she was certain she had a one-hundred percent chance of not getting caught. The group was silent for a moment, each to their own thoughts. Suddenly, Chad reached to his neck, removing the St. Chad pendant from around it. With the silver medallion dangling from his fingers, he held his hand out to Luke. "You know what to do."

With a nod, Luke took the medallion and left the room. Dani watched the exchange, her curiosity piqued, but she said nothing. The group continued to talk for several more minutes until Luke walked back into the room, handing the medallion to Chad.

Chad would have preferred a private moment, but was aware that Dani watched every move. He turned and slipped the St. Chad necklace around her neck. Her face scrunched in question, but before she could speak, he explained, "Luke has fitted the medallion with a tracer. If, and I pray to God you never need it, but if you are ever in danger we can find you."

Cupping his face once more, she leaned in and

said, "I'll never do anything to put myself or the baby in harm's way, I promise. But the only thing I'm one-hundred percent sure about in life is my love for you."

With a heartfelt kiss in front of the other grinning Saints, Chad agreed.

26

For three days Dani had watched Jahfar as he went about his business, seeing nothing alarming. Neither had she found the opportunity to sneak into his office. With her division working on a project, most of them had worked through their lunch break and he never left early.

On Wednesday, near the end of the day, Chad sent a text indicating he would be working late. Making the decision to use that time to try to outstay Jahfar, she waited impatiently. He suddenly poked his head in her office door, causing her to jump.

"I'm sorry," he said, "I didn't mean to startle you."

"Oh, don't worry. I was a million miles away," she answered, forcing a smile.

"Then perhaps you should call it a day also," he replied. "I'll be happy to walk you out."

"I...uh...thought I'd finish this report before I left."

Nodding, he wished her a good night and she watched as he walked down the hall. Tiptoeing over to her door, she peeked around the doorframe, observing as he entered the elevator with others. *Don't rush. Take your time, girl,* she told herself. Sitting back down at her desk, she fiddled with the report for fifteen more minutes, watching as the rest of the employees left their offices and headed home.

Stealthily, she checked the hall, seeing all of the office doors closed. Listening intently, she heard no voices at all. Looking two doors down, she saw his closed door. *I go up and down this hall all day long...so why am I fearful now?* She took a deep cleansing breath before ordering her feet to move. With her fingers on his doorknob, she let out the breath as the cold metal turned. Pushing the door open slightly she saw his office appearing just as it always was—neat, clean—orderly. Thinking of her own somewhat messy office, she wondered how he kept it so neat. *Does he actually do any work?* Immediately chastising herself, she knew he did.

With a last, nervous glance over her shoulder, she closed the door and moved to his computer. Texting Luke, she got his go-ahead. Placing the thumb drive into the computer, she texted Luke again to inform him she had done so.

The next five minutes passed at a snail's pace. While waiting, she looked around his office but found little to hold her interest. A family photograph was framed on his credenza. A wife and two children. *Are they his? Is his family real or a front? Is he—*

"Mollie? You gonna clean the ones at the end of the hall now or wait?"

Jumping at the voice, Dani ran to listen at the door and heard the voices of the night cleaning crew. *Oh shit, I didn't realize they got here at this time.*

"With Sally out sick, I'm gonna start in the conference room and hall bathroom and then make my way down the offices."

Dani's phone vibrated, causing her to jump again. Heart pounding, she thought, *Little one, your mama is going to have a heart attack. I've got to get out of here!* Checking her phone, she saw that Luke was finished so she raced over to jerk the drive out of Jahfar's computer. Making sure his office was left exactly as she found it, she moved to the door. Opening it slightly, she heard noises around the corner. Slipping out unnoticed, she walked a few steps toward her office when the two women from the cleaning crew came around the corner.

"Ms. Turner, we didn't know you were still here."

"Oh, I needed to get some files copied before I left. I'll be leaving as soon as I can grab my purse."

"When's that baby coming?"

Her hand automatically going to her stomach, she smiled. "Not for several more months."

"Well, have a good night, Ms. Turner."

With a smile and a wave, Dani walked into her office and slipped the drive into her purse. Closing her computer, she headed out to her car. The parking lot was far from empty with the shift workers filling many spaces. As she pulled out, she noticed another car leaving at the same time. *Oh, my God, not again!* Before she could panic, the other car turned to another street soon after leaving the parking lot. *Oh, baby girl, your mom is truly becoming a nervous Nellie!* Driving to Jack's compound to drop off the drive, she wished once again for the investigation to be over.

The cloudy night cloaked the two men in total darkness as they made their way inside Jahfar's house. Reconnaissance proved the whole family had left for the evening. Bart searched the rooms while Cam inserted the drive into the computer in the office.

Bart slipped back into the room and said, "Both kids have laptops and it appears there's a desktop in the family room."

"Get 'em all," Cam said. "No reason to think that he only uses this one."

Within ten minutes the men were finished with the computers and continued to look around. The house appeared precisely what it looked like from the outside—a family's home, filled with photographs, kids' drawings on the refrigerator, clothes in the closets, toys scattered around, and a cat wandering the rooms. As Bart and Cam left, they remained silent until driving away.

"What are you thinking?" Cam asked, noting Bart's quiet, circumspect demeanor.

"House was just what it should be. Not one thing that gave the indication that he's not what he says he is. Nothing that says that isn't a real family."

"You think we're wrong about him?"

"Don't know. We do know he's been in contact with Fazan and there's no doubt he's in with the big terrorists."

"Something bothers you, though, I can tell."

"If that house was a front, they did a damn perfect job making it look right."

"Hopefully, with these drives and what Dani got from his office computer, we'll get a better idea of who we're dealing with."

The two men continued to drive in silence for several more minutes until Cam pulled into Bart's driveway.

"You know, I really love investigating...but I hate like fuck some of these long-ass cases that seem to have no end...and make no fuckin' sense," Bart confessed.

Nodding, Cam agreed. "Yeah, this one keeps going in too many directions for me. But maybe it'll be over soon."

The two friends parted, each with the uncomfortable feeling that the investigation would become worse before getting better.

Swush, swush, swush...the baby's heartbeat sounded loud and strong as Chad and Dani looked toward the sonogram monitor. Unable to keep the smile off her face, her hand gripped his. Turning away from the monitor for only a moment, she sought Chad's face, catching his expression of wonder.

"All right, everything is on schedule. Baby's size is good, head size is within the normal range, and as you can see, there are the fingers and toes."

Dani and Chad looked on in amazement at the limbs and digits waving about.

"Is it still a little girl?" Dani asked.

Laughing, the sonographer replied, "Sex doesn't change, sweetie."

Dani blushed and explained, "Well, last time they were pretty sure but not absolute."

"Oh, gotcha. Well, yes, by now we can see she is definitely a girl."

Feeling her fingers squeezed, she looked over at Chad once again. "You okay?" he whispered.

She nodded, smiling. "Yeah, I'm great. Perfect, in fact. I've got a perfectly healthy baby girl growing in me...a man I love by my side...and a future together."

Chad sat silently, his heart in his throat as his

eyes poured over the woman lying on the table and his daughter waving from the monitor. *My daughter...yeah, Adam's and my daughter.* He stood, his large body towering over Dani, as he touched his lips to her forehead. "You're my world, you know," he whispered. "Both of you...my whole, fuckin' world."

Her smile widened as his proclamation washed over her, filling the empty corners of her being. Lifting her fingers, tracing his face from his hairline down to his jaw, she smiled. The only blip on her happiness was the thought of Adam having had contact with terrorists. Looking back to her daughter on the monitor, she thought, *Oh baby. How will I ever explain this to you?*

"I can tell what you're thinking," Chad said, drawing her eyes back to his. "It'll be okay, babe. We'll find out what was going on and then we'll decide together what to tell our daughter when the time is right. So don't worry about it now...just concentrate on her and us."

As the sonographer wiped the gel off Dani's stomach and assisted her to sit, Chad kissed the top of her head and said, "Come on, little mama. Let's get you and baby girl fed."

Dani's eyes danced as she moved off the table. "Oh, good. I'm starved!"

Driving home in the truck, she moved over the bench seat and placed her hand on his thick thigh. As they got closer to his house, she silently began moving her hand toward his crotch.

"Dani," he growled, his rough voice sending a jolt of need straight to her core. "I'm losing my concentration."

"You're on your street," she pouted. "I've been patient the whole way home and I hardly think you'll wreck turning into your driveway."

"Babe, with your hand on my cock, I'm liable to run straight through my garage door."

Giggling, she moved her hand back but found it captured in his much larger one. He linked his fingers with hers and brought them to his lips. The warmth of his touch inflamed her more, but she knew they would soon be inside and able to quench their thirst.

Setting the alarm after getting home, Chad gave Dani a nudge toward the stairs. "Go on up and I'll be up as soon as I check the house."

Exhausted, she nodded and walked upstairs into the master bathroom. Stepping into the shower, she let the warm water pound her aching back.

"Babe, I'm coming in!" Chad shouted, knowing her propensity for startling and not wanting to frighten her.

Laughing, she said, "Did you think I'd jump out of my skin?"

Stepping into the shower with her, he grinned,

"It wouldn't be the first time." His eyes roamed over her curves, loving each and every one. Noticing the water aimed at her lower back, he grew concerned. "Your back hurting?"

Dani stood, entranced with the male specimen standing in front of her. Michelangelo could not have carved a more perfect embodiment of the male form. Tall, broad shouldered, defined chest and tight, washboard abs. A narrow waist that led to his strong hips and tree trunk legs. His arms reached toward her, their muscles speaking of their power. She loved everything about him, finding not one inch undesirable. He could be standing on the bow of a pirate ship, on horseback leading the Roman armies, wearing a kilt deep in the Scottish Highlands. He was every romance cover all rolled into one...*and mine. My very own gentle giant.*

His arms moved to her shoulders as he leaned down to peer deeply into her eyes. "Babe, are you okay?"

"Huh? What?" she stammered, blushing. "Oh, yeah, I'm fine. Just a little backache."

He pulled her front to his as his arms moved down to her lower back. Still allowing the warm water to hit her muscles, he pressed his hands expertly on her pain, rubbing and massaging.

Relaxing against him, she rested her cheek against his chest as her arms wrapped around his waist. Moving one up, she felt the hard muscles of his back quiver under her touch. The other hand dropped to his ass and she realized that as she had categorized his delectable body traits, she had missed his ass. *How could I have forgotten his exquisite ass?* Giving it a squeeze, she suddenly sensed a rumble deep in his chest against her face.

"Babe," he growled. "You gotta stop that, or I'm gonna to want to do more than you need right now."

His fingers had her lower back relaxed and she leaned back to look into his face. "I think I know exactly what I need right now," she purred, moving both hands to squeeze his ass, feeling his erection now pressing against her stomach. Just then, the baby kicked and Chad jumped back.

"Baby, little girl can kick." Chuckling, while rubbing his hand over his face, he said, "And how weird was that to have her kick me right in the balls."

Sliding her wet hand around to his front, Dani grasped his swollen cock and said, "Guess we'd better get busy to make sure she didn't do any permanent damage."

"Babe, you know what you're doing?" he rumbled again, cocking one eyebrow.

"Oh, I know exactly what I'm doing. The question is, what are you going to do about it?" she teased.

Grinning, he grabbed the body wash and squirted it on his hands, rubbing them together to create scented suds. He started at her shoulders and massaged the bubbles into her skin before sliding them down to her full breasts. Her fingers grasped his arms for support as her knees grew weak at the sensations. Paying equal attention to each breast, he then gently tweaked each nipple. Throwing her head back, she moaned in delight.

He continued her shower massage as he washed her round stomach, laughing as he felt the baby kick once more. "Turn around, little mama," he ordered gently. They moved so that the spray hit him and her back was now presented. Running his soapy hands over her shoulders, he worked out the kinks before moving them to her lower back where he paid special attention.

Boneless, Dani groaned with pleasure. "Honey, I need to take care of you. If you keep this up, I'll just be a relaxed puddle on the floor."

"This isn't about me, babe. This is all for you."

"Bu—"

"Uh uh," he interrupted. "Believe me, taking care of you will take care of me." With that, he flipped the water off and reached for a towel. Drying her off carefully, then quickly moving the towel over his body, he carried her bride-style into the bedroom.

"What have you got in mind, big boy?" she whispered, nibbling on his earlobe.

"Grrrrrrh," he groaned, her lips on his ear zipping right to his cock. He bent, laying her on the bed, sliding in next to her. Leaning on his arm, he trailed his hand down her body from her breasts to her mound and back again. Agonizingly slow, as though he had all the time in the world. His cock jumped at the tortuous pace, but he willed it to wait.

The warm shower, combined with his massaging hands, had Dani relaxed and pliant. As he teased her nipples, the electricity pulsated to her core. He kissed her shoulder, then continued placing wet kisses on her skin toward her breast before pulling her nipple deeply into his mouth. Sucking hard, he swirled his tongue around the taut bud, elongating it as he grazed his teeth over the sensitive flesh.

Sliding his finger into her folds, he felt her arousal. "Babe, you're wet for me. So fuckin' responsive. It's as though all we have to do is think about sex and you're ready to go."

She cupped his face and said, "I know you think this is just the pregnancy hormones, but I've never been like this. Never."

He held her gaze, understanding the gift she was giving him. Smiling he moved his mouth back to hers, searing her with his talented tongue.

Moving down her body, he slid between her legs, the scent of her sex intoxicating. He lapped first before plunging his tongue inside. With one hand splayed over her stomach, the other slipped under her ass, lifting it for easier access. He had read about pregnancy hormones, but was still surprised at the evidence of her need.

She reached down, tangling her hands in his hair as she watched him feast intimately on her womanhood. Moaning, she raced toward the precipice, lost in her desire.

Nipping on her clit and sucking hard, he felt her hips jerk as her orgasm rushed over her. Lapping the juices, he moved up her body, kissing his way from her mound to each breast, to the wildly pulsing point at the base of her neck.

She pleaded, "Now. Please, I need you now."

Rolling her body over so that her back was tucked into his front, he lifted her leg as his cock stood at attention at her entrance. He slowly pressed his cock into her slick channel an inch at a time until he was fully seated, holding his head up so he could watch her gaze the entire time. Seeing the gradual curve of her lips forming a smile took his breath away.

"I'm yours, Chad. Always and forever," Dani whispered into the night.

With that promise ringing in his ears, he pulled back out and immediately plunged in again, this time harder and faster. Her inner walls grabbed him back in every time he moved out, as though her body needed the contact. Her breasts bounced with each thrust and he kept one hand firmly on her waist, his thumb caressing her stomach. She lifted her leg, opening herself up more to him, allowing him to plunge deeper and deeper.

His balls tightened and knew he was close. She recognized it also, feeling his cock grow even thicker than imaginable. Sliding his hand down from her waist to her clit, he tweaked the swollen bud bringing the desired result. Her sex grabbed his shaft, squeezing it in a rhythm as she cried out his name. With a few more thrusts he emptied himself into her, his muscles corded in strain as he felt the orgasm down to his toes.

Once again boneless, first from the massaging shower and now by two orgasms, Dani felt his arms surround her, enveloping her in his large body. For several minutes they lay, legs tangled in the sheets and each other, the coolness of the night slowly penetrating their warm bodies.

With her head on his upper arm while that hand circled around her chest, she felt his other hand come over her middle, his fingers splaying over her stomach. Just then, baby girl woke up, giving another hard kick before moving around as though stretching.

"Oh fuck, babe," he said, surprise in his voice. "Did you feel that?"

Laughing, she replied, "Uh, yeah. It happened inside of me, so believe me, I felt it!"

"Does it hurt?"

"No," she said, softly, her hand resting on his. "It feels like...life."

Kissing her neck, he whispered, "I love you, Dani. And this baby girl."

Closing her eyes tightly to keep the stinging tears from sliding out, she smiled. Swallowing hard, she said, "I'm so lucky. So lucky."

As his now flaccid cock slid out of her body, she twisted in his arms so that she was facing him, cupping his strong jaw with her fingers. Peering deeply into his eyes, her chin quivering, she said, "Months ago, I thought everything in my life was gone. Lost. My husband and friend. You. My job. My home. But more than that...my security, faith, self-confidence, happiness. When Adam died, I felt as though I lost everything. But now...here with you...where I always wanted to be...I'm found."

He watched as a tear slid down her cheek to land on the pillow and he leaned in, kissing her lips. "Life could have been so different if I hadn't waited too long to tell you how I felt. I think of that every day, Dani. Every fuckin' day."

She shushed him with her fingers over his mouth, offering a small smile. "Life is choices, Chad. We make them, figure out what was good or not so good. Then we make more."

"Yes, but if Adam had not died, we wouldn't be here right now."

She bit her bottom lip as she pondered his words. "There's no way of knowing where we'd be, honey. We have no idea what would have happened...but we're here right now. And that's all I can think about."

Smiling, he tucked her silky, auburn hair behind her ear and leaned forward, kissing her lightly. "You're right. Life goes on, life changes. But however it had to happen, we're here. We're having a baby. Starting a family. Moving forward. Together."

Pulling the sheets over their bodies, he tucked

her in tightly to his side. “Sleep, little mama,” he ordered gently as he listened to her breathing slow.

She’s going to be my wife. She’s truly, irrevocably mine. Mine to love. Mine to protect. His hand moved down her body, resting on her stomach, fingers splaying out. *And so are you, little one.*

27

"What have you got?" Jack asked Luke as he met him in the command center.

Luke looked up, his face showing his surprise. "You're not going to believe it, but I've got nothing on Jahfar's computers that indicate he's had any contact with any of our known terrorists other than two with Fazan. Not his work...nor his home computers. And neither one of those emails have anything incriminating in them. I ran them through decoding programs...nothing."

"So the only thing the FBI's got is that his name was mentioned with Fazan's and he's had a couple of emails."

"Yep. So whatever he's doing, he's hiding it well."

"The connection's too much to ignore...Jahfar having any communication Fazan, a known associate of a terrorist. And Jahfar works in an ammunition plant."

Nodding, Jack poured some of Luke's high-octane coffee in his cup and said, "Get whatever you've got to Mitch."

Luke leaned back in his chair and said, "You think we're getting this all wrong?"

Blaise, turning the corner at the bottom of the stairs, stepped into the room hearing Luke's comment. "Getting what all wrong?"

Shaking his head, Luke said, "I don't know, but the puzzle pieces aren't fitting together at all. That usually means we are missing a piece."

"Or something is staring us in the face and we just haven't figured it out yet."

The other Saints trickled in and they meticulously reviewed the intel again, moving the players around on the large board on the wall. Jahfar. Fazan. Muhammad. Abdul. Marsden Energy Systems. Adam.

As Chad stared at the board, it was the last two that caused his heart to pound. *Too many unknowns...too fuckin' close to Dani.*

Aaron and Cybil sat in Dani's office, discussing the new project. "Are you going to be able to finish before you go on maternity leave?"

Dani looked up, seeing Aaron smiling in his teasing way. "Yes, boss. I promise to have all my homework done."

The trio laughed as they continued to work.

"I have to admit I'm envious, Dani," Cybil said. "I know you suffered tragedy before you came to us, but now you have your baby to look forward to and a man who wants to love your baby as much as if he was his own."

Smiling, she admitted, "He's really good for me." Staring at Cybil, she said, "But what about you and Ethan?"

"Oh, we're fine...just no wedding bells yet."

Dani noted Cybil sounded wistful and cast a glance to Aaron, but his attention was at her door. Looking up, she noticed Jahfar standing there. *He is so sneaky!* "Can I help you?" she asked, trying to keep the snarkiness out of her voice.

"I was just wondering if you had any information on the latest detonators. I am working on my report, and could use any insight you have."

"When we're finished here, I'll come see you."

Nodding, he bowed his head in a conciliatory motion as he left her office, his heels sounding his retreat on the tile floor. She looked back at Aaron and Cybil, seeing both of them staring at her strangely. "Um...what is it?"

"You just seem out of sorts when talking to Jahfar," Cybil said.

"No, no, um...I just hated being interrupted." Forcing a smile back on her face, she was determined to keep her suspicions to herself. Cybil accepted her explanation but she felt Aaron's gaze stay on her.

Before they were able to continue, Ethan

popped in, asking to speak to Aaron, who excused himself. The two men headed down the hall as well.

Cybil huffed, "See what I mean? Ever since Ethan became Head of Production Security he barely has time for me…and certainly not at work."

"I think he's just protecting his professionalism. His promotion is really important and I'm sure he doesn't want it to look like he only got the job because he's dating the company owner's daughter and Vice President."

"You think?" Cybil asked, a thoughtful expression on her face. "Well, thank your lucky stars that you and your man don't work together. Workplace romances can be tricky."

With that, Cybil left as well, leaving Dani reminiscing about when she, Adam, and Chad had all worked at the ATF. *What if I had worked in the same field office as those two?* Sighing heavily, she wondered how different her life would have been. *Would Chad have approached me sooner?* Shaking herself, she realized it was pointless to wonder how the past could be different. *Take your lot in life and make sure it's the best it can be,* her grandmother used to say.

Standing, she headed to Jahfar's office to find out what he needed. Knocking on the doorframe, she entered as he motioned.

"I am so sorry to bother you, but I am working on the latest report for triacetone triperoxide and wanted your input. You had some experience with this when you were with the ATF, I believe."

"Why are you looking at it?" she asked, a burning sensation beginning in the pit of her stomach, as she recognized the material.

"I think its potential is unlimited," Jahfar replied, his eyes lifting to hers.

Her voice halting, she continued holding his gaze as she said, "It's often used in terrorist attacks. Easy to create in rough form, the destruction from such a small amount makes it worthy to those who wish to do ill."

"But think of the potential for the military?" he insisted.

Pressing her lips tightly together, she just nodded, afraid to speak. *Yes, but whose military?* "I did have some experience with it when with the ATF, but I'll have to look to see if I can find it."

"There is always someone who will use something for ill, Danielle. But you may be surprised to know who the enemies are." His words, now filled with innuendoes, slithered over her.

Turning, she walked out of his office, fuming as she made her way back to hers. Halfway down the hall, she stopped. *No, I'm going to tell him straight up that I'm uncomfortable with what he's proposing. That compound is too volatile.*

Approaching his door, she noticed it was almost closed this time. Lifting her hand to knock, she heard him on the phone.

"I think I pushed too hard. I'm sure she suspects

something. Yes, yes...I'm being careful, but will still keep an eye on her."

Backing away soundlessly, she tiptoed back to her office. Heart pounding, she sat heavily in her chair, her hand protectively on her stomach. Checking her watch, she decided to leave. *It's only fifteen minutes until the end of my day, anyway.* Heading out, she entered the elevator, seeing Ethan.

"Hey, are you all right?" he asked. "You seem rather pale."

"Yes, I'm fine. Just not feeling well, so I thought I'd go ahead and leave." She hesitated, chewing on her lip in indecision. *Do I say anything about my concerns?*

"Dani, I can tell you've got something bothering you."

Looking up into his concerned face, she said, "What do you know about triacetone triperoxide?"

A surprised expression crossed his face. "TATP? Peroxide-based chemicals are highly unstable and are extensively used by terrorists to make bombs; they're too volatile to handle safely. Why?"

"It's just that Jahfar is asking me about it, so I wondered since you're now Head of Production Security, if it was something we were moving into. If we were working on either TATP or HMTD, I was just surprised that I hadn't heard of it yet."

"Or...you're also wondering if Jahfar has something going on the side?" Ethan asked pointedly.

Hanging her head, Dani stared at her toes for a

silent moment, her thoughts rushing. Lifting her head, facing Ethan squarely, she said, "Something's going on, and I'm trying to figure it out. I'm not saying Jahfar is doing anything wrong, but you confirming that MES is not actively working with TATP, has me now convinced more than ever that he's up to something. What, I don't know."

"Do you think I need to talk to him?"

"I've got no proof that anything is happening and to throw around false accusations would be professionally, as well as morally, wrong."

As they reached their cars, Ethan placed his hand on her arm. "Take care of yourself, Dani. If things are happening, make sure you stay safe." He glanced back toward the building they just left. "I think I'll keep a closer eye on Jahfar as well. I won't say anything to Cybil or Todd yet. But if he's working on TATP, we need to be aware of that."

Smiling, she added her own warning. "Ethan, I know what they're capable of. You make sure you're safe as well."

Parting, the two walked to their cars. Eyes watched from a window above, before making a phone call.

Mohammad walked into the small neighborhood house with Abdul and Habib, finding Fazan overseeing the two men and woman in the kitchen with supplies all around.

"How are they working out?" Mohammad asked.

"Good," Fazan answered. "The material is difficult, but I've been training them on how to handle everything carefully. They have zeal...not always patience."

Mohammad glared at the trio of recruits. "If you cannot do the job properly, we will find someone else who can...and you will not live to see the morning sun."

Their eyes widened in fright as they nodded emphatically, babbling quickly. Mohammad silenced them with a raised hand, then turned and moved from the room. Abdul, Habib, and Fazan followed him into the living room, silently waiting to hear what their leader wanted to discuss.

"I've heard from our friend at MES. We hope to get more detonators soon, but they have to be extremely careful. We don't want any problems there or our special materials pipeline will dry up. Our computer recruits have started working on the codes for long range detonation with what we have so far."

"What about the Turner woman?" Habib asked.

"She's becoming a problem and may have to be eliminated. It appears she is now getting curious. I'd rather not have anything happen...the time is not right for our publicity, but I won't have the infidel bitch create a problem. I have given our contact the go-ahead to take care of her, if needed.

And if necessary, we'll take care of her by making a big statement."

The other three men nodded, knowing Mohammad was deadly serious. Deadly.

Early the next morning, Luke stared at his computer screen, blinking, uncertain for a moment at the information. Running emails through several decoding programs finally produced a hit. Picking up the phone, he called Jack. "We've got to meet. Now. Yeah, everyone. Including Mitch."

An hour later, the Saints sat at their conference table as Monty pulled Mitch up on the screen. As soon as the FBI agent was patched in, Jack turned to Luke and said, "Okay man, it's your show."

"There was nothing about Jahfar's computer records that turned up anything concrete, other than the two emails to Fazan, and they did not mention anything that would seem out of the ordinary. I kept running them through various decoding programs because I was certain there had to be something. I finally got a hit. But you're not going to like it."

Chad, on pins and needles knowing Dani worked with Jahfar and was in his presence every day, growled impatiently, "Just tell us."

"One email when decoded mentioned Adam's name. And that was from his home computer... before he started working at MES."

Fucks were heard around the table as the Saints reacted to that.

"He knew about Adam?" Chad bit out. "Dani said he acted like he didn't know anything about her life before they were employed at MES."

"I've got to get hold of Roscoe at ATF again," Mitch said. "He needs to be apprised that one of his men was compromised for certain."

"Wait on that, man," Luke said quickly. "There's one more thing you need to know first." Seeing the rapt, and impatient, attention of everyone, he added, "I discovered another email from about a month ago from his home computer, and when decoded it mentioned Roscoe's name."

The silence was deafening for a moment until the sudden uproar began. *Fuckin' hells,* combined with growls of *Holy shit, what the hell, you've got to be shittin' me,* and *goddamn terrorists* rang out from all of the men around the table.

"You're telling us that a man, who I might add, works with Dani…knew about Adam before he went to work at MES, and has had some contact with a known terrorist…and has had contact with a lead ATF agent?" His voice rose with each word until he yelled the end. "Mitch? What the hell do you know about this?"

Shaking his head in shock, Mitch admitted, "Speechless. Absolutely fuckin' speechless. I'm not going to contact Roscoe directly. I've got to go up my chain and find out what the fuck to do."

Jack, rubbing his hand over his face, looked

around the table before setting his sights on Mitch. "So, there's the possibility you've got a major problem with the ATF?"

"Not saying anything, Jack," Mitch admitted. "Until I find out what the hell is going on, I'd advise everyone to stand down."

"What about Dani?" Chad asked. "I don't even want her to be at MES until we have more information."

"Is she at work today?"

"Yeah, but I could call and ask her to take the afternoon off. Since it's Friday, she could be out of there until Monday."

"Might not be a bad idea," Marc agreed.

Chad pulled out his phone and dialed Dani. It went straight to voicemail. *Fuckin' hell...can this day get any worse?*

28

Once more, Dani's thought as she walked out of her final meeting for the week was *TGIF.* Looking forward to the weekend she stood up straight, stretching her back as her fists kneaded the kinks out.

Jahfar walked up behind her. "I hope you are well."

Jumping, she grimaced before forcing a smile. "Yes, thank you."

"I've been meaning to ask if you were able to find any of your materials on TATP?"

"I'm sorry. I did look, but must have gotten rid of my research when I left the ATF," she lied smoothly, holding his gaze.

"Yes, yes, of course. I realize you left at a time of great tragedy. Well, I wanted to check, just in case."

Stepping to the side to let the rest of the meeting occupants move by down the hall with *Have a good weekend* ringing in the space, she turned back to Jahfar. "I'd like to know what information you have about the explosive and why you think it would be good for the military if MES produces it?"

"I don't have any pre-conceived ideas about how the military would use it right now, that is why I'm looking into it."

"I just know that the material has been used by terrorists overseas, but not necessarily to their benefit. It's very unstable. I'd hate to see it get into the wrong hands."

Jahfar held her gaze for a long moment without looking away, before speaking. "And who determines the wrong hands? Do you not realize some of the explosives we make and sell to the military end up stolen...or even sold...to terrorists worldwide?"

Eyes wide, she retorted, "Yes, I do. Is that what—"

"Hey guys," Ethan's voice rang out, directly behind her. He and Cybil were the last to leave the conference room.

Jumping once more, she willed her heartbeat to slow. Turning, she smiled up at him and, with a nod toward Jahfar, she moved down the hall to her office. As the rest of the employees left the building, most eager for their weekend plans, Dani decided to stay. She closed her door so that it appeared she was already gone. The next thirty minutes crawled by, and then she slipped out, noting the silent hallway.

Moving stealthily, she walked straight to Jahfar's

office and slipped inside, shutting the door behind her with a soft click. Orderly. Neat. As always. She padded around to his desk, sitting in his chair. Pulling open a file drawer, she rifled through its contents. *So easy,* she thought, as her fingers landed on the file labeled peroxide-based explosives. Pulling it out, she flipped through article after article on the volatile explosives. *He's certainly doing his research, but for what?* Not finding anything of interest, she moved through the next drawers. After almost twenty minutes, she had discovered nothing untoward. Frustrated, she checked the room making sure to leave the contents the way she found them and slipped back to her office.

Leaving the building, she noticed Cybil and Ethan over by Cybil's car. Throwing her hand up in greeting, she halted calling out to them when she noticed they were arguing. Cybil jumped in her car, slamming the door, and pealed out of the parking lot.

Ethan, his face a mask of frustration, looked up at Dani. He walked over to her but his eyes were on Cybil's taillights.

"I would ask if you're all right, but I can see that you're not," she said.

"I've got something to do tonight and she doesn't understand that the world doesn't revolve around her. I want it to. I'm trying to keep her happy, but there are other demands."

Dani nodded, although she loved how Chad always made her feel first in his life. *Ethan reminds me a little of Adam...caring, but not as into the relationship as I was.*

"So, why are you working late?" he asked.

She pondered her answer for a moment, then took a chance knowing Ethan never seemed to trust Jahfar. "I'm going to tell you something, but I need it to stay between us."

Ethan eyed her carefully, curiosity in his expression. "Okay," he agreed. "Just between us."

"I was actually snooping. I was in Jahfar's office, seeing what I could find out."

Ethan reared back, his face morphing between surprise and anger. "Dani, you need to stay out of the situation," he barked. "If you find things you don't need to, then you're in the crosshairs."

"Crosshairs? What are you talking about?"

"You just don't want the attention of someone who doesn't want you to discover anything," he groused. "You didn't find anything did you?"

"Not in his office, but I did obtain a sample of his handwriting. You see, I came across an order for some acetone peroxide, but when I looked, it did not appear to be his handwriting on the bottom of the order. I'm going to keep snooping."

"Jesus, you're crazy," Ethan said.

"I worked on this when I was with the ATF," she replied. "I'm not some amateur sleuth."

"I know, I know." He ran his hand through his hair in frustration. "Listen, I'm in a bit of a pickle. Cybil and I rode together this morning and now I have no ride. I think she forgot that when she high-tailed it out of here. I need a lift to the city."

"Charlestown? Sure, hop in."

Chad, ready to leave Jack's, looked at his phone as a text came in. **Leaving wrk late. Checking something.**

Damn, Dani, stop investigating. Frustration poured off him as he felt the effects of the brick wall they kept running into.

Marc yelled out of the door of the compound. "Hey, Chad. Come back in here. Mitch is back and says he's got important info."

The Saints quickly settled in, noting Monty and Jack's hard expressions. Mitch came on the video-conference, his face red with anger. "Guys, I'm fuckin' sorry, but I had no idea. I just found out that the ATF had a sting operation going, in league with the FBI. I wasn't in the know since it wasn't my division, but Roscoe has been leading the task force."

"What does this mean for us?" Chad bit out, wishing he could get hold of Dani.

"Jahfar isn't working with terrorists. He's been recruited by the ATF to work in their sting. He's an undercover agent. And the terrorist that he's been in contact with, Fazan Darzi—he's also an undercover agent."

"So what about Dani's suspicions?" Chad asked.

Mitch's face, still red with anger at not knowing

about the operation, said, "It's got to be someone else at MES. Not Jahfar."

"So, what do you think is going on?" Ethan asked as Dani drove toward Charlestown.

"I think Jahfar's in league with someone who's wanting to obtain detonators that will work with TATP. He's got the ability to get his hands on it, and I now think he may be in league with someone else at MES. Someone who he had sign his name. My fiancé is an investigator who used to work for ATF. I'm turning everything I've been thinking over to him since he's working on this case anyway."

"Turn left here," Ethan directed.

She glanced around at the modest neighborhood of small, neat houses. Somehow the area did not fit the picture in her mind of where he lived. She knew Cybil lived in a large condo and wondered about their differences.

"It's this one here," he said, pointing to a house at the end of a cul-de-sac. The one-story, white house sat back just a little from the road. Several cars were in front of the house and one car was in the driveway.

"Um...do you have company?" she asked, as she navigated to where he indicated by pulling into the driveway.

"You need to come with me," he said.

Looking out the front windshield at the house,

she said, "Oh, thanks, but I need to get home."

"No, you will come with me," he said again, this time, his voice carrying authority.

"What are you—" Her voice halted as she glanced his way and saw a gun pointing at her. "Ethan? What...what are you doing?"

His handsome face contorted with fear. "I'm going to open my door and will keep my gun on you as you crawl over and come out on my side also. If you attempt to escape, Dani, I will shoot you. I've got no choice."

Heart beating erratically in her chest, she watched as he opened the door and exited the Jeep, then jerked the gun at her to indicate she should follow. With no choice, she crawled over the console, made more awkward with her pregnancy, and joined him on the passenger side.

"Walk," he ordered.

"Ethan, talk to me. What's going on?" she begged, forcing her voice to remain calm.

"Just go. Go to the front door," his voice shook.

Given no choice, she moved ahead of him, eyes alert and darting back and forth. *Nothing. Not one damn way out.*

The door swung open and Dani stepped across the threshold, the cold gun barrel pressed between her shoulder blades.

Entering, she moved into the first room, seeing four men all staring at her. Middle eastern. Cardboard boxes opened on the floor. A woman stepping into the room from the kitchen.

One man walked directly to her, his eyes darting between her face and Ethan's. "What is going on?"

"Mohammad, she knows too much."

"You weren't given orders to bring her here."

"What else was I going to do?" Ethan whined. "I never wanted to get this deep, now I can't get out."

"No, no you can't," Mohammad agreed.

Dani refused to look down, moving her gaze around the room, memorizing the faces of those there. The woman appeared frightened and stepped back slightly out of the room. The two men standing over the boxes glared at her with unadulterated hatred. The last man peered at her speculatively.

"You have compromised where we are now... but, perhaps we can make a statement from here. Fazan and Habib, move these boxes into the van in the garage. Sabah, pack your things and be ready to leave with the others. Abdul, you know what to do."

"What about me?" Ethan asked, his voice shaky.

"Leave. Just leave. Say nothing. Do nothing. Take her car and move it somewhere out of sight. I'll contact you as soon as you are needed again," Mohammad said.

Dani turned to look at Ethan's pale face, his eyes full of regret. "I trusted you," she said. "You've betrayed us all."

Pain slashed across his face at her words. "I'm sorry, Dani. I...I never meant for anything like this to happen."

"Bullshit, Ethan. You knew the minute you brought me here you were signing my death warrant."

Wincing, he started to speak again but Abdul bit out, "Get out of here, *alkalb la qimatan laha*." With a parting grimace toward Dani, Ethan walked out of the house, jogging to her jeep, her keys in his hand."

"Sit," ordered Abdul.

Eyeing him defiantly, she watched as he pulled out a long, curved knife. "Have you ever seen what a janbiya can do? Slicing off the skin of an infidel would be nothing to me."

Licking her lips as her chest heaved while she sucked in air, she dutifully sat down in the hard-backed chair. Abdul slipped behind her, securing her tightly with tape.

Oh, Jesus help me. Somehow let Chad find out where to find me. She watched in horror as Abdul began placing plastic bags of white powder in her lap and taping them to her as well. Glancing down, she noticed the pendant. *The tracer! I forgot the tracer. Chad will know where I am...if he realizes I'm gone in time to look for me."*

"Do you know what this is?" Abdul asked.

"TATP," she replied, her voice barely above a whisper.

Chuckling, he said, "Yes. But it has another name...one that I am particularly fond of. It is called the Mother of Satan."

29

"So the goddamn ATF and FBI have an undercover sting operation going and have the balls to ask us to help investigate without putting us in the know?" Jude bit out.

"It sucks, but having been undercover before, you gotta keep a lid on it," Cam explained, although his face had the same irritated expression as his fellow Saints.

"So what about the recruits we investigated?" Bart asked.

"According to Roscoe, everything we've done was legit. It was only the undercover agents that we did not know about. They could not obtain the detonation info that we got, so your efforts were necessary," Mitch replied.

"And our investigations into the materials they're using," Blaise growled. "Fuckin' hell, did we do it all?"

Jack looked around the table at his men, all angry, and in his opinion, rightfully so. Before he could speak, Mitch looked off screen. "Guys, hang on. Roscoe knows that I'm telling you and he's come to the FBI regional office. Let me get him up here."

A minute later and with some minor jostling of the conference cameras, Roscoe appeared alongside Mitch.

"Gentlemen, I understand that you're pissed, but we have no time to go into the intricacies of undercover work. Right now, we've got a bigger problem on our hands. We've located the local cell's house that has been busy with TATP. We've been watching them, wanting to find out what they're doing. We've got someone on the inside. He's sent a signal that something's up. He can't tell us and we've got no fuckin' idea right now."

"You've got a man there and don't have cameras or audio on the inside?" Marc asked, throwing his hands up in irritation.

Roscoe grimaced, replying, "They move around and for fuck's sake, they're not stupid! They've got ways to detect recording devices. These terrorists have money...organization...and determination. It's been a two-year process to place a man on the inside."

"So all you can tell us right now is that your agent at that house says it's been compromised? What does that mean?" Blaise asked.

"We don't know. We've got visual that a man

and woman went inside and the man was the only one to come out so far. I assume they'll be on the move soon. But with the TATP inside, we can't just send someone in."

"This is one of the reasons I had to leave the agency," Chad said under his breath to Monty, sitting next to him. "Too many cock-ups."

"Tell me about it," Monty agreed. "FBI was the same way. The fuckin' right hand had no clue what the left hand was doing."

"Fazan Darzi is your man inside, right?" Luke asked.

Roscoe looked shocked for a second, then covered it well. "What makes you say that?"

Mitch jumped in. "I told them!"

"If Jahfar isn't working with the terrorists and the only person we know him to have had communication with is Fazan, then it stands to reason they work together," Luke added.

Roscoe, tight-lipped, nodded. "Yes, Fazan is our man inside and as soon as he can, he'll report in and let us know what's going on."

Roscoe stopped talking as he took a call, his face changing as he listened. Disconnecting, he looked straight into the camera and said, "Chad—a jeep registered to Danielle Turner was seen at the house we have under surveillance. She was positively identified as going in, but not coming out. The person leaving in her vehicle was Ethan Petit of MES."

Chad stood quickly, his chair tipping back, slamming onto the floor. "They've got Dani?"

"I'm sorry, but it appears so—"

Mitch interrupted, saying, "Jack, my office is on it. We're going to coordinate with ATF to get there."

"Fuck that!" Chad roared. "ATF's fucked this whole thing up and now those bastards have Dani in a house with fuckin' explosives."

Roscoe said, "You don't know where to go and I'm not giving you that information."

"Don't need it, asshole," Chad said. Turning to Luke, he barked, "Pull her up on your monitor. She's got a chip in her necklace."

The other Saints stood in solidarity. Jack looked at Mitch and said, "My guys will be there...you can count on that."

"You cannot go charging in," Roscoe pleaded. "I'll have bomb squad members at the location. Everything's going to have to be played by the book, or these bastards'll get away."

Slamming his hand down on the table, Chad roared, "I don't give a damn about them right now. I'm going in to get Dani."

"If you're not careful, you'll end up just like your former partner. Adam wouldn't listen either."

With those words, the silence in the room entombed them. Chad's mind blanked for a moment as he tried to reconcile what Roscoe's words meant. "You...Adam? What the fuck did you mean by that?"

Mitch was looking at Roscoe, his face mirroring

the Saints' disbelief. Roscoe growled, "We don't have time for this!"

"What did you mean?" Chad asked, with deadly calm.

"Adam came across evidence after he jokingly set up a fake account on a dating site. He came to me. We used him to keep an undercover profile to find out what he could. He dug. Deep. Then he became afraid that Muhammad Hakim was on to him and he didn't want anything to blow back on his wife. He backed off with us, but he still kept notes—that he did not turn in to me. They must have figured out he knew something and eliminated him when he walked into a trap."

"He was a hero and you let his wife think he was working with terrorists? You goddamn fucker!"

Mitch, interrupting the escalating argument, said, "Get to the location and we'll meet you there."

Signing off, Jack nodded to the Saints. "Men, suit up. Luke, let's get the van ready."

Chad stood for a moment, his legs refusing to carry him anywhere. Feeling a hand on his shoulder, he turned. Marc stood behind him, his sympathetic expression hitting Chad in the gut.

"Let's go, man. Let's get your girls."

Girls...Dani and the baby. Hell yeah, I'm going to get my girls, Chad vowed, his face set in anger.

Dani sat perfectly still as the duct tape wrapped around her ankles and knees. With her hands taped behind her, she was afraid to move with the TATP in her lap. Her chest heaved as her breaths came in pants, but she forced herself to slow her breathing in order to keep her movements to a minimum.

Abdul finished and smiled down at her. "Good, good. Stay very still, woman, while we finish what we need to do." He stood, then looked back down and smiled. "It's fitting, you know. You will die the same way your husband did. He tried to be a hero and look where it got him."

She lifted her gaze, piercing him with her hate. "Adam? What about Adam?"

"He tried to find out what we were doing. Tried to play at being undercover. He wasn't very good at it and paid the ultimate price."

"Adam…was—"

He interrupted her as he walked out of the room and out of her sight.

Adam? Adam was a hero? Not a...

A trickle of sweat slid down the side of her face as she looked around, desperate for anything to use. *Nothing. Oh, my God...I'm going to die here.*

One of the other men came back into the room, picking up a box near her. As he leaned over, he whispered so softly, she almost was not sure she heard him. "I'm trying to help."

Her eyes darted over to him, watching the expression on his face. He mouthed, *ATF.* Eyes widening, her chest heaved again before she reminded herself to stay calm. Glancing down at the explosives in her lap, she bit the inside of her cheek to still the trembling.

Mohammad walked back into the room, his dark eyes sharply assessing. "Leave her," he ordered to Fazan. "Go help the others and then take the van to the next location."

"I can stay here, if you like," Fazan offered. "I'll make the sacrifice and stay here to make sure everything goes as planned."

Mohammad eyed him for a long minute, then a slow smile spread across his face. "You seem taken with the woman."

"No, I just thought—"

"Your job is not to think. Your job is to follow orders."

Fazan nodded as he stood, flashing a look of regret Dani's way. He walked out of the room slowly as her mind scrambled for a new hope.

By the time the Saints arrived at the entrance to the subdivision, their way was blocked. The ATF and FBI had cordoned off the area. Roscoe met them as they charged toward him.

"Got the residents out of the house next door and my guys are still in the other house at the end of the cul-de-sac. That's how we knew what was going on. She's still inside, but it looks like they are on the move. We hope to detain them as they leave without letting them tip off one of their remote incendiary devices."

"They go to another house, they'll blow this one or set it up to blow," Chad said. He looked over to one of his former ATF buddies that was suiting up. Walking to him, he asked, "What are your orders?"

"Get in close. Send in the robot, see what we can find out. If there's a hostage inside, we've got to then work on eliminating the risk first." The man looked at him in curiosity before asking, "What's got you here?"

"There is a hostage inside...my woman...carrying my baby," he managed to choke out.

"Damn, I'm sorry, man." Looking around, he said, "I'll keep you informed."

"You won't have to," Chad added. "I'll be inside before you can make it that far."

The agent's eyes were wide as he shook his head, but Chad had already turned and walked away. The Saints moved away from the crowd of ATF agents and were huddled by their van. Luke was on the inside with his bank of monitors and computers.

"What's the plan?" Jack asked Chad, turning the mission over to him.

"I'm circling around and checking it out from behind. I'm going in when we've determined there are no outside triggers." He noted the incredulous expressions, then explained. "If she goes, then I go too. Either we both get out or we both die...but I'm not living without her."

He felt Marc's hand on his shoulder, squeezing the emotion when words would not suffice. "We got your back, man. Tell us what you need."

"If the task force is going to wait here to grab whoever comes out, then let me know what they say. I'm heading to the back of the property." He already had his earpiece in and his Kevlar on. Securing his weapons in his holsters, he looked up, seeing Marc and Blaise doing the same. He did not need to ask. They were going too.

"Luke, when we move in close and determine if there are no outside trip wires, I'll snake in the camera. You monitor it from here and let me know what you see."

The three men eyed the others before jogging down the road in the opposite direction. Roscoe saw them leave and marched over to Jack. Glancing into the fully equipped van, he halted for a moment before turning on the Saints.

"You cannot interfere with my operation," he barked. "Chad's a civilian now and not part of this."

"Got a private citizen going after his woman. Don't see that you're gonna stop him," Jack growled back.

Roscoe's tirade was interrupted when the call came through that a van and an SUV had left the house. He turned and continued barking orders to his men. As the two vehicles came into sight, they were rushed by the combined task force agents.

The two vehicles were surrounded with guns pointing directly to them.

Jude, Bart, and Cam took the opportunity to follow Chad's group that had now circled to the back of the house, to provide support and continued intel.

Jack and Monty headed over to the halted convoy, watching as the men were hauled out. Mohammad's face was stone as one of the men in the van held a weapon against his head. That man yelled to Roscoe, "I've got his phone! He can't call in the detonation, but the hostage is inside."

The agents rushed to secure Mohammad, Abdul, Habib, and the two others with them. Fazan stepped outside, chest heaving as he looked at Roscoe. "I tried to get her out, but couldn't. She's taped to a chair in the front room. TATP is taped to her lap. There are no outside trips. Nothing in the house but her."

As soon as the words were out of his mouth, Jack relayed the intel to Chad and the other Saints.

Mohammad glared at Fazan, saying, "You whoreson traitor. You're worse than the ones we fight. You were one of us."

Fazan walked up to the man, now in handcuffs. "I was never one of you." Turning, he walked away.

Jack and Monty, done with the events outside the house, ran to the van, pulling themselves in. Driving around the barricade while the agents were busy with their arrests and processing, they stopped three houses away from where the other Saints were approaching.

Chad, armed with the information from Fazan, approached the house. Carefully stepping onto the front porch, he peered into the window, his heart stopping at the sight. Dani was not just taped, but almost mummified to a chair with duct tape. A lump was in her lap, taped to her as well.

"Dani!" he yelled, "Don't move. Stay very still. I'm coming in the front door."

Dani's teary eyes jumped to the window, stunned to see Chad standing so close. Still processing his appearance, she heard the front door lock jiggling. The doorknob turned and she saw Marc swinging the door open gently.

Suddenly, Chad was in front of her. His large body, bulked with the Kevlar vest, filled the door-frame. Her gazed jumped to the window where she saw ATF agents in full ABS gear in the yard.

"Why aren't you suited? Why are you here?" she whispered as he approached her. "Please don't sacrifice yourself for me."

Squatting in front of her, his eyes captured hers. "Nowhere else I'd rather be than with you...in this world...or another." He watched as her chin quivered, a silent tear sliding down her cheek. "But don't worry, babe. We'll be together in this world for a long time."

Luke, busy in the van, spoke to the other Saints. "He's gonna need oil...something like WD-40." Cam ran to the neighbor's abandoned house and broke into their garage. Coming out, he brought two bottles of oil, hustling them over to Marc, who met him at the bottom of the porch steps.

"Babe, I want you to keep your eyes on me," Chad ordered gently. "I'm going to cut away the tape from your body as best as I can. Then I'll work on the package taped to you. Do you know what it is exactly?"

"I'm sure it's TATP," she whispered. "They left, but one of them was—"

"We know. The task force captured them and it was Fazan who was on the inside as undercover."

"Ethan Petit brought me here—"

"They're picking him up too, babe. Now shush and let me work."

Dani sucked in her lips, continuing to still their quivering. Her eyes roved over the man squatting in front of her. His dark hair, mussed from his hands moving through it. His face, masculine and youthful, now a study in concentration. Focusing on him, she remembered the first time she saw him when he and Adam walked over. The first time she knew she had fallen for him. Burying the old hurt of his leaving and the many mistakes she made after that, she forced her thoughts back to when he showed up at Adam's funeral...holding her hand during the service. *My hand in his always felt like...home.*

Chad focused all his attention on the careful slicing of his knife through the tape. First around her ankles, then pants. *Thank God she's wearing pants or the tape would be attached to her bare legs.* He left her thighs for the moment, not wanting to jostle the package in her lap. He moved to the back of the chair, swiping the back of his hand over the sweat dropping off his brow. Slicing the tape at the back of the chair, she was now free of the seat, although he ordered her to stay as still as if she were still taped to it.

Squatting in front of her again, he held her gaze. "You know I need to get oil onto the TATP to stabilize it as much as possible. As soon as I can do that, I'm getting you out of here and the ATF can take care of the house. Got that?"

A barely perceptible nod was his answer.

"Okay, tell me how they taped the explosive."

Forcing her mind back to her former agent days, Dani meticulously divulged the steps. "They taped me first then taped the TATP to my lap. It's in a plastic bag, laid on my taped lap with tape put over it."

"Good, good. That's the first break we've got. That means that if I can get the tape off of you, then the package comes off with it. The trick will be to move slowly."

He stood and moved to the door where Marc handed him the oil. Looking at the road full of emergency vehicles he cast his eyes to the ATF agent in full ABS gear.

The agent walked to the porch, standing at the bottom of the steps. He called to Marc, saying, "Let me take your place, man. I can be of more help to Chad right now."

Marc looked at Chad, accepting his nod, and moved down the steps carefully as the ATF agent walked up. "I'd suggest you let me take over, but I've got the feeling you'd tell me to go to hell," the agent said, trying to lighten the tension.

"You'd be right," Chad agreed.

"I've got part of a uniform you can use and something for her head." The agent handed the headgear to Chad, who slipped it on, providing protection to his face. He watched as the agent moved behind Dani, placing the headgear on her as well. He then looked to Chad for more instructions. "What do you need me to do?"

"I'm going to work to cut the tape off her midsection. Put the oil in a bucket and, when I release it, I'm putting the whole package into the oil and we're getting the hell out of here."

The agent left and returned a minute later with a container full of oil, placed close to Chad's kneeling body. "I'll set it here for you and when you're done, we'll take care of it while you get her to safety."

The next ten minutes crawled as Chad methodically sliced the tape from her midsection. Looking down, Dani said, "Chad, cut my pants and blouse. Just take them away so that you don't have to pull the tape back."

Nodding, he knew it was a good plan, but felt his hand shake slightly as his knife passed through the cloth. This made the work quicker and within a few more minutes, he had the taped package, with the material clinging to the back, in his hands.

Looking into her eyes, he whispered, “Don’t move. Stay with me.”

A tear slid down her cheek as she fought to hold it back. Yearning to reach out to touch his face, she simply nodded. “Always.”

30

Dani watched as he stood, ever so carefully, and placed the package into the container full of oil. The agent then walked steadily to the door where he was met by another agent. They took the container out to their explosive storage container.

As soon as the agent passed through the door, Chad scooped Dani in his arms and, shielding her from prying eyes, moved to a protected area of the yard. Monty had already set up a safety perimeter for them, keeping the media in the background.

Tossing his helmet to the ground, Chad carried Dani to the Saint's van, where Blaise was waiting with a blanket. Her arms wound tightly around his neck and his arms, shaking, refused to let her go.

"Come on, brother, at least sit down with her so I can check her out," Blaise ordered gently.

"Her clothes were cut away. Get another blanket."

Sucking in a deep breath, Chad watched as the other Saints formed a protective circle around them, keeping any prying eyes away. Marc grabbed a blanket from his SUV and jogged over to wrap it around her.

"I'm fine," she protested as Blaise shown a light in her eyes. "I'm not hurt."

Blaise looked her over, but with some of the tape still attached to her body, it was difficult to ascertain any injuries. "We've got to get this tape off. Do we still have some WD-40?"

Bart ran to his vehicle and came back with an aerosol can of the spray lubricant. Blaise looked at Dani and explained, "I'm so sorry, honey, but this is going to hurt no matter what I do. I'm going to let Chad keep holding you while Marc sprays it around the ends. As we lift up the end of the tape, we'll keep spraying."

She smiled weakly. "I think if Chad was willing to sacrifice himself to save me...I can sacrifice a little skin."

Chuckling, they arranged themselves and began working on the tape on her arms. The process took over thirty minutes, during which she clung to Chad's arms as he held her tightly, offering his strength to her.

Roscoe made his way over to the van, his progress halted by the semi-circle of Saints. He stood toe to toe with Jack, his jaw set. Finally, giving in, he looked around at the group, saying, "You did good. You don't follow orders for shit, but you did good."

"Not our job to follow your orders," Jack clipped, his taciturn voice hard.

With a sharp nod, Roscoe turned and walked away. In his place, Mitch came over. Nodding to Jack and Monty, he said, "She okay?"

"She will be," came the answer.

Nodding, Mitch dropped his head, staring at his feet for a moment. Finally, lifting his gaze back to the Saints, his eyes settled on Jack's. "I'm sorry. Really, fuckin' sorry."

"Wasn't your fault, man. Don't take that on."

"A fuckin' task force working out of D.C. and they don't bother to tell me when a cell is sitting in my back yard. I fuckin' understand need-to-know, but I promise you, heads will roll over this one."

Jack clapped his hand on the agent's shoulder and said, "You do what you've got to do, but this was not your fault." He waited a moment, letting the words sink in, and then smiled as Mitch stared back. "It's been great having a friend at the FBI as we work together, but if you ever get tired of the bureaucratic bullshit, you know you'll have a place with the Saints."

Chuckling, Mitch nodded, seeing acceptance in the eyes of the others around. Looking over Jack's shoulder into the van, he smiled at Chad and Dani. "You know you'll have to be interviewed, but that can wait until tomorrow." With a slight wave, he headed back to his team.

The tape finally off her arms and legs, Blaise added cream to her skin, telling Chad to have her keep out of the shower for at least a day to give the ointment a chance to work on her abraded limbs.

Jack gave the nod to his men, and said, "You did good. Everyone. We need to debrief tomorrow. I suggest we meet at Chad's place to make things easier on Dani." Getting the nods from all around, they moved to their vehicles.

Luke, from the driver's seat, said, "I'll take you two home."

As the van moved away from the house at the end of the cul-de-sac, now swarming with ATF and FBI agents, Chad tucked the blanket tighter around Dani.

She reached one arm out, sliding her hand through his hair and down to cup his jaw. Holding his gaze, their eyes remained locked on each other.

"You're safe, babe." He moved his hand down to her protruding stomach, saying, "You and our baby girl." His thumb captured the tears flowing down her cheeks, before leaning forward to kiss them away. Moving his mouth over hers, he sealed his vows with his lips.

The next day, the Saints met for their initial debriefing at the compound before heading to Chad's house. Mitch was present, Jack having taken him into their conference room.

"So Jahfar and Fazan were working undercover for the ATF," Mitch said, still shaking his head at being kept out of the loop.

"I get that it took Fazan two years to be placed with Muhammed's group," Chad said, "but what about Jahfar? Was he at MES because of Dani?"

"According to what I finally got out of Roscoe, it was pure coincidence that Jahfar and Dani were hired by the same company and about the same time."

Doubtful expressions appeared on every Saint's face at the same time. "No fucking way," Chad cursed.

"I know, I know," Mitch agreed, "but according to Roscoe, Fazan had discovered that Ethan Petit at MES was in contact with Muhammed. So the ATF planted Jahfar at MES to see what he could discover. It appears that even Roscoe and Jahfar were surprised to learn that Adam's widow was there also."

"What was Ethan's motive? What was he doing?" Cam asked.

"Looks like he'd been targeted by the terrorist group...they have their eyes and ears open for anyone that might be of assistance to their cause. Ethan fell for the oldest trick in the world," Mitch explained.

"Holy hell," Jude bit out. "He screwed around and was blackmailed."

The others looked to Mitch for confirmation and were greeted with his nod. "Yep, he stepped out on Cybil, who was not only his girlfriend but also his boss. It seems he was more than willing to do what he could to keep that piece of information hidden."

Marc, his expression thoughtful, asked, "You think he had any idea of the scope of what he agreed to?"

Shrugging, Mitch answered, "I've got no idea. Probably not. Probably panicked and, once in, always in."

"And Adam?" Chad asked.

"It's like what you heard from Roscoe. It appears that Adam entered the dating site as a joke, but when he realized what was happening with the recruiter, he went to his superiors at the ATF. They had him continue to play along to acquire as much information as possible. That was supposed to be his only involvement with the task force, according to Roscoe. But then, things began to heat up and Adam got nervous."

"Nervous? Adam nervous?"

"Yeah. It seems he became afraid that the recruiters would catch on to what he was doing and he was afraid of blowback on Dani. So, he resorted to an attempt to leave clues for her to believe in him if things went wrong."

"The key. The note in the safety deposit box. The notebook," Chad stated. "Any one of those things might have easily been missed by her."

Mitch and the others nodded. "Yeah, it seemed as though he had watched one too many bad mystery movies. But he desperately wanted her to know that he wasn't one of the bad guys...and certainly didn't work for terrorists."

Jack glanced at Mitch and said, "Why didn't Roscoe speak to Dani when Adam was killed? He could have alleviated a lot of her angst."

"Got no idea, man. I'm so disgusted with the taskforce right now. I'm afraid it's tainting everything I'm feeling about my government job."

Chad sighed heavily, shaking his head, gaining the gazes of everyone in the room.

"You okay, man?" Marc asked, looking into the tired face of his friend.

"Gotta tell you, my mind's still reeling," Chad admitted. "I felt all along that the Adam I called friend would have never become involved with terrorists, but when the evidence began to pile up, I wondered what the hell he was doing." Rubbing his hand over his face, he continued, "But no matter what a cock-up he was with his marriage, the truth of the matter was...he was a good man."

The Saints were quiet a moment before Monty asked, "How's Dani?"

Chad leaned back in his chair, the fatigue evident from having been up all night with Dani. He gazed around the table, noting the concerned faces of every person there. Smiling despite the exhaustion, he replied, "She's fine. The baby's fine. I took her to see her doctor early this morning and everything's good." Sighing, he admitted, "We didn't sleep much last night. The events continued to play over and over for both of us, so rest was elusive."

He looked over to Mitch and added, "She's going to want to know everything he was doing, but I don't know what the taskforce will allow."

Shaking his head, Mitch grimaced as he replied. "We'll tell her anything she wants to know. Fuck the taskforce!"

That drew laughter from the group along with sounds of *Hell, yeahs* calling out. As the Saints completed their debriefing, Jack nodded toward Chad and said, "How about we continue this meeting at your house. The women are there with Dani already."

Eyeing his boss, Chad gave him an appreciative chin lift. "Thanks, man. I know she's anxious to hear everything." Looking over at Mitch, he added, "Come on over and join us at my house."

Breathing easier having the case close successfully, the Saint adjourned, smiles all around.

Later that night, after everyone had left, Dani and Chad lay in bed, processing everything they had learned. Utterly exhausted, she lay her head on his chest, enveloped in his strong embrace.

"It's all over, babe," he said, his hand stroking her lustrous hair, easing the tension from her body. "I want you to have sweet dreams for our baby and know that I will keep you safe."

"I know," she murmured, "thanks to your willingness to sacrifice yourself for me."

"Dani, I would walk through fire for you. Live and breathe and die for you. I've felt this way a long time and refuse to let one single day go by that I don't tell you...show you...prove to you that my heart is yours."

31

FIVE MONTHS LATER

The sound of a cry filled Chad's ears, as he supported Dani's back during her final push. He had stayed by her side during the long labor, his body aching while knowing her body had done all the work.

The doctor held up their daughter, red and squalling, her little arms and legs moving with indignation before being taken by the nurse. Chad wiped the perspiration from Dani's face, peering into her green eyes, sparkling with happiness as well as unshed tears. Kissing her lips, he said, "You did it, babe. God, I love you so much."

Laughing through her tears, she turned her gaze over to the corner where the nurse was weighing and measuring their newborn, before bringing her over.

"Is she all right?" Dani asked, suddenly nervous. She eyed the nurse carefully, her hands reaching instinctively for her baby as they laid the infant on her chest.

"She's absolutely perfect," the smiling nurse answered. "She's seven pounds, eleven ounces and nineteen inches long."

The baby blinked at the lights and Dani could have sworn she looked right at her. Chad lowered his head, gazing at his daughter. Hesitantly he reached out his large hand, placing it on her back. A blanket was brought and wrapped across the back, allowing their daughter to snuggle tightly to her mother.

The nurse smiled at the new family and asked, "Do you have a name picked out?"

Dani cooed to the baby, lost in the world of new mothers, as Chad glanced up at the nurse. "Her name is Amanda," he replied. "It means *beloved*." He leaned over, placing his lips on the top of his daughter's head and whispered, "And you are, little one. Beloved."

Four years later

Amanda sat on the couch, her reddish hair glistened as the sun shone through the window, shining on the silver framed picture held in her chubby hand. Staring at the three, smiling faces in the photograph, she grinned. She knew their story by heart, having heard it so many times as her favorite bedtime story. Her little finger reached out to touch each figure.

First was the tall man on the left, with dark hair and a big smile. Amanda thought he looked as though he had just told the others a joke. Or maybe thought of something funny but had kept it to himself. Adam, her father. *Strong and brave, mommy tells me. He was a hero and would have loved me very much.*

Her gaze moved to the pretty woman standing between the men. *Mommy.* Grinning, Amanda loved seeing her mother's smiling face between her two favorite men. She thought her mommy was the prettiest girl in the world. *I want to grow up to be just like you.*

Next, her finger moved to the tallest of the group...*daddy.* His eyes were not focused on the person with the camera, but were glancing down at the woman in the middle, a small smile curving his lips. Amanda loved that expression. She saw it many times when her daddy would look at her mommy. Grinning, she realized he looked at her with the same smile.

Her heart leaped, just then, as she heard his old truck pulling into the driveway. Yelling in delight, she gently tossed the picture frame onto the sofa as she barreled out of the door, running to greet her daddy coming home from work. Waving her hands wildly in the air, screaming her greeting, she giggled when he swooped her up into his strong arms, swinging her around.

"Hey, baby girl," he greeted, kissing his daughter's head before seeing Dani walking out onto the porch. Her titian hair, pulled back from her face, showcased her porcelain complexion, the sprinkle of freckles still across her nose. Black leggings hugged her legs as a long blue shirt hung below her ass. Chad's eyes immediately dropped to his wife's arms, where she held a small, dark-haired baby. *His son.* Hugging his daughter tightly in his arms as he walked to Dani, not stopping until he moved directly into her space. Continuing to hold Amanda with one arm and wrapping the other around Dani and his son, he surrounded his family in his embrace and in his heart...*and life was now complete.*

Don't miss the next Saint!
Protecting Love

Don't miss any news about new releases! Sign up for my Newsletter

ALSO BY MARYANN JORDAN

Don't miss other Maryann Jordan books!

Lots more Baytown stories to enjoy and more to come!

Baytown Boys (small town, military romantic suspense)

Coming Home

Just One More Chance

Clues of the Heart

Finding Peace

Picking Up the Pieces

Sunset Flames

Waiting for Sunrise

Hear My Heart

Guarding Your Heart

Sweet Rose

Our Time

Count On Me

Shielding You

To Love Someone

Sea Glass Hearts

For all of Miss Ethel's boys:

Heroes at Heart (Military Romance)

Zander

Rafe

Cael

Jaxon

Jayden

Asher

Zeke

Cas

Lighthouse Security Investigations

Mace

Rank

Walker

Drew

Blake

Tate

Levi

Clay

Cobb

Hope City (romantic suspense series co-developed

with Kris Michaels

Brock book 1

Sean book 2

Carter book 3

Brody book 4

Kyle book 5

Ryker book 6

Rory book 7

Killian book 8

Torin book 9

Saints Protection & Investigations

(an elite group, assigned to the cases no one else wants...
or can solve)

Serial Love

Healing Love

Revealing Love

Seeing Love

Honor Love

Sacrifice Love

Protecting Love

Remember Love

Discover Love

Surviving Love

Celebrating Love

Searching Love

Follow the exciting spin-off series:

Alvarez Security (military romantic suspense)

Gabe

Tony

Vinny

Jobe

SEALs

Thin Ice (Sleeper SEAL)

SEAL Together (Silver SEAL)

Undercover Groom (Hot SEAL)

Also for a Hope City Crossover Novel / Hot SEAL...

A Forever Dad by Maryann Jordan

Letters From Home (military romance)

Class of Love

Freedom of Love

Bond of Love

The Love's Series (detectives)

Love's Taming

Love's Tempting

Love's Trusting

The Fairfield Series (small town detectives)

Emma's Home

Laurie's Time

Carol's Image

Fireworks Over Fairfield

Please take the time to leave a review of this book. Feel free to contact me, especially if you enjoyed my book. I love to hear from readers!

Facebook

Email

Website

ABOUT THE AUTHOR

I am an avid reader of romance novels, often joking that I cut my teeth on the historical romances. I have been reading and reviewing for years. In 2013, I finally gave into the characters in my head, screaming for their story to be told. From these musings, my first novel, Emma's Home, The Fairfield Series was born.

I was a high school counselor having worked in education for thirty years. I live in Virginia, having also lived in four states and two foreign countries. I have been married to a wonderfully patient man for thirty-five years. When writing, my dog or one of my four cats can generally be found in the same room if not on my lap.

Please take the time to leave a review of this book. Feel free to contact me, especially if you enjoyed my book. I love to hear from readers!

Facebook

Email

Website

Made in the USA
Coppell, TX
21 January 2022

72059548R00236